JAI

By

Rob Ashman

Print ISBN 978-1-912986-25-5

Also By Rob Ashman

The DI Rosalind Kray Series
Faceless (Book 1)
This Little Piggy (Book 2)
Suspended Retribution (Book 3)

The Mechanic Trilogy
Those That Remain (Book 1)
In Your Name (Book 2)
Pay The Penance (Book 3)

Praise For Rob Ashman

I have discovered a new Favourite Author in Rob Ashman! Wow! What captivating books he writes. I've read four of his in three days and have my fifth waiting to start. They have all contained amazing stories with very well drawn characters it's easy to visualise. I became attached to each one, including the serial killers! But I put this down to Mr Ashman's writing, rather than any character flaw of mine. His books are dark, disturbing, fast paced and gripping, Faceless had me in the first two sentences, "The Mechanic" trilogy in the first paragraph. **Anne – Amazon Reviewer**

Well what can I say... for a start this book so deserves more that the maximum 5stars can be given. I was immediately thrown into the rollercoaster ride of this story and my word what a ride. Once again I am raving about Rob and his books to anyone who will listen. If you have not tried this authors books I STRONGLY recommend you to do so **Nikki Ayling – Amazon**

If I could award more stars for this one I would. Absolutely gripping from start to finish - was incapable of putting this down. Roz's character is so well thought out you really feel you get to know her, whilst getting in the head of a really sick killer at the same time. It barrels forward at an impressive rate resulting in a mouth-dropping, detailed finale. Brilliant. Now on to This Little Piggy.... **Kodakai – Amazon Reviewer**

Faceless is a gritty, compelling and thrilling serial killer thriller that kept me utterly engrossed and I look forward to seeing what Rob Ashman comes up with next! **Eva – Goodreads Reviewer**

Rob is the author of quite a few amazing books and I think I've read most of them. His thrillers are always fantastically written, unusual and quite dark which combined makes for a great read. I really look forward to reading more from him in the future. **Joanna Park – Goodreads Reviewer**

For my mum, who never got to read this one.

Preface

'Apart from killing the occasional person, I consider myself a good man. A fair man. A man with principles.

'When I was young I learned an important lesson – taking a life is fine so long as you've given the matter due consideration. Spur-of-the-moment murder is for the rude and bad-tempered, and there is no excuse for that.

'I also learned that to maintain the façade you need two things: You must not get caught and you must have someone to blame. I'm fortunate in this regard. I have so many personalities there is always someone there to take the fall. Besides, I'm always careful.

'As you travel through life there will be those who threaten to disrupt your plans, and when that happens it is perfectly acceptable to remove them... after due consideration, of course.

'That is, unless you've made a promise.'

Chapter 1

Michael Ellwood was bobbing around on a boat in the Irish Sea, which under normal circumstances would have made him sick, but spitting his teeth onto the deck was taking his mind off it.

A gloved fist smashed into his jaw again; his head snapped back, then recoiled onto his chest. He felt another foreign object in his mouth. A dislodged tooth joined the others at his feet.

'We can do this all night if we have to, though I think you'll run out of teeth before we run out of steam. What were you going to do with the shipment?' The man in the balaclava spoke with a gravel voice, pitched somewhere between Barry White and Chewbacca. He grabbed a handful of hair and yanked his head back. Ellwood gazed into the cold, black eyes staring out of the ragged holes cut in the wool.

Ellwood was strapped to a chair on one of the lower decks. The lounge and kitchen blurred in and out of focus. His assailant was right in his face.

'I keep telling you, I don't know what you're on about! I don't know about any shipment. My name is Michael Ellwood, I own a garage in Salford Quays, Manchester. I fix cars, I can't tell you–'

The gravel-voiced man slammed his fist into his chest. A torrent of air and blood burst from Ellwood's mouth. He coughed and gagged. The man hit him again, blood peppering the air.

'You're starting to piss me off with this Manchester bollocks. Tell us what we want to know and it all stops.'

Four hours earlier Ellwood had boarded a train at Manchester Piccadilly and found a seat for the one hour and twenty-six minutes journey to Blackpool North Beach. He had read a newspaper and ate a pasty, both of which he purchased from a kiosk on the main concourse at the station. He had a knot of anxiety in the pit of his stomach which he'd never felt before, a sense that something wasn't right. It was as though this time was going to be different – he got that right.

The boat lurched to one side and a second man stepped up, grabbing Ellwood from behind. He wrapped his forearm around his neck, crushing his windpipe. Ellwood's hands strained against the ties binding them to the arms of the chair, blood seeping from the wounds as the rope lacerated his wrists.

Ellwood's eyes popped from their sockets like a cartoon character. His tongue protruded from his bloodied mouth. Apart from the sound of the chair legs rattling against the wooden decking as Ellwood's body jerked and spasmed, the room was silent. His face turned purple and the tiny blood vessels in his distended eyes began to rupture.

'We know you work for Berkley. Who else is behind this?' the gravel-voiced man snarled.

Ellwood's face looked like it was going to split wide open. The man released his hold. Ellwood rasped air into his burning lungs, choking and coughing. Tears streamed down his cheeks, mixing with the blood stains on his chest.

'Please believe me. I… I… I don't know what you're talking about. My name is–'

'Yeah, we know.' The gravel-voiced man left the room, followed by two other men each sporting the same style of headwear.

Ellwood had his head bowed. He could hear a heated conversation coming from the next berth. Then silence. He had no idea how long he'd been holed up in this cabin, he could remember alighting from the train and heading for the taxi rank. He had taken a short ride in a cab and paid the driver. As he was walking up the road a stranger had called him over, asking for help – something about not being able to find the Hilton Hotel. The man was standing at the entrance to a side road, holding a map. He remembered going over to speak to him when a Transit van pulled out of nowhere and someone stuffed a bag over his head and bundled him into the back. He heard the doors bang shut and the screech of the tires on the road as they drove away. He'd struggled and yelled at the top of his voice, then a series of heavy blows rendered him unconscious. He woke up on board the boat, in the middle of God knows where.

The gravel-voiced man came back, flanked by the two gorillas.

'Did you know that Tehuacán is the second largest city in the Mexican state of Puebla, with a population of a quarter of a million people?' he said circling around him to the kitchen.

'What?' croaked Ellwood, trying to lift his head up.

'It's a volcanic region famous for producing mineral water. And do you know what's amazing about it… it's carbonated from the geological activity. Fascinating that, don't you think?'

Two pairs of hands grasped him by the shoulders, toppling the chair backwards. Ellwood crashed onto his back, his head bouncing off the wooden floor. He stared up at the ceiling, flashbulbs of light popped in his head. The gravel-voiced man came into view, towering above.

'But the most fascinating thing is the fizzy water is used by drug cartels to extract information from people, they even call it the Tehuacán technique.' The man was unscrewing the top of a two-litre plastic bottle of soda water. 'Now you are probably wondering what's so terrifying about a fizzy drink, right? But those South Americans know a thing or two about extracting information.' He removed the top from another smaller bottle and emptied a red substance into the plastic bottle. Ellwood could see the red liquid swirling around. 'They like their food hot out there and have a ton of this stuff.' He waved the smaller bottle at Ellwood. 'Red hot chilli sauce.'

Ellwood struggled against his bonds.

The gravel-voiced man placed the bottles onto the worktop and fished a wallet from his pocket.

'Recognise this? It's yours.' Ellwood squinted his eyes in an attempt to focus. 'I have a problem with this. Do you know why?'

Ellwood shook his head. 'I have a problem with it because it contains eighty pounds in cash, two rail tickets and a ticket to the cinema, and that's it. No credit cards, bank cards, driver's licence, receipts – nothing. Now who the hell doesn't have those things in their wallet?'

'I... I don't know,' croaked Ellwood.

'No, and neither do I. A grown man with a ticket to watch *The Lego Movie*, there's got to be something wrong with that. The other thing I have a problem with is... where's your phone?'

'I... must have dropped it.'

'Nope, don't think you did. We've turned the van inside out and checked the snatch site – no mobile. Now why would someone not have a mobile phone?'

'I–'

The gravel-voiced man seized Ellwood's face.

'Why don't you save yourself a world of pain and tell me what you're doing in Blackpool, and what the plans were for the shipment?'

'I don't know what you mean! My name is Michael Ellwood and I fix cars. Check it out, for fuck's sake, check it out.'

One of the men crouched down and clamped his hands either side of Ellwood's head, while the other tore a length of duct tape from a roll and stuck it across Ellwood's mouth. The gravel-voiced man upended the bottle of soda water and forced the opening over Ellwood's nostrils. He squeezed the bottle.

The pain in Ellwood's head exploded with the searing heat of molten lava. He screamed against the gag as the liquid burned its way down his nasal passages and into his throat. He was drowning in fire. His body bucked and twisted in the chair but the strong hands held him firm. The gravel-voiced man squeezed again.

A column of pain tore through him. Water squirted out the sides, scalding his eyes. He felt the fluid scorching its way into his lungs.

The gravel-voiced man removed the bottle and ripped away the gag. Ellwood coughed a torrent of pink water into the air and gargled a scream. Everything burned.

'You work for Berkley. Now what were you planning to do with the shipment? We're not interested in you, we want to know who was the next in the chain.'

'Agghhh!' Ellwood couldn't speak. He coughed and barked, spitting water over the floor.

The gravel-voiced man nodded and another secured a fresh length of tape across Ellwood's mouth. He jammed the bottle over Ellwood's nose and forced the liquid into his nasal passages. Blood flowed from Ellwood's wrists and ankles as he tried to free himself from the chair. His body bucked and jerked. Then he was still.

'Roll him over,' the gravel-voiced man said to the other two as they ripped away the gag and turned Ellwood onto his side, striking his chest – pink water gushed from his nose and mouth, fizzing on the floor. Ellwood gasped for air.

The gravel-voiced man beckoned to the other two men who followed him out.

'I don't think he knows anything,' said one of them.

'Neither do I,' said the other.

'But what about the wallet and the phone?' asked the gravel-voiced man.

'That's strange. It doesn't make sense.'

'Any ideas?'

'I'll make a call.'

Ten minutes later all three entered the cabin, Ellwood groaning on the floor, still coughing up blood and water.

'Okay, let's get you up.'

The men righted the chair and one of them took a knife from his belt. Ellwood was too far gone to react to the blade. The man edged the knife under the rope and cut it free.

They put their arms under his and heaved him up, dragging him across the cabin and up the stairs to the top deck.

Ellwood felt the cold sea breeze on his face; he began to come round. He struggled to hold his footing as they threw him onto the fibreglass hull. He lurched forward and fell flat on his face then managed to haul himself onto all fours. The rocking motion of the boat seemed more pronounced up on deck, making his head swim. Looking one way he could see the twinkle of orange lights in the distance, dancing on the shoreline, glancing the other way he could see nothing – it was pitch black.

The two men lifted Ellwood onto his knees and the gravel-voiced man blocked his view of the lights. He drew a gun and pushed it into Ellwood's forehead.

'One more time,' he said.

'No, no, please…' Ellwood stared up at the barrel, silhouetted against the sky.

'What were you going to do with the shipment?'

'I don't know what you're–'

The muzzle snapped upwards as the round entered Ellwood's skull and blew out the back of his head. The men either side dragged him across the deck and threw him overboard.

Chapter 2

Three weeks later

Detective Inspector Rosalind Kray felt like shit, and the fact that she had stopped smoking and given up alcohol had nothing to do with it. The fact that she was two months pregnant, however, had everything to do with it.

For a woman in her late thirties, who had the body fat percentage of an elite athlete without going anywhere near a gym, drank like a fish, and barely ate enough food to keep a small child alive, skipping the odd period was not an uncommon occurrence. Her menstrual cycle had been a mystery for years, so what made her go to the chemist to buy a test kit was beyond her. Since then she had bought three more with the same result every time – the two thin blue lines screamed *Yes*.

She fished around in her bag for a tissue, her fingers found the glossy pamphlet she had picked up at the health centre. She pulled it from her bag and opened it up. A parade of earnest, smiling faces greeted her from the pages. She scanned the words, knowing exactly what they said.

Kray had no doubt the reception staff would be welcoming, fully expected that the clinicians would be sympathetic and understanding, and that the aftercare team were highly qualified. But she couldn't bring herself to come to terms with the fact that they were there to take the life of her unborn child. Not from any puritanical, moralistic perspective. This had nothing to do with thinking abortion was wrong. For her a little voice inside her head said, *termination is not for you.*

She tore the leaflet lengthways, then turned it and repeated the process. Soon she had a cluster of confetti in her hand which she dropped in the bin.

DC Duncan Tavener burst into her office like a kid coming home from school with a gold star.

'Hey, Roz, are you busy?'

'For you, Duncan, never. What is it?' Roz Kray didn't have favourites, but if she did, the young Scotsman with the boy band looks and stature of an international lock forward would be top of the list.

'I have good news and bad news.'

'If you've come in here to wind me up you can piss off, I'm not in the mood.'

'Okay, good news first. Do you remember that body that washed up on the beach a few weeks ago?'

'Of course I remember, I attended the scene. He'd been beaten up and shot in the head before ending up in the water. We've still not been able to identify him and the case remains open. What of it?'

'I think we have a name. Michael Ellwood. His wife reported him missing when he failed to return home after attending a football match, he supposedly went to see Man United playing at home. The interesting thing is, he never went to the game. Greater Manchester Police did a trawl of public transport CCTV and caught him boarding a train out of Manchester Piccadilly bound for North Beach. We have him arriving on the platform and exiting the train station.'

'So why the football cover story?'

'Search me. All I know is he ended up here and the next we see him he'd been in the water for two days feeding the fish. They ran DNA and dental records and got a match, though four of his teeth were missing.'

'Was he on his own in the CCTV footage?'

'Yeah, he was.'

'Didn't the results of the post-mortem say his respiratory and digestive tract were burnt with a corrosive liquid? Something about it having the hallmarks of a South American drug cartel murder?'

'Yes, that's the guy.'

'Next of kin?'

'His wife and two grown up kids. He'd been married for twenty years and ran a small garage business in Salford Quays.'

'What was he into?'

'How do you mean?'

'The guy gets tortured, executed, and his body is dumped in the Irish Sea. He must have been into *something*?'

'Not according to GMP, not even a parking ticket.'

'I don't believe that.'

'That's what they say.'

'We'll need to interview the wife.'

'Ah, and that brings me to the bad news.' Kray gave him one of her death stares, daring him to continue.

'Well?'

'She's downstairs, interview room two.'

Thirty minutes later Kray and Tavener were sitting opposite a petite woman with long brown hair and a face that matched the colour of the whitewashed walls. Her body seemed crumpled in the chair.

What the hell must she be thinking? Kray thought as she eyed her across the table.

A PC handed her a cup of coffee, the woman shook her head and pushed it away.

'Any more coffee and I won't sleep for a week. But who am I kidding, I don't sleep these days anyhow.'

'Mrs Ellwood, we are sorry for your loss,' Kray said.

'If I had a pound for every time…' she replied staring down into her lap. She dug her thumbnail repeatedly into the palm of her hand as if she was trying to gouge away the pain.

'My name is DI Roz Kray and this is DC Tavener. I believe you have–'

'Identified the rotting corpse of my husband? Yes, I identified him. I've known that man almost twenty-five years and the only thing I could recognise was two rings. Two fucking rings!'

'I'm sorry, Mrs Ellwood.'

'My name is Miriam, DI Kray, please call me Miriam.'

'Okay, please call me Roz.'

'I suppose you want to ask me some questions,' she said, still digging a hole in her hand.

'We do, but you've had a traumatic enough day already, we can reschedule if you would prefer.'

'Ask away, Roz. You can't possibly have as many questions as me, so be my guest.'

'Thank you. You said that your husband was attending a football match on the day he disappeared. Did he normally go to games?'

'He occasionally went when they played at home, but he seldom travelled to away matches. Unless it was Everton or Liverpool.'

'Did he go with friends?'

'No, he went on his own.'

'This is a tough question but I need to ask. Your husband was murdered in a particularly violent manner, was there anyone who would want to hurt him?'

'No, nobody. Michael was well liked, he had loads of mates, and was a popular bloke. Who the hell would want to do this?'

'I don't know, Miriam, that's what we need to find out. He ran a garage; did he owe anyone money? Was the company in debt?'

'I kept myself out of his business affairs but we didn't owe money. Our house is paid for and the garage was doing well. We have a loan on the pickup truck but that's about it.'

'Your husband was seen on CCTV boarding a train to North Beach, here in Blackpool. Can you think of any reason why he would make that journey?'

'No idea.'

'Had he travelled to Blackpool before?'

'Look, I've never been to *fucking* Blackpool, is that clear enough for you!' Ellwood spat the words at Kray from across the desk. 'I don't know why he would want to come here, maybe he had a woman on the go, or maybe a fancy-boy, or maybe he rented himself out, or maybe he liked the view from the tower, or maybe he liked to eat Blackpool rock and have rides on the donkeys… I don't fucking know why he was here!'

'I know this is difficult, Miriam, but we have to ask.'

'Sorry, you're only doing your job.' Tears rolled down her face and onto her lap.

'Did Michael ever do drugs?'

'What sort of a question is that? No, he never took drugs. Christ, he was bad enough when he drank beer let alone anything else. Three pints and he was on his back.'

'How many times did he go to watch the football?'

'Every now and again, when a game took his fancy.'

'And they were always home matches.'

'I said that already.'

The scar on Kray's cheek tingled.

'Yes, you did.' Kray paused. 'The coroner and pathologist have released the body so we will transfer it to a place of your choosing. Thank you for your time, Miriam, I'm sure we will have an opportunity to speak again and right now I suspect you just want to go home.'

'Is that it?'

Kray rose from the table and extended her hand. Miriam gave it a fingertip shake. Kray tilted her head at Tavener, who took the hint.

Outside in the corridor Kray stopped in her tracks, spun on her heels and bobbed her head into the interview room.

'On second thoughts, Miriam, I wonder if I could impose on you for a little while longer? I'm sure we could stand you lunch in our canteen, after all you've had a traumatic day and it's a good two-hour drive back to Manchester. Can we talk again in an hour?'

Ellwood shrugged her shoulders. 'I suppose so.'

'Thank you.'

Kray marched out with Tavener in hot pursuit.

Tavener asked, 'What are you doing? I thought–'

'There's something not right about this.'

'Where are you going?'

'I have to go to a meeting now, Bagley has a weekly get together. It normally lasts about forty minutes. I want you to go around the houses again and turn over everything you can about Michael Ellwood before we sit down again with Miriam.'

'Okay, but for what it's worth, I felt really sorry for her.'

'So did I…' Kray chewed her bottom lip. 'Right up until she started lying through her back teeth.'

Chapter 3

I'm an extreme example of what a crazy person can achieve. Some days, when I wake, I have so many personalities inside me I can't decide which one to choose. It's a macabre game of pick and mix, a morass of people, each one crafted for a reason.

I would like to say that being me is shit and that's the reason I choose to be other people, but that isn't strictly true. I ghost through life pretending because I can no longer remember what being me looks like.

My father died when I was six in a car crash and mum fell apart after filling her veins with alcohol and her head full of skunk. A concerned neighbour reported her to social services and they came to take me and my brother into care. We never lived with her again. Supervised visits were the closest we came to being a family. Then she died. Choked on her own vomit in a drug and vodka fuelled bender.

I remember there were ten people at her funeral and that included the vicar and a woman from the council. It was pitiful.

My younger brother and I were catapulted into a toxic procession of children's homes and foster parents. Each one intent on doing us harm in the name of proxy parenting, which set me on a path of permanent self-loathing. Sometimes, I would force myself to be sick after eating breakfast because in my head I didn't deserve a good start to the day.

We were placed with one couple who were Bible-bashers, church of the something-or-other it was called. I remember when we went to worship there was a big fat book which took pride of place on the altar, the summary of the one thousand page tome seemed to be 'If it feels good, it's a sin'. Our time with them felt like a different form of abuse, one being conducted by a higher calling.

When the donations plate came around on a Sunday I would pretend to put money in and took coins out. One for me and one for my brother. It seemed only fair – we had to endure the rigours of a religious upbringing – and the church roof seemed fine to me.

However, what was not fine was when our foster mother caught me pilfering cash. We were back in the children's home faster than you could say, 'Thou shalt not steal'.

I learned fast that you either fitted in or felt the back of somebody's hand – it was up to you. And fitting in for me entailed working out what they wanted and adapting my personality and character to suit. Life was all about survival. I became a social chameleon, blending into my surroundings while pandering to the quirks and vices of those in charge.

I always knew I wasn't right in the head. I would look at the other kids and think, *that's not me*. While they were developing into boisterous young adults with all the problems that came with it, I was ghosting through life pretending; pretending to be in love, pretending to rebel, pretending to be heartbroken, pretending… everything.

I slipped into adulthood copying those around me. I became a master at blending into my surroundings, fitting in so no one saw the join. Occasionally, I would glare at my reflection in a mirror and wonder, *who is the real me?* And the answer that came back was always the same – *there is no real you*.

I'm a composite picture of everything I've ever seen and everyone I've ever met. Capable of shape-shifting in an instant to meet any given circumstance. It's a real talent.

But a talent with a drawback – because there is no real me, there's no empathy. I look at others and think, *I don't know what that feels like*.

While I was busy blending in, my brother was hell-bent on making himself a square peg in a round hole, getting into trouble and being punished on a regular basis. I became fiercely protective and did everything I could to keep him safe, but he would insist on putting himself in the firing line.

I remember at one children's home there was an older lad who bullied him mercilessly. We tried to get help from the grown-ups but they did nothing and made matters worse. I was fourteen and my brother was twelve. The boy in question was called Barry Canning.

Canning was the freak of the bunch. You know the type – he'd been shaving since he was fourteen, had hairs on his chest, stood a foot taller than everyone else and swung his dick around in the showers. I don't know what my brother did to upset Canning so much but he hated him with such a passion that you could taste it in the air.

The home nestled comfortably in its own grounds which were maintained by a handyman. He worked out of a large, windowless building where he stored his tools and equipment. The lady who managed the admissions and placement process was called Mrs Macklam. She was a forty-year-old peroxide blonde with enough cleavage for three women and a liking for short skirts. She played the lead role in many a teenage boy's night-time fumbling and Canning boasted to anyone who would listen that he was shagging her. A likely story. The other boys were in awe of him and believed every word, whereas I thought he was talking bollocks.

His attacks on my brother were getting worse.

One day I wrote Canning a note and slipped it under his pillow while he was out peddling his testosterone-fuelled lies. It was supposed to be from the lovely Mrs Macklam, inviting him to join her in the handyman's shed for a night he wouldn't forget. There was an immediate change in Canning's behaviour when he found the note. He strutted around the home with a pronounced swagger and adopted a benevolent, almost presidential, air about him, which was more disturbing than his school bully routine. To my amazement he kept the forthcoming liaison a secret. It must have been burning a hole in his pants.

I had miscalculated the degree of preparation necessary to carry out my plan which resulted in many late nights working by torchlight, trying to figure out how to hold down the handle so the machine would start. Fortunately, it was old and not fitted with a fail-safe device – God only knows what I would have done otherwise. My elaborate plan would have fallen at the first fence.

On the night in question I stole the key from the main office and hid in the equipment shed. It was cold and I can remember my teeth chattering. My eyes became accustomed to the dark and I used a stepladder to remove the starters from the fluorescent fittings to ensure the place remained in darkness. The last task was to leave the lock on the latch. Everything was ready.

Then I sat back and waited.

The hands on the luminous face of my watch were approaching midnight when I heard the door creak open – it was Canning.

'Mrs Macklam?' he hissed. 'Mrs Macklam, it's Barry.'

The door swung shut and I could hear him feeling around, bumping into things in his search for the light switch. He found it and the fluorescent fittings above our heads flashed staccato bursts of light as the gas in the tubes failed to ionise. It was like a badly timed strobe show in a nightclub. The pitch black punctuated with pulses of bright white light. I watched the faltering figure shuffle to the centre of the room, his arms outstretched, groping at the space in front of him.

'Mrs Macklam, it's Barry,' he repeated himself. 'Are you there?'

I kept my eyes fixed on Canning, reached up with my gloved hand and flicked the switch. The big industrial lawn mower roared into life, filling the room with a cacophony of sound.

'Mrs Macklam?' Canning called out. He took a few tentative steps towards the noise. 'Is that you?'

I ran forward and shoved him in the back with all my might. He toppled forwards, flailing his hands in the air to arrest his fall.

Later that night, Canning left the home in an ambulance and never came back. The upturned mower removed all but three of his fingers, his right ear and most of his cheek. And almost severed his right arm at the elbow.

There was a police investigation and we were all questioned, but I had a watertight alibi – I had been playing chess with my brother. We received a sound telling off from the housekeeper because that time of night was way past our bedtime, but the police left us alone after that. My brother and I never spoke about the events of that evening, we didn't have to. The only thing that mattered was Barry Canning never bothered us again.

Chapter 4

My name is Billy Ellwood or Billy Raymond or Billy Osmond… take your pick. I answer to any of them, or at least I did once upon a time. Now, I'm Billy Wright; a fifty-year-old man with a mind-numbing job, no wife, no kids and no significant other – whenever it looks like someone is in danger of becoming *significant*, I break it off.

I'm sitting in my car in an open-air car park which looks like a bomb site. Potholes the size of lunar craters pepper the surface. I glance into the rear-view mirror, Jade glares back at me.

'You're having second thoughts, aren't you,' she sneers through her black painted lips.

'There's a lot to think about.'

'Rubbish! There's nothing to think about.'

'I'm just saying…'

I shake my head and stare out of the window at the Birmingham skyline shrouded in light mist and rain. The same shitty weather as the day I left.

Jade's heavily made-up eyes narrow to slits. It's a look she tends to adopt when she's annoyed with me, which at the moment is most of the time. 'Don't bloody bottle this.'

'I have no intention of bottling it, all right!' I snap back. 'This is not straightforward, that's all. There's a lot to think about.'

'The only thing you're thinking about is that damned promise. That was eighteen years ago. Eighteen bloody years ago! Now I know moving on is not your strong suit… but… really?'

'Piss off.'

'Charming! Don't get angry with me, get angry with them.'

'I am angry.'

'Doesn't look like it. You look like a rabbit caught in headlights, like a kid who's sulking cos he's not been picked to play football, like a–'

'Shut the fuck up, Jade.' I yank on the door handle and step from my car, tugging my collar around my ears. It feels strange being back on my old stomping ground and not in a good way.

The buildings cut a very different silhouette against the skyline to what I remember. It would appear a team of architects have had a field day creating structures that look more like works of art rather than places to live and work. I try to block out the memories of the last time I was here – it's not working.

I stomp across the car park, avoiding the puddles, and enter The Mailbox. A fabulous building filled with shops, restaurants and bars. Something for everyone. It's a country mile from the time when it served as the Royal Mail sorting office. And another country mile away from the building I last saw when I got in my car and drove north all those years ago.

Two sets of escalators carry me to the second floor and I spot Caffé Nero on the right. I check my watch, I'm early. My heart is thumping in my chest. I'm out of practice.

I clock him, walking up the steps at the far end, heading towards me. He hasn't changed a bit. A little greyer around the temples and thicker around the waist, but other than that he looks the same. He still walks with the aid of a stick, the product of falling from a roof which shattered one of his knees. His eyes are bright and alive, raking the faces of the people milling about. He sees me and looks away. I weave my way between the shoppers to the café. He gets there first and joins the queue at the counter. I walk past to find a table at the back, picking up a newspaper as I go.

I pretend to read the headlines, all the while checking out the customers around me. After five minutes he pushes a black coffee across the table and slides into the seat next to me, both of us facing the door – old habits die hard.

'Hey, Rick,' I say, reaching for the cup.

'Hello, Billy. Are you wearing the same coat?' he replies, removing his own.

'Cheeky bastard.' I fold the paper and place it onto the empty table next to us.

'Good to see you.'

'You too.' Our eyes lock and it's like it all happened yesterday. The years melt away and a shiver runs through me, I feel the onset of tears stinging my eyes.

'This is not a good idea,' he says.

'Since when did that ever stop us.'

'Ha, yeah, you're right there. How have you been?'

'I have more good days than bad. How did you get on?' I waste no time.

'Christ, is that the end of the pleasantries?'

'You and I were never pleasant.'

'Right again.'

'So?'

'You got to understand I've been out of the game for five years now, it's not that easy.'

'Don't give me that bollocks. You can pull in more favours than a ten quid hooker. What have you got?' I ignore his preliminary excuses.

'It's not them.'

'Go on.'

'The Critchley firm is non-existent. The younger brother is serving out his time in Wakefield prison and the elder brother is dead. He developed cancer and when he died the whole enterprise fell apart. The clubs have either been taken over by new owners or flattened to make way for developers. The foot soldiers have dispersed into other gangs or disappeared altogether. They've not done any serious business for years.'

'Shit,' I say under my breath. 'Are you *sure*?' My companion looks at me with his very best *fuck off* face. It was a stupid question.

'It's my turn,' he asks.

'Okay.'

'How do you know it's him? My sources tell me the body hasn't been identified.'

'I just know. It made the local news and was picked up by the nationals, as soon as I saw the report… I knew.'

'Does that mean you've been in touch?' he asks, which is my cue to give him *my* very best *fuck off* face. 'Jesus Christ, Billy, what were you thinking?'

'I was thinking I'd given up enough and didn't want to go through the rest of my life not seeing him. We were careful.'

'How did it work?'

'I would book a couple of seats at the cinema for a specific date and time and mail him a ticket. If he couldn't make it he'd send it back, if he didn't we would meet and chat for a couple of hours, then he'd go home.'

'Did anyone else know?'

'No.'

'How did you–'

'He didn't carry anything with his name on it and no phone. Cash only, public transport, you know the drill.'

'Well someone knew he was there.'

'That's why I thought of them.'

'What was the last thing I said to you?'

'I remember it well, but it was easy to say, difficult to do. And besides, that was a lifetime ago.'

'I didn't say it would be easy, I said it was the right thing to do.'

I stare at him. I'd seen that look in his eyes before. 'What is it?'

'Nothing.'

'Spit it out. I've known you too long.'

'I don't want you to get hurt.'

'Thank you for your concern… now what is it?'

'The Critchleys are gone but not all the foot soldiers disappeared. Do you remember they had a cocky shit working for them? Really fancied himself as an old-style gangster.'

I crook my head to one side. 'Where are you going with this?'

'He fell off the grid and resurfaced a few years back. He's now the enforcer for another gang.'

'I'm listening.'

'He's turned up in Blackpool.' The comment stops me in my tracks. My face must have said it all.

'Where?'

'Billy, you need to be careful.'

'Where do I find him?'

'It won't be him.'

'Where do I find him?'

'You know I can't–'

'You owe me.' I lean in close and spit the words into his ear.

'I can't say.' He drains his mug and folds his coat over his arm. 'I told you once before and I'm telling you again – don't.'

He shakes my hand and when I pull away he's deposited a square of folded paper in my palm. I wait until he leaves and unwrap it.

Fucking hell.

I head back to Blackpool with Rick's words ringing in my ears.

Chapter 5

DCI Dan Bagley had been parachuted into Lancashire's CID unit from GMP to assist with a murder case. Though Kray preferred to substitute the word 'assist' with the phrase 'almost fuck up'.

He wasn't a Detective Chief Inspector when he arrived but with the help of his buddy Assistant Chief Constable Mary Quade he quickly gained promotion. A promotion which should have gone to Kray. She didn't bear grudges but on this occasion she made an exception.

Bagley's relationship with Kray had descended into open hostility, ever since she had decided not to heed his advice and move to another department. It made for a fractious existence which Kray was willing to suffer, because she knew that every day she came to work it pissed him off.

Bagley checked his watch, impatient to start the meeting, but Kray was late. She was in her office with Tavener who looked like he'd been awarded a D for his homework.

'Lying!' Tavener screwed up his face.

'Oh, come on, Duncan, what's wrong with your radar today?'

'I didn't think anything was wrong with it. Why do you think she's lying?'

'We are being asked to believe that her husband has a ton of friends and yet he goes to football games on his jack. I mean, when you go to the pub with your mates what do you talk about?'

'Erm, I don't know, it depends.'

'I bet you talk about women and football.'

'Excuse me, but isn't that a little stereotypical? We talk about the state of the economy and discuss our feelings, if you must know.'

'Okay, okay, let's not use you as an example in case you report me to HR. Hypothetically speaking, a typical bloke will say, "I'm off to the footie, does anyone fancy it?" and if he doesn't offer, one of them will say, "I'll come along".'

'I suppose they might.'

'And when I asked her what her husband might be doing in Blackpool she answered "*I've never been to Blackpool*" and then went on a rant, hoping I would drop that line of questioning.'

'That's right, she did.'

'Have we got our hands on the CCTV from the areas surrounding North Beach train station?'

'Not yet. I've put in the request and we should have it later today.'

'Let's revisit the enquiries we made with the yacht and boating clubs when we first found the body on the beach. Whoever turfed him overboard had an ocean-going vessel. We have a mugshot of the victim now and a better timeline, it might jog someone's memory.'

'Okay, I'll pull the files.'

'What the hell was he doing here?'

'And what has Miriam Ellwood got to hide?'

'I don't know but I'm going to find out. I have to go to this bloody meeting with Bagley. See what you can dig up.'

Kray pushed open the door to Bagley's office and took her seat. This was a gathering of his direct reports, where they discussed their current caseload. For Bagley, it was his way of maintaining a command and control management style while creaming off the good news to feed into the ear of ACC Quade.

He opened the meeting with, 'Nice of you to join us, Roz.' Kray ignored the dig. 'Okay, let's go around the table, starting with you, Colin.'

Kray hated Bagley's office, not solely because it contained Bagley, but his desk was always a mess. Papers, pens and pencils littered the surface. She had to steel herself from stacking the papers into neat piles while gathering the pens on one side of the desk and the pencils on the other.

Everyone knows you don't mix them together.

She tried to avoid looking at the clutter of boxes and files in the corner, but her eyes were drawn to it as if it were a car crash. Sitting in Bagley's office sent her OCD off the scale.

DI Colin Brownlow was not so much coasting to retirement, rather he was approaching it with all the vigour of an injured snail. These meetings were a challenge for him because he had to make the equivalent of three days' work sound like a packed to-do list.

Brownlow plodded through his report; the drone of his voice caused Kray's concentration to drift. She pictured herself walking along the promenade in the sunshine. A gurgling bundle of joy was cooing at her with a shock of dark hair that stood straight up, Gary Rhodes style. Chris had one arm around her waist and the other pushing the pram. He was smiling, she was smiling…

'Thanks, Colin. Judith, what have you got this week?' Bagley always called Kray last, yet another subliminal dig.

Kray snapped back to the present and found she was unconsciously rubbing her belly under the desk. The next two people gave succinct accounts of what they were working on while Kray fixated over the muddled position of the pens and pencils.

'Right, Roz, what do you have?'

'We're wrapping up the last of the loose ends with the Alex Jarrod case.' The mention of the name made Bagley wince. It was the last big case the department had handled and it had not gone well.

'Can't we make short work of that? It's been going on for months,' he said.

Yes, with good fucking reason. If you'd listened to me in the first place, instead of having us chase our arses, we might have…

'Yes, sir, we are on the final stretch now.' Kray refused to rise to the bait. 'We also have a development with the unidentified body that washed up on the beach. His name is Michael Ellwood, he comes from Manchester and his wife identified his body this morning–'

'Wasn't he the guy who'd been tortured and shot in the head?' Bagley asked.

'Yes, that's him. He came up on GMP's missing person list and they joined the dots.'

'What did the wife have to say?'

'She said her husband was supposed to be at a football match on the day he disappeared, but for some reason which she cannot explain, he winds up taking a train to Blackpool.'

'What do you think?'

'She's hiding something. The way she answered our questions–'

'It will be drugs.'

'What? There was something not right, sir, but I'm not sure–'

'Mark my words. Whoever did it subjected him to the carbonated chilli treatment, which is a copybook technique. She'll be covering for his involvement in drugs.'

'I'm not sure about that…'

'What did he do for a living?'

'He ran a small garage.'

'Perfect for laundering money. I'm telling you, get the Drug Squad up to speed.'

'But sir, I'm going to interview her again shortly and she may throw new light on why he was here.'

'That's fine, have your interview, then get drugs involved. That's our best course of action.'

'I think we should–'

'Is there anything else from anyone?' Bagley scanned the faces around the table, avoiding eye contact with Kray. 'Okay. Let's have a good week.'

The others rose from the table. Kray remained seated and stared at her notebook while Bagley gathered his things and left.

Kray met Tavener on his way to the interview room.

'How did you get on?' he asked.

'Not good. Bagley is convinced there is a drug connection. I understand why he would jump to that conclusion but Miriam doesn't fit. What did you find out?'

'Not much more than we already know. Michael Ellwood has been running his garage for twelve years. It makes a modest profit. He's got two teenage kids that live at home, both are in college and Miriam works in an admin job at the local primary school.'

'GMP said he was clean, did you find anything to suggest he was up to no good?'

'Nothing.'

'Social media?'

'Again, nothing out of the ordinary. Sorry, Roz.'

They entered the interview room to find Miriam Ellwood sitting in the same seat they had left her in earlier.

'Did you grab a bite to eat?' asked Kray.

'I did thanks, I think I needed it,' replied Ellwood. 'Am I... am I under arrest?'

'No, Miriam, you're helping us with our enquiries into your husband's death.'

'I've told you everything I know.'

'Can you start from the beginning. I hate to be a pain but I want to get it straight.'

Ellwood let out a sigh and repeated what she had said about the football game and how she had no idea why her husband should have ended up in Blackpool, even less why someone would want to kill him. Kray leaned back in her chair when she had finished.

'Thank you for going through that again, Miriam. I wonder if you could help me further?'

'I'm not sure there's anything more I can add.'

'You see, I have three big unanswered questions: Why was your husband killed in a manner that looked like a drug cartel execution? And what was he doing in Blackpool?'

Ellwood looked at Kray and swallowed hard. 'As I said before, I have no idea.' She paused, then said, 'That's only two.'

'The third one is… what are you not telling us?'

'What! I've told you everything.'

'So you said, Miriam, but I think you're holding out. I think you know more than you're letting on.'

'This is absurd.'

'I think you know why your husband was in Blackpool. You know because this wasn't the first time he made the trip, was it, Miriam?'

'How dare you! I've told you all I know and you are calling me a liar – on the day I identified the body of my dead husband.' Ellwood jumped to her feet.

'I'm sorry, Miriam, this must be difficult. But surely you want to help us catch the people who killed him?'

'Of course I do.'

'Then tell us what Michael was doing in Blackpool.'

Ellwood picked her coat off the back of her chair and leaned over the desk.

'I… don't… fucking… know.' She marched out of the room and clip-clopped her way down the hallway.

Tavener and Kray watched through the window as she crossed the concourse to her waiting car.

'You're right,' said Tavener.

'About what?'

'She's lying through her back teeth.' Tavener's phone rang. 'DC Tavener… Oh yes, thanks for calling back… that would be fine… thank you, we'll see you then.'

'Something good?'

'Get your coat, we're off to see a Commodore.' He gathered up his things and hurried out of the interview room.

'Off to see the Commodores?'

Chapter 6

I *graduated* from the care system and, after a series of downbeat jobs, joined the army at the age of eighteen. They didn't care that I had more personalities than a jobbing stage actor. It hurt to leave my brother but he had got himself a handful of qualifications and wound up with an apprenticeship to become a motor mechanic. He was settled – I wasn't. The army was like a breath of fresh air. It felt weird to meet people who welcomed me with open arms.

Signing up heralded the only period in my life where I didn't feel the need to blend in to protect myself. They didn't give a shit who I was and keeping myself safe was easy – they gave me guns to play with.

Who knew I had a talent for weaponry? From handguns to assault rifles, grenade launchers to mortars, if it went bang – I was good at it. Then one day our commanding officer summoned everyone together and declared that Operation Granby had kicked off in response to Saddam Hussein invading Iraq. From that moment I became one of the fifty-three thousand British troops shipped off to liberate Kuwait City.

I was dispatched to Saudi Arabia to live in a Portakabin just outside Jubail to acclimatise, and was later flown into Iraq. I loved it. After all, getting up in the morning into an environment where people wanted to do me harm was what I was used to. Even the fear of someone shouting, 'Gas… gas… gas!' I took in my stride.

I made friends with a guy from Bristol called Speedy. You know how some people have a trembling leg, that pumps up and down even when they are relaxed? Well Speedy's whole body did that. I swear the only time Speedy would be at rest is two weeks after his death. And having a conversation with him was like watching a chicken peck at corn.

I liked Speedy because, like me, he was different.

We muddled along happily, then everything changed when we had a new guy join us – Captain Mark Wilkins. He was a bright young thing not much older than me, a product of Oxford and Sandhurst, and determined to make a name for himself – a regular go-getter. He was as keen as English mustard and expected everyone else to be the same.

Me and Speedy had other ideas: *Bollocks to that.*

Wilkins was assigned to our team and started throwing his weight around straightaway. We received fresh orders and were deployed to guard a group of prisoners of war. The Iraqis were surrendering in their droves due to them being poorly equipped and on the brink of starvation.

It took us two and a half days to reach the makeshift camp. Two and a half days of being bounced around in the back of a truck, listening to the incessant drivel of Captain Whiz-Bang who insisted on giving us our orders over and over again, even though we had not reached our destination. This guy was getting on my tits.

We arrived, tired and travel-sick at the compound. The site housed two hundred and twenty Iraqi soldiers. They were in bad shape, having spent months living in holes in the ground. Some were nursing infected wounds, others were sick and they were all malnourished. Our job was to look after them until the Americans built a POW camp in which to house them, but that was some way off into the future. The deployment was looking like it was going to be a walk in the park, the POWs were no trouble. They had had enough of war and at least they were being fed.

I could see weeks of happy boredom stretching out in front of me. A time spent sorting out our kit, writing letters home and getting a tan. But Captain Whiz-Bang had other ideas. He said we had to go out on patrol – which was not only a complete waste of time but took a lot of preparation and was fucking dangerous. The place was littered with anti-personnel mines and there had been reports of rogue groups of Iraqis in the area. This was not good. I remember thinking, as I geared myself up to leave the compound for the third time in three days: *The way this is going, Captain Whiz-Bang is going to get me and Speedy killed.*

Then one day, two interesting things happened: I found something sticking out of the earth while out on one of our walkabouts and learned an interesting fact about Whiz-Bang.

I hatched a plan with Speedy, which proved to be more of a challenge than I had anticipated.

'Tell me what I have to say?' Speedy asked for the umpteenth time.

'Not a lot, let me do the talking,' I replied.

'Okay. Run it past me again.'

After pulling out most of my hair, Speedy had it sorted. We were both sitting in the shade with our backs to a wall, drinking tea. Whiz-Bang came over.

'I'm telling you, Speedy, I heard it and then I saw it,' I said.

'You are fucking joking me,' Speedy replied right on cue.

'I'm telling you it was a Grey Francolin, I swear to God.'

'You lucky bastard.'

'I know, right? A Grey Francolin, it was as close to me as you are now. Oh, good afternoon, sir,' I said as Whiz-Bang approached.

'Hi guys, what was that you were saying about a Grey Francolin?'

'I saw one when I was out on patrol,' I said.

'You sure?'

'At first, I heard it calling, *tee… tee… tee*, and I thought, *No way*! Then I saw it. I couldn't believe my eyes. The boys back at the club are going to be so jealous.'

'That's amazing,' said Speedy, remembering his lines.

'But the Grey Francolin is indigenous to north west India and Pakistan. Are you sure you saw one all the way down here?'

'Scout's honour.' I gave a three-finger salute. 'Are you a twitcher, sir?'

'Man and boy. I would love to see a Grey Francolin, because…'
He was hooked.

An overheard conversation and a few calls back home, and I had Captain Whiz-Bang eating out of the palm of my hand. He rabbited on about the rare birds he had seen and how he had his own hide. He banged on for ages. Then he said the words I wanted to hear.

'I don't suppose you could take me out to where you spotted it, could you?'

'I'd be delighted. It's a real treat to share this with a fellow bird enthusiast. Do you fancy coming along, Speedy?'

'To what?'

'To see if we can find the Grey Francolin?'

'The Grey what?' Speedy had reached the end of his useful contribution. I stepped in quickly to avoid blowing the charade.

'That would be great. When do you want to go?' I said, leading Whiz-Bang far away from Speedy. We made arrangements to head out later that day when it was cooler.

Captain Whiz-Bang was like a kid on Christmas morning as we kitted ourselves with binoculars and field gear and walked out of camp. He talked incessantly about his hobby; there was no need for me to contribute at all. Which was just as well because I only knew about one bird. Who would have thought it? A degree from Oxford, a family lineage in the armed forces as long as your arm and a die-hard twitcher. What were the chances?

We walked half a mile across rough terrain, criss-crossed with shallow trenches. I sunk into a crouch position.

'Did you hear that?' I whispered.

'No.'

'I'm sure I heard it.'

'Trouble is the damned things are so well camouflaged.' He crouched down beside me and we scanned the ground.

'Maybe it was just wishful thinking.' I stood up and pressed on. I could feel my companion fizzing with excitement.

The sun was casting long shadows across the shale and sand, and the heat of the day was fading fast.

'Shit!' I hissed under my breath.

'Can you see it?'

'I can see movement.'

'Where, where?' He grabbed his binoculars.

'Fuck, not the bird. Iraqis. I think they've spotted us.'

'Where are they?'

'Towards that ridge.' I pointed into the middle distance. 'We need to find cover.'

'In here.' Captain Whiz-Bang launched himself into a trench that ran to our left and scurried along the bottom. I sunk to the floor and covered my head.

The dull thud of the pressure wave hurt my ears. Rocks and soil showered around me. The explosion sent Whiz-Bang cartwheeling in the air – his torso one way and his legs another.

Then there was silence, apart from the ringing in my ears.

I had spotted the exposed tops of mines while out on patrol. They had briefed us not to enter into enemy trenches because many of them were booby-trapped. I guess Captain Whiz-Bang hadn't got the memo.

The sound of the explosion alerted the camp and I called it in. As I waited for them to arrive it occurred to me that I'd had enough of army life and decided it was time to do something different. When they reached us, they were shocked to find that Whiz-Bang was dead.

We got back to base and I gave a stellar performance, recounting the unfortunate events that had led up to the untimely demise of Captain Mark Wilkins. By the end of the following week I had worked out what I wanted to do when I left the army – in the end it was a relatively easy decision. My mind was made up.

Then me and Speedy settled down and spent the rest of our time at the detention camp checking our kit, writing letters and getting a tan.

Chapter 7

I waved goodbye to the army and kind of fell into the police. It seemed a natural progression at the time, though in hindsight, I think that was just me lying to myself... again.

I worked a couple of years in uniform, passed my exams and progressed into CID. I enjoyed detective work, it kept my mind busy – leaving me less time to obsess about whether or not I was fitting in.

That's when I met Blythe.

She worked in a police staff role and we clicked straightaway. You know how sometimes you can look at a member of the opposite sex and go, 'Hell, yes!' Well, up to then I had never experienced that feeling. But when I clapped eyes on Blythe it went off in my head like a grenade.

She was bright, funny, pretty and way out of my league. And that's when my demons came back with a vengeance.

How the hell am I ever going to be good enough for her? Being me isn't enough.

I began to morph into the person I thought she would find interesting, creating a new 'Please like me and be my girlfriend' persona. To my surprise it worked. Not only did we start dating but I enjoyed being the new me. I became bright and funny too, though I could never match her in the 'looks' department.

We moved in together and got married. I was happy, she was happy. I got promoted a couple of times and after a few years ended up in the Drug Squad. A motley band of individuals, each of us sticking our finger in the dyke trying to stem the tide of heroin, cannabis and cocaine washing through our patch. It was a thankless job. Then my Superintendent came to me one day and said, 'They're setting up a new team, Ellwood, and I think you should go for it.'

'Oh, why's that, guv?'

'Because you're a scruffy git.'

'A scruffy git?'

'Yeah, I haven't read the briefing properly but that seems to be one of the main selection criteria.'

'Okay, as I'm so well qualified, why not?' And that was it – two weeks later my transfer came through.

Nowadays, candidates go through a rigorous selection process, which includes psychological suitability testing, security vetting, an assessment centre, along with a variety of written and role play exercises. How times have changed – I got the job because I was scruffy.

Nevertheless, I was like a pig in shit. For the first time my talents were being put to good use and I could legitimately create a new persona and get paid for it. I was a rising star.

I was deployed on several operations and got the reputation for being the best in the force. Then I landed the biggest job they had on their patch – the Critchley brothers. It was *the* big-ticket investigation and I was going all out to make it a success.

But the Critchley job was different. Little did I know my life was about to be torn apart at the seams.

It was the winter of 1998. A time when the fashions were different, the music was better and video games didn't scare the shit out of you. The late nineties heralded a period in society where the gulf between the haves and have-nots grew to become a chasm, and the north–south divide kicked in with a vengeance. Needless to say, I found myself playing on the side of the have-nots.

I was standing inside the club entrance when I saw them coming and I can remember thinking *this is gonna hurt.* I had been expecting a return visit but had not expected the main man to show up in person.

His name was Winston Carlyle but he was known as Ton-Up due to his passion for racing cars around housing estates. He was exactly like the photographs I had seen, dressed in a sharp suit and cowboy boots, looking more like an extra from an eighties pop video rather than a mid-level drug dealer with his eyes on the big time. He was flanked by two burley men, both of them sporting an exaggerated gangster walk, shaven heads and sunglasses. They looked like a pair of caricature bookends.

A gaggle of young women were making a right racket outside, waiting for more of their friends to show up. It was too early for any serious clubber to avail themselves of our entertainment. I glanced at my watch, it said 10.38pm.

'Yo bro, you said no!' Carlyle sang the words at me, emphasising the rhyme as he approached. The two gorillas rolled their heads back with laughter.

'Come on, Ton-Up, we don't want any trouble,' Eddie Marshall said in his croaky voice, walking out to meet them with his arms outstretched. Eddie and I had worked together for six weeks. He was in his late twenties and built like a Marvel comic hero. He was an obnoxious, mouthy shit with one major flaw – his personality.

'My man TJ was polite and he said please, but your "new boy" said no. That's not nice,' Ton-Up said as one of the bald heads nodded in agreement.

I remembered TJ from the previous week. At the time, he told me he'd be back and I believed him.

'You know the rules, no drugs in the club,' Marshall said, blocking their path.

'Are you shitting me? I could walk in there now and get whatever I want. I was paying you the courtesy of asking permission. I always believe in doing business in a courteous manner.'

I pushed the red button behind the door and stepped out to join them. The tight knot of women had stopped cackling, choosing instead to gawp at the floorshow unfolding before them while putting a safe distance between themselves and the mounting tension.

'TJ *was* polite when he asked permission,' I said, 'and I was *equally* polite when I declined his offer. So it seems to me we were both polite.'

Ton-Up slid his sunglasses down his nose and glared at me. 'I was talking to this gentleman. It's rude to interrupt.'

'No one else was speaking, so I hardly interrupted.'

'I think "new boy" is being rude again,' the big guy with the Uncle Fester head growled at me.

'Not at all, I was merely pointing out that I hadn't interrupted, in the same way as I pointed out to you last week that we had a zero drugs policy at the club. In a polite way of course.' I stared at TJ.

All three removed their sunglasses.

'Now you're being insolent,' Ton-Up said, turning to face me. 'You said *no* to TJ, so I'm going to ask you nicely. I want–'

'The answer is still no,' I said, not waiting for him to finish. 'Now that… was an interruption.'

Ton-Up shoved me and TJ grabbed my shoulder. I took half a step back and stamped my foot into TJ's knee, sending him crumpling to the ground. He yelped, grasping at his buckled leg. Uncle Fester threw a haymaker which landed high on Marshall's head, but he failed to see the fist arcing upwards to connect with a crack under his chin.

Ton-Up blindsided me, punching me in the face. My nose went snap. His arms were windmilling in the air, landing blows on my back and shoulders. I can remember thinking *for a big guy he hits like a girl.*

I straightened up and crunched my elbow into his jaw. A torrent of air rasped from his mouth when my knee drove deep into the pit of his stomach.

TJ was back on his feet, staggering around on one leg. My right foot swept his good leg from under him and he once more clattered to the floor.

The women started shrieking as their sideshow took a turn for the worse.

Marshall had Uncle Fester in a headlock trying to wrestle him to the ground. But the big guy was too strong. He picked Marshall up and tossed him over his shoulder like a kid's toy.

Ton-Up was crouched down, trying to catch his breath. My knee slammed into his face and he catapulted backwards, landing in the road like he'd been laid to rest on a mortician's slab, his glazed eyes staring up at the streetlights.

Uncle Fester was standing over Marshall, blood running from his gaping mouth, stomping for all he was worth. Marshall was rolling on the floor trying to avoid the piston-like movement of the size thirteen boot.

The inside of my forearm caught Fester full in the throat and he staggered backwards. The sole of my shoe smashed into his chest, sending him toppling over. I leapt on top, my fists bouncing off his skull.

I felt a pair of hands grip my shoulders, dragging me off.

'That's enough, Billy, he's had enough.' The hands pulled me back to the club. I saw three other guys dressed in suits, one helping Marshall to his feet while the other two were attending to Ton-Up and TJ.

'You get inside, we'll deal with this.' Rolo was head of security, an older guy with a fearsome reputation. I did as I was told.

I shot through a set of double doors; the room pulsated to the sound of synthetic drums, a handful of people were propping up the bar. The dance floor was empty. I turned right up a flight of stairs to the offices on the first floor where there was a small kitchen area. A man was sitting drinking tea. He jumped when he saw me.

'Here, let me get this.' He cleared coats from a hard-backed chair and I dumped myself onto it. He left his drink and disappeared downstairs. The door opened and Marshall entered, looking dazed. I got up and swilled a couple of tea towels under the tap, handing one over.

'Hold this tight,' I said, pointing to his bloodied eye.

Marshall winced as the material rubbed against the open wound.

'Good job your beak was already broken,' he said, checking me out.

I hung my head over the sink and pinched the bridge of my nose; blood ran onto the stainless steel and spiralled down the plughole.

Rolo appeared in the doorway. 'What the hell happened?'

'They were out for a fight,' replied Marshall.

'I know that, I mean what happened?'

'The guy called TJ showed up last week and asked if I would allow him into the club with a pocket full of tabs if I took a cut from the proceeds. I told him the club had a zero tolerance for drugs and ordered him to leave,' I said, trying to stem the bleeding.

'What happened then?' asked Rolo.

'He got shitty and flounced off saying he'd be back. I told him he wasn't fucking Arnold Schwarzenegger and that was it. Then he turns up today with his mates. Don't know who they are but they didn't like what I'd said.'

'And you didn't think to let me know?' asked Rolo.

'Sorry, I didn't think much of it at the time.'

'Look, you're new and learning the ropes. The next time anything like that happens, I want to hear about it right away, is that clear?'

'Yup, sorry.'

'We will keep the police out of it, none of us wants that.'

'Hey, thanks for that,' said Marshall, mopping his eye.

'For what?' I asked.

'For getting that big guy off me.'

'It's nothing.'

Rolo flicked his head to the side and said to Marshall, 'Can you give us a minute?'

Marshall nodded and walked out, closing the door behind him.

'You handled yourself well,' said Rolo.

'Yeah, I've done a bit in the past. Who the hell were they?'

'The man with the big mouth is called Ton-Up, he's a dealer who thinks he's the Cali Cartel. The other two are his strong men. You did the right thing telling him to take a hike.'

'That's good to hear, I was beginning to think I hadn't.'

Rolo clicked his tongue against the roof of his mouth.

'Do you want to earn some extra cash?'

Chapter 8

Kray parked in a slot marked for visitors and they both got out. The breeze was coming off the Irish Sea, hurtling up the river Wyre from Fleetwood with the sole intention of chilling them to the bone. The metallic clanking of rigging striking against the tall masts filled the air.

In front of them stood a modern two-storey building with the words Blackpool Marina Yacht Club emblazoned across it. Kray was showing her frustration, having just spent the entire journey trying to justify her earlier confusion.

'So, when you said–'

'Nope, never heard of them,' repeated Tavener.

'You must have. They sang "Three Times A Lady".' Tavener pursed his lips, shaking his head. 'I can't believe you've never heard of the… ah, I give up, what's the name of the guy we've come to see?' Kray said over the roof of the car.

'Commodore Chuck Bateman, he runs the club.'

They walked across to the main entrance, Tavener pointed to the CCTV cameras. 'That's a good start.'

They pushed open the door and stepped inside. The place was open plan with pale laminate wood covering the floor and whitewashed walls. Plaques and award certificates adorned the walls along with a roll of honour announcing the committee membership. To the right there was a large hall with a bar at one end and tables clustered around a dance floor.

Tavener reached for his phone, but before he had a chance to dial the number, they heard footsteps coming down a flight of stairs. Their eyes widened as the man strode towards them.

'Hi, I'm Commodore Chuck Bateman. You must be the police officer I spoke to earlier.'

Tavener regained control of his bottom jaw. 'Hi, Mr Bateman, thank you for seeing us at short notice. This is DI Kray.' Kray nodded hello.

'Welcome to our yacht club,' Bateman continued. 'We had you chaps around a few weeks ago, something to do with that terrible incident of a man washing up on the beach.'

'Yes, it is connected, Mr Bateman. Can we ask you a few questions?'

'Of course, I have an office upstairs, follow me.'

Bateman was a rotund gentleman in his fifties with a white beard and white hair, tufts of which protruded from beneath a sailor's cap with gold braiding on the peak.

Tavener mouthed the words, *Captain Birdseye.*

Kray mouthed the words, *don't you dare.*

Bateman's office was sparsely furnished with a huge panoramic window looking out onto the boats moored against the jetties. He ushered them to take a seat.

'How can I help?'

'Have you ever seen this man?' Tavener held up his phone showing a picture of Michael Ellwood.

Bateman shook his head, causing his hat to wobble. 'No, sorry.'

'Have you heard the name Michael Ellwood? Maybe one of your members might have mentioned him?'

'No, never heard that name before. Sorry.'

'How many members do you have, Mr Bateman?' Kray asked.

'About eight hundred.'

'That's a lot.'

'We cater for all types of vessels from dinghies to cabin cruisers and everything
in-between. Our membership is growing.'

'We noticed you have CCTV, does it cover all the moorings?'

'I'm afraid not. We have over three hundred boats here now and have not upgraded the system to cover everywhere.'

'If I remember correctly from your previous statement, you don't keep logs detailing when owners take their boats out?'

'That's right, but what we do have are these.' Bateman pushed a stack of paper across the table towards Kray. 'This is a register of our members, the names of their boats, the types of vessel and how long they have been a member of the club. You're welcome to take it with you.'

Kray scanned the sheaf of papers. 'Thank you. Are all the boats listed here capable of going out to sea?'

'Oh no, many of them are strictly river vessels.'

'Could you indicate which ones are ocean-going?'

Bateman frowned and reached for a highlighter pen. 'I suppose so.'

While he had his head down working through the list, Kray took the opportunity to slope off in order to look around. There were two conference rooms on the first floor plus a small kitchen area. The rooms were decked out with modern tables and chairs. She poked around, finding nothing of interest.

Tavener was looking out of the window at the wooden jetties protruding out into the river like bony fingers; each one had a boat moored against it. To the right was what looked like an engineering works where boats were sitting on massive cradles. In the centre was a huge cabin cruiser.

'What's that boat?' asked Tavener.

'Which one?'

'The big one, out of the water.'

'Oh, that's the Marine Blue, a forty-footer. The biggest boat in the club.'

'It looks like it. How much would that cost?'

'That depends on how she is fitted out, but you would expect to part with the thick end of a quarter of a million.'

'Wow! Why is it in dry dock?'

'She's having her bottom cleaned.'

'What?'

'Sorry, it's a nautical joke. Every year vessels have to be cleaned below the waterline, the only way to do it is to have them on dry land.'

'How long does it take?'

'Depends on how dirty she is.'

'How long has that one been in dry dock?'

'She had to undergo repairs and maintenance so it's been about a month and a half now. Here, I've marked the vessels suitable to sail into open waters.' He slid the wad of papers across the table.'

Kray appeared and picked it up. 'Thank you.'

'Is there anything else I can help you with?'

'No, we have to go, Mr Bateman.' Kray passed her phone to Tavener for him to read what was on the screen. 'If we think of anything we will give you a call.'

'Always glad to help,' he said, showing them out.

They shook hands in reception and walked back to the car. Kray fastened her seatbelt.

'You okay to tag along?' she asked.

'Yes, I could do with getting out of the office for a while. Do you know the phrase they use when they clean a boat below the waterline? It's really funny.'

'I doubt it.'

Kray sped from the car park heading for Manchester. The warrant had come through to search Ellwood's garage.

Chapter 9

I'm back in Blackpool, trying to ignore Rick's parting words while lurking on a street corner with a good view of the Paragon nightclub. It's spelled with the middle A denoted as a capital letter and inverted in the centre of the word, another piece of genius marketing that goes right over my head.

The pubs are rammed and there must be twenty people in the queue waiting for their chance to get in. I can't believe how busy the place is. Since when did Thursday stop being a school night?

Seeing Rick again was a distraction I could do without. I need to focus. The problem is, try as I might, Marshall keeps barging his way into my thoughts.

In his day, Marshall was a handful. Long before it was popular to put two men in a cage and tell them to kill each other, he had forged a formidable reputation through bare-knuckle fighting. He had first appeared on our radar when he killed a man; a Romany who went by the name of Tyrol. He was a monster of a human being with a four stone advantage over Marshall.

A thumping left hook to the head dislodged Tyrol's optic nerve in the first round which meant he didn't see the punch coming in the second. It slammed into the side of his head and his brain did a little dance against the inside of his skull. He died eight hours later in hospital. Marshall went home with the one hundred pounds prize money and, two weeks later, Tyrol went home in a casket.

When the police investigated the death, they were greeted with a wall of silence; no one had seen anything and Marshall walked away to fight another day. That was until a bunch of Tyrol's relatives came to visit and smashed him in the throat with a pickaxe handle. He survived but never fought for money again – well, not in the ring anyway.

I drag myself away from thinking about Eddie bloody Marshall and assess my position. This is proving to be a challenge. The difficulty is I need to be in two places at once. My car is parked around the back facing the rear entrance, where there is an area of hardstanding for the delivery wagons to pick up and drop off the booze, plus a set of huge bins along the side. The problem is, while I'm watching the front, I have no idea what is happening around the back.

It's cold and the wind whips through the streets plunging the thermometer down further. Still, at least it is not raining.

The door staff are dressed in their regulation bomber jackets and black trousers with fluorescent identification badges around their arms. They are kept busy by the raucous line of people, who for some reason are dressed like it's the middle of summer. The grand entrance is a dazzling display of lights to entice people inside. I scan the faces of the door staff, none of them are him. I take pictures anyway – it's strange how fieldcraft never leaves you.

Shit, it's started raining.

I push myself off the wall and head around the back, getting into my car. The back of the club looks dirty and worn out, a façade quite at odds with the glitz and glamour of the front.

'I'm freezing my tits off.' Jade is hunched up in the back. I swivel the rear-view mirror to catch her face. Her bobbed black hair frames her jawline. She's wearing a thin coat with the sleeves rolled up and enough make-up to garnish the cast of an entire fashion show. Her teeth shine brilliant white against her black lipstick.

'Yeah, well it's cold,' I reply.

'Smart guy.'

'If you had a better coat then–'

'Give it a rest.'

The minutes tick by as we sit in silence. 'What are you waiting for?' She leans forward, placing her tattooed forearms on the back of the seat.

'Don't know yet.'

'Oh well, just so long as we're not wasting our time then?'

'You can be such a dick.'

'Err, excuse me, in case you haven't noticed I've got one of those vagina things.'

'You know what I mean.'

Jade slumps back in her seat and folds her arms. 'You must have some kind of plan?'

'Shhh, I need to concentrate.'

'On what? All I see is bricks and mortar and sod all happening. You've lost the plot. You need to–'

A shaft of light cuts through the darkness as a door opens on the mezzanine walkway of the second floor and the silhouette of a man appears in the doorway. He's carrying a kitbag and chatting to someone over his shoulder. He steps out onto the landing, closing the door behind him and blends into the black of the brickwork. He scampers down the steps to the yard below and gets into a car.

This is more interesting than watching a queue of drunk people.

'Game on, I reckon,' says Jade, leaning forward again, running her tongue across her lips in expectation.

'Shhh!'

Headlights come into view as he noses a dark-coloured Astra out of the gates and heads off. I wait a few seconds before filing in behind.

The roads are empty, which means I have to keep my distance to avoid being spotted. Several times he deviates from the main roads and my heart stops when I think I've lost him, though I catch up each time. After twenty minutes he draws the car over to the kerb and stops. He steps out into the night air. He's not wearing his bomber jacket nor his identification. He slings the bag over his shoulder and marches off.

I watch as he turns a corner and jump from my car. He has about thirty yards start on me. I reach the corner and poke my head around; I can see him up ahead. I fall in behind. The sound of his heavy brogue shoes striking the pavement reverberating in the narrow street.

I'm gaining on him. Suddenly he darts into an alleyway that runs along the backs of two sets of houses. I start counting his footsteps, *1, 2, 3, 4…*

I arrive at the alleyway and he's still going, *15, 16, 17, 18…*

He stops at *21* and I hear the sound of a bolt being drawn across. I set off after him, counting as I go. The walls either side of me are eight feet high and the further into the alley I go the less the street lighting penetrates the darkness.

I count my steps, *11, 12, 13, 14…*

The place stinks of mould and stagnant water.

19, 20, 21. I stop and look around. There is a gate to my left and nothing but a brick wall to my right. I can't see a damned thing. I jump up, putting my hands onto the top of the wall and heaving myself up. A small garden opens up onto the back of a two-up, two-down house. The light is on and I can see through the kitchen window; two men are stood chatting. I struggle to maintain my grip on the slimy bricks. Suddenly the back door springs open and my man steps out clutching the holdall.

'See ya!' he says and the door closes behind him.

Shit, where do I go now?

I drop to the floor and hurry further into the alleyway, crouching down. The gate creaks open and the man with the bag comes out, striding back the way he came to the main road.

This is perfect.

I straighten up and fall in behind, closing the gap. The noise of his shoes echo in the confined space.

'Got a light, mate?' I say. He jumps out of his skin.

'Err, you what, mate?' he says over his shoulder.

'A light, have you got a light? Sorry if I startled you. There's a woman who lives here and she doesn't like me leaving by the front door, if you get my drift.'

I narrow the distance between us. I'm weighing up the options.

Will I? Won't I? Shall I? Shan't I?

He turns to face me.

'No mate, I don't–'

'Fucking stick him!' Jade yells.

I plunge the diver's knife into the side of his neck and rip it across. His eyes pop from his face as he slumps against the wall, dropping the bag, both hands clasped to his throat. His mouth is opening and closing but no sound comes out. I step aside to avoid the arterial flow.

His legs give way and he slides down the wall to settle on his haunches. He's rocking back and forth, gargling. Then he's still.

I lean down and wipe the blade on the shoulder of his jacket, returning it to its sheath on my belt. The rain pitter-patters onto the pavement as I walk back to my car. The bag feels heavy as I drop it into the passenger footwell. I head back to the Paragon, to park up and wait.

I catch Jade's reflection in the rear-view mirror. She gives me a half-smile and mouths, *Nice one*.

They must be going berserk by now. I've been sat in my car watching the back of the club for forty minutes. I can imagine the frenetic activity taking place inside. They will have called the bloke at the counting house who would have confirmed that the bagman had left. They would have called him too.

The head honcho will be stomping around telling everyone what he's going to do to the bagman when he returns. Or at least that's what I was used to, maybe this operation is different.

The door leading out onto the top mezzanine walkway bursts open and six guys pile out. They scurry down the stairs into two cars and a Transit van. I can hear the engines revving and the squeal of tyres. The first car shoots out of the gate, closely followed by the second with the van bringing up the rear.

I catch a glimpse of the man sat in the front of the lead car. He has less hair than when I saw him last and has put on a few pounds, but there's no doubt in my mind… the man in the passenger seat is Eddie Marshall. My camera goes *click*.

Chapter 10

'I don't give a toss, find him and bring him to the club.' Marshall was barking orders into the hands-free set in the car. 'He should have been back ages ago and his phone is ringing out. When you find him, call me.'

'Okay, boss, will do.' The line went dead.

'That fucking Tommy… I gave him a simple job to do and he screws it up.' The man in the driver's seat said nothing, choosing instead to focus on the road. The car behind them turned left and sped off. The car in which Marshall was travelling carried straight on with a Transit van following close behind.

'He knows we have a shipment tonight, and an auction tomorrow, and he does a moonlight flit. When I get my hands on him…'

'Tommy's normally a solid guy, maybe there was a problem with the pickup,' said the driver.

'And what's the first thing you do if there's a problem?'

'Call you.'

'Exactly. I've heard jack shit from him.'

The urban roads gave way to the blue signs of the motorway. Marshall shifted in his seat to look out of the back window.

'They're still there, boss. Don't let this situation with Tommy distract you.'

'I'll distract the little shit when I get hold of him.'

They peeled off the M55 motorway onto the M6 and made their way across the M58 until they reached a sign saying, Bootle: All Docks. Marshall opened the glove compartment and pulled out a handgun. He ejected the magazine to check the rounds, snapping it back in place.

'Nearly showtime,' he said.

Fifteen minutes later the driver buzzed down his window and spoke to the security guard who handed him a visitor's badge. He hung it from the rear-view mirror and, when the barrier went up, drove through and pulled over to wait for the van.

Both vehicles trundled across the tarmac into the yard. A vast expanse of shipping containers stretched out in front of them, looking more like a small city rather than a storage facility. They turned this way and that, threading their way between the metal skyscrapers. Then came to a halt. Fifty yards away, two stationary vehicles were facing them with their lights on.

Marshall's car reached there first, closely followed by the van. Before long, five men were standing shoulder to shoulder in the glare of the headlights. An Asian man in a sharp suit stepped from his car and walked towards them, at his side was a brute of a guy wearing a boiler suit. Marshall and his driver met them halfway. It was like a Mexican standoff in no man's land.

Marshall extended his hand, the Asian man shook it.

'I trust everything is in order, Mr Zhang?' Marshall said.

'Of course, would you like to inspect the merchandise?'

'Would you like to see the money?'

The men separated; Marshall went with Zhang, while the boiler-suited brute accompanied the driver back to the car. The boot lid opened and both heads disappeared inside.

Marshall arrived at a rusty container and Zhang opened one of the doors. They both stepped inside.

'As you can see, the delivery matches the shipping manifest.'

Marshall flicked the torch on his phone and inspected the goods. 'It does, you will find our money is in order, too.'

They walked back to no man's land to find the brute in the boiler suit holding a briefcase. He nodded to Zhang. Marshall gave a signal and the van backed up to the container. The back doors flew open and the men began to load the cargo.

'Good doing business with you, Mr Marshall,' said Zhang, holding out his hand.

'We will be in touch.'

They shook hands and Zhang got into his car and drove away, leaving Marshall and his crew to finish up.

Ten minutes later they had returned their tags to security and were driving towards the M58. The phone rang.

'Yeah,' said Marshall.

'Boss, I found Tommy.'

'Good, have you taken the fucker back to the club?'

'No, boss.'

'I told you–'

'Boss, he's dead.'

'What?'

'Someone stuck him with a knife and took the money.'

'Shit!' Marshall slapped his hands against the dashboard. 'Where are you now?'

'I'm in Spencer Street about thirty yards from the alleyway where Tommy's lying.'

'Okay, now listen to me carefully, Josh. There are things you need to do. Are you listening?'

'Yes, boss, I'm listening.'

'I want you to go back to Tommy and take his car keys, phone and wallet. Be careful not to step in the blood. You got that?'

'Yes – get the keys, phone and wallet.'

'The next thing is to go to the counting house and tell the counter he's going to get a visit from the police. They'll conduct house-to-house enquiries, so he's going to have a copper turn up at his door at some time. He needs to be prepared for that. Then remove any money from the premises. Counted or not counted, it doesn't matter. Got it?'

'Yes, boss – tell the counter he's gonna get a visit and clear the place of cash.'

'And finally, I want you to drive Tommy's car back to the club. Stay off the main roads and only use the back streets. We will be back in about an hour, wait for us there and we will sort out your car later. Have you got that?'

'Why can't I use the car I came in? Why do I have to drive Tommy's car back to the club?'

'Because, dummy, it isn't Tommy's car. It's a pool car and registered to the club. Now stop thinking and get it sorted. Call me if anything else happens.'

Marshall disconnected the call. It's fifty-eight miles from Liverpool to Blackpool. He swore at the top of his voice for fifty-five of them.

Chapter 11

Kray opened her front door and had never been so pleased to see the inside of her house. It was late and she was shattered.

The trip to Manchester had been a waste of time. Miriam Ellwood made them as welcome as a cactus in a nudist camp and refused to accompany them to the garage. She simply threw them the keys and said, 'Knock yourselves out. Post them back through the letter box when you're done. Oh, and don't bother knocking.'

The premises were precisely what you would expect. Ramps, lifts and maintenance pits combined with an Aladdin's cave of motor parts and tools. The place smelled of engine oil and grease which turned Kray's stomach. She managed to hide her nausea from Tavener but she was sure she had turned an ugly shade of grey.

The office was located on a mezzanine floor set in the corner. Kray opened the door and her OCD went into overdrive. It was a mess of paperwork, manuals and boxes of parts. You couldn't see the surface of the desk for the debris. This, coupled with the turmoil in her guts, forced her to hit the eject button and leave.

The team seized a desktop computer and a few ledgers to examine back at the station, but that was it. Kray's closing thought as she burst into the fresh air was, *Drugs connection, my arse.*

The warmth of her home wrapped around her as she threw her bags down and kicked off her shoes. She was on autopilot and headed straight for the fridge. Two bottles of wine screamed out to her. She cursed under her breath.

I'm going to have to put those somewhere else.

She shook her head. This pregnancy was getting in the way of her indulgences. The bar of chocolate would have to suffice. She closed the fridge and went upstairs to run a deep, foamy bath.

Kray undressed and stood sideways on in the mirror. She examined the profile of her belly. It was flat. Her eyes wandered onto the red scars, criss-crossing her body like a London tube map. Scars made by the vicious knife attack which left her lying in a warm pool of her own blood and her husband dead, Carl Rampton's Stanley knife embedded in his neck. She drew her fingers across the puckered skin, it tingled beneath her touch.

What the hell am I going to do?

She had been in a relationship with Dr Chris Millican for a while now. He was the Home Office pathologist, with a penchant for wearing a waistcoat and tight trousers, who first caught her eye when she was on her way to the mortuary. Well, parts of him caught her eye. Who says romance is dead?

She had not visited her husband's grave since she'd buried her wedding ring at the base of his headstone when deciding it was time to move on. After all, sharing her life with a dead person was not a healthy thing to do. Sharing it with someone who was alive had to be the way forward – and that's where Chris Millican came into the picture.

Kray traced her finger along the scar that started to the left of her navel, traversed her stomach, and ran up her chest to bisect her nipple. Her summation was: she was borderline anorexic, had galloping OCD, drank way too much and had a boss that she would gladly kill. Being pregnant was the last thing she needed right now and laying off the drink was definitely not helping. She padded into the bathroom to sink beneath the blanket of foam.

When the blue lines informed her she was pregnant, Kray had gone into free fall. An unplanned baby is what happened to other people, not her. After peeing on two more test kits she had spent the next three days ghosting through the day job while avoiding Millican. Every advert on the TV seemed to be about babies, and when she left the house the outside world was awash with mums pushing prams, and even bus stop posters declared the benefits of one type of nappy over another.

On the morning of day four, the fog cleared, and she decided to get a grip. She announced to Millican that she was embarking on a health kick, which meant cutting down on the wine and stopping smoking. Looking back on it now, that announcement probably came as more of a shock to him than saying, 'Hey, Chris, you're going to be a dad.'

Kray had pretended to drink the occasional glass of wine to maintain the charade but tipped it down the sink when he wasn't looking. Taking a sip only made matters worse, it made her want to tear the bottle from his hand and neck it in one go. Giving up altogether was a daunting prospect – but it was the only way.

She had ripped up her last packet of fags and dumped them in the kitchen bin. Forty-five minutes later she had been sorely tempted to pull them back out and puff away on the pieces that were left. But she resisted.

Her emotions were all over the place. Crushing feelings of guilt threatened to swamp her very existence. When married to Joe she couldn't conceive and now it was wham-bam-thank-you-ma'am – why not have a baby?

Millican had swallowed the line about the health kick and suggested she joined a gym.

Why don't you go and slam your bollocks in the car door?

Fortunately, she resisted the temptation to give her thoughts airtime, choosing instead to utter the words, 'Mmm, I'll think about it.'

It was then she came up with her genius idea of having a water infection. A course of antibiotics would buy her a week to sort herself out and would provide her with a legitimate reason to give up the booze while feeling like shit. She was now on her second course of fictional medication and was running out of options. The deceit of not telling him was burning a hole in her. Her eyes began to close when she heard the front door open.

'It's only me,' the voice drifted up the stairs.

'I'm in the bath,' she called down. She had agonised over whether it was too soon in their relationship to give Millican a key, and while she was churning the matter over in her head, she – one day – just handed one over to him. The key to his flat was in her bag. She heard a clunking noise coming from the kitchen, then footsteps coming up the stairs. Millican entered the bathroom carrying a pizza, a wine bottle and two glasses.

'Hey, pizza boy has arrived.' He placed them onto the floor, bent over and kissed her on the mouth. His lips were cold. Millican had healed well following the injuries he had sustained at the hands of Alex Jarrod, the vigilante ex-soldier who Kray had sought to bring to justice in her last case. His right eye drooped a little at the corner where they had to reconstruct his cheekbone, but other than that he was as good as new – almost.

'How was your day?' she asked, not getting up.

'Oh, you know. I cut up a few dead people, weighed their internal organs, and then came home. How about you?' He unboxed the pizza, tore off a slice and handed it to her.

'Well, let's see. I got an interesting lead on a case, wanted to punch Bagley in the throat, met Captain Birdseye, drove to Manchester and then came home.'

'Pretty good all round then?' He munched on the pizza and poured the wine, offering her a glass.

'None for me. I'm still on these bloody antibiotics. This infection will *not* clear up.'

'Maybe you're having too much sex, DI Kray.' He leaned over and kissed her again.

'Maybe.'

'You okay? You look a little green around the gills.'

'Yeah, I've not been feeling so good today. Maybe I'm hungry. Thanks for the pizza.'

She hauled herself out of the foam by leaning her forearm on the bath top. It was her turn to kiss him.

'Okay if I stop over?'

'If I wasn't in this bath you'd already be in the bedroom.'

'Promises, promises.'

Kray munched on the pizza and began to feel better. The aches and pains of the day soothed away into the hot water and her body relaxed. Besides, Dr Ding Dong was here, and everything seemed better when he was around.

They talked for the best part of an hour before Kray announced, 'The water's cold. Help me out, I need to go to bed.'

'I thought you'd never ask.' Millican held her hand as she stepped from the bath and he folded a towel around her. She melted into him. 'Come on, Detective Inspector, you've had a busy day.' Kray allowed herself to be led into the bedroom and into bed. Sleeping naked next to him felt right. She no longer felt the need to cover her scars in layers of nightwear. The best thing about Millican was he had never tried to fix her. With all Kray's obvious hang-ups, he wanted her – wreckage included.

Kray lay with her head on his chest. 'Chris, there's something I need to tell you.'

'Oh, what–'

Kray's phone buzzed angrily at the side of the bed.

'Ignore it,' he said.

'You know I can't do that.' She rolled off him and picked it up. 'Kray.'

The voice on the other end was slow and deliberate.

'Okay, where is this? …I'll be there in half an hour.' She hung up and rolled back into Millican, planting a kiss on his lips. 'I gotta go.'

'You were about to say–'

'Sorry, I gotta dash. They've found a guy with his throat slashed in an alleyway. You can stay, I'll wake you when I get back.'

'Promises, promises.'

Kray pulled up at the blue and white tape drawn across the entrance to Spencer Street. She got out and signed the clipboard held for her by the uniformed PC and then looked up to see a handful of residents peering from their front room windows.

She cast her eyes to the sky, letting out a sigh of relief that it had stopped raining, and pulled on the white coverall and overshoes.

'Who's the crime scene manager?'

'That's Sergeant Cullum – he's the guy talking to the two people next to the patrol car.'

'Thanks.' Kray ducked under the cordon and made her way over to where he was standing. He saw her coming and met her halfway.

'Sergeant Cullum? DI Roz Kray.'

'Evening, ma'am.'

'What do we have? And please call me Roz.'

'A white male, mid to late twenties, severe laceration to the neck. The coroner's office has dispatched a doctor. No witnesses.'

'Who called it in?'

Cullum nodded in the direction of the couple chatting to an officer by the car. 'They were walking home when the man gets taken short and needs a pee. He disappears down the alleyway to relieve himself and finds the victim lying dead against the wall. He calls three nines, and they were both still on the scene when the officers arrive. The couple are giving their statement now.'

Kray looked over to the alleyway which was lit up with powerful LED lamps. A white glowing tent could be seen close to the entrance.

'I've taken the precaution of covering the scene, ma'am, in case the weather turns against us.'

'Do we have a name?'

'Not yet, we've not moved the body to see if he is carrying any form of ID.'

'Shall we take a look?' Kray marched over to the alleyway, stepping on the metal checker plates covering the floor. Cullum followed suit.

'That's where he took a piss.' Cullum pointed to a pool of urine on the floor that had drained across the concrete.

'Lovely.' Kray wrinkled her nose.

She then reached the tent. Inside was a man sitting with his back against the wall and his legs outstretched; his arms hung by his side. His head was tilted forward and his chest and legs were awash with blood. The paving slabs were stained dark brown.

Kray bent down. 'The blade entered his neck on the left-hand side. There are signs of arterial spatter on this side of the victim.'

'I agree, Roz, I've put in a request for a forensic biologist to examine the blood pattern.'

'Good idea.' Kray stared at the body, then at the blood spatter and back again. The scar on her left cheek began to tingle. She leaned forward with a gloved hand and tapped the dead man's pockets. 'I don't think he's got anything on him.'

'A mugging, perhaps?'

'Maybe – the killer wiped the blade clean on his shoulder.' Kray pointed to the red smears on the jacket. 'Okay, let the CSI team go to work.'

They both retraced their steps back into the street. Kray chewed on her bottom lip, something bothering her. She walked over to the couple who were finishing their statements.

'I'm DI Kray, did you find the body?' she asked the man.

'I did. I went into the alley for a wazz and there he was, sitting in a pool of blood.'

'What did you do then?'

'I ran back out to Kelly and called the police.' The woman next to him nodded in agreement.

'Did you touch the body at all?' asked Kray.

'Shit no! It was obvious from the amount of blood he was dead, so I legged it.'

'But it must have been dark in there, how could you see?'

'My eyes got used to the dark, cos I was in there a while, I was proper bustin', wasn't I, Kell?'

'Proper bustin' he was.'

'And I could see this bloke sitting on the floor. I called over to see if he was all right and he didn't answer, so I got out my mobile and turned the torch on and there he was... dead.'

'Okay, thank you.'

Kray walked back to Cullum.

'Did you get what you wanted from them?' he asked.

'Yeah, I did. Can you direct the CSI team to focus on the position of the victim?'

'Why is that?'

'I reckon someone moved the body.'

Chapter 12

At the time I had always assumed Rolo got his nickname from his body shape. He was, after all, like an egg on legs. It was only much later when I discovered his name was Roland. He never looked like a Roland, he looked like an egg on legs.

I remember sitting in that kitchen at the club with a towel pressed to my face when Rolo crooked his finger. 'Come with me,' he said, walking out of the room and down the corridor. He unlocked a door and disappeared inside. I followed, still clutching the tea towel to my nose.

'Come in and close the door.' He sat behind a big oak desk. The room was set out like a modern office with a couple of laptops and wooden filing cabinets around the walls.

'I've never been in here,' I said, standing in front of the desk.

'No, you haven't. We keep it locked because this is the nerve centre from which we control our operations.'

'Oh, okay.'

'I've had my eye on you since you arrived and I've been impressed.'

'Thank you. I like working here. Well… tonight didn't go so well but…' I raised the blood-soaked towel to emphasise my point.

'Sometimes that happens. Comes with the territory.'

'I suppose so.' There was an ominous silence. 'What's this about, Rolo?'

'You did the right thing telling that TJ wanker to piss off.'

'Yeah, but I should have let you know.'

'We don't want his drugs in our club.'

'No, we don't.'

'That's because we want people to buy our drugs.'

I allowed the comment to sink in. 'But I thought we had a zero tolerance?'

'We have to, it's the same shop window that everyone has. But in reality, we allow our own softer, recreational drugs to be available in the club because that's what punters demand and that way we can control it.'

'I had no idea.'

'Of course you didn't. I've had you working the door since you arrived.'

'I don't know what to say.'

'I'm hoping you'll say yes.'

'Yes to what?'

'Yes to becoming part of the family. We need guys like you who can not only handle themselves but also have a good head on their shoulders. Anyone can throw a punch. That's not what we need. Guys like you… that's what we need.'

'Umm, thank you. I do my best. Who else…?'

'All of them – you are the only member of the team who isn't in the family.'

'Bloody hell, so Eddie is–'

'Eddie's a good guy, a little on the gobby side but he knows the score. What d'you say?'

'They're all–'

'Yup, every one of them.'

'Shit, no one said a word.'

'That's because you weren't in the family.'

'You said something about extra cash?'

'I did and that's an important part of the deal. You'll be well paid in return for carrying out simple, but critical tasks, and demonstrating loyalty.'

'What kind of tasks?'

'Things like… taking a taxi ride, carrying a bag, looking after someone. Things that are well within your skill set.'

'I don't understand.'

'No, Billy, you don't, but you will. But first of all, you need to pledge your loyalty to me because that is very important. Without loyalty there is nothing. Do you agree?'

'Yes, loyalty is important.'

'No, Billy, it's crucial. And any breach in loyalty will result in the harshest of penalties. Understand?'

'Yeah, I understand.'

'Go on then. If you want to accept my offer you'll need to pledge your loyalty.'

'Okay, Rolo. I pledge my loyalty.'

'That's good, Billy, but that's not how it's done. Come around my side of the desk.' I did what I was told. 'Now kneel down.'

'What?'

'To pledge your loyalty you have to be on your knees.'

'But…'

'Do it, Billy.'

I sank to the carpet, looking up at Rolo. He leaned over and slid open the desk drawer. Reaching in, he pulled out a handgun.

'When you say it, Billy, you need to mean it.' He levelled the gun at my head. 'Because any breach in loyalty will bring with it the harshest consequences.'

'I…'

'Do you pledge loyalty to the Critchley family?'

He stared at me down the barrel. I could feel my right eye twitching.

'I pledge my loyalty to the Critchley family.'

A silence washed between us that set the hairs on the back of my neck on edge. Rolo's eyes were dead, not a flicker of emotion.

'That's good.' He jumped up from his seat, waving the gun in the air. 'I do like a good pledge.'

I gasped. A zing of exhilaration sprinted down my spine.

What a rush.

'Welcome to the family, Billy.' He extended his pudgy hand and pulled me up. 'Clean your face up. I've got a job for you.'

Chapter 13

With the pledge completed I became part of the Critchley family, I was on the payroll and going places. But to fully understand the significance of this, you need to understand the context to the story.

The nineties was a golden era for organised crime, mainly because they did just that – got themselves organised. In the previous two decades the normal portfolio for any gangland crew would include prostitution, protection, drugs, gambling, smuggling, high-end robberies, extortion… that kinda thing. It was an extensive menu of wrongdoing which meant resources were spread thinly and, in many cases, required specialist skills. Then it became apparent that there was only one game in town for any serious gangster – drugs.

Whether it was cocaine from Columbia, heroin from Afghanistan or a bit of everything from Venezuela, the supply was plentiful – and demand was going through the roof. The markup was eye-watering and the law enforcement agencies didn't have a clue. The creation of the Serious and Organised Crime Agency was still years away and it was playtime for everyone. It was left up to local drug squads, the National Crime Squad, HM Revenue and Customs and a few other disparate organisations to police what was happening. But when you could ship one hundred kilograms of heroin into Liverpool Docks and turn that into twenty-two million pounds on the street, the authorities didn't stand a chance. It was drug-fuelled chaos on an industrial scale.

The best example I have to indicate how big the problem had become is that a drug lord from Liverpool catapulted himself into the *Sunday Times* Rich List at the same time that he topped Interpol's most wanted list. I rest my case.

The gangs in London were being squeezed out by a firm called the Adams Family, which meant they spilled over into other regions. Liverpool and Dublin had more than enough homegrown talent so they headed to Nottingham where the Critchley brothers ruled the roost.

The drug business is all about cash, which brings with it a couple of major problems. Firstly, that much money is difficult to move around and store. Whether you vacuum pack the notes into bricks or roll them into bundles, it is heavy to cart about. Secondly, you can't spend it. If you start buying fancy houses and flash cars when you supposedly work as an office clerk someone is going to raise an eyebrow. The money needs to be laundered through legitimate businesses. And the businesses of choice for the Critchley brothers were nightclubs.

The Critchleys owned four clubs for that very purpose. Nightclubs are perfect for turning dirty money into clean money. They are cash intensive, provide a wide variety of services and are highly subjective. From entrance fees to VIP tables, from vintage champagne to inflated till receipts and promotional nights – who knows how many people are in the club? Who knows how much cash is changing hands? The dirty money is mixed with the clean money. You pay taxes on the profits and hey presto! You got cash to burn. But the best thing about nightclubs is they can take years to become successful, so it is fine for you to make small losses. That avoids paying tax altogether! It's kinda genius.

Anyway, back to the story; my nose had stopped bleeding and Rolo had instructed me to go to a flat above a travel agent called Lazy-Day Travel, located on Carrington Street.

'At this time of night?' I said, looking at my watch.

'He's expecting you. It's got a bright red front door, tell him Rolo says *hi*.' He tossed me a set of keys.

I used the back entrance to the club to avoid bumping into Ton-Up and his mates who were still being dealt with out front.

I hit the bar on the emergency exit leading out onto the car park and checked the licence plate number on the key chain. It was a battered, white Transit van.

Great, now I really look like a criminal.

It started first time and I headed south across town. The streets were filled with drunk people falling over, having a good time. Saturday was always a busy night for us at the club and I was beginning to understand why.

I turned off the main drag, parked up and took in my surroundings. All was quiet. I smiled to myself when I remembered that a short distance away, on the other side of Castle Boulevard, they had just started building the new HM Revenue and Customs offices – the irony was a foot thick.

I walked the short distance to Lazy-Day. The place was in darkness apart from a light in the flat above. To the side there was a metal staircase bolted to the exterior wall leading to the first floor. The wrought iron creaked under my weight as I reached the top. I rapped on the red door. Nothing. I rapped again and a man in his mid-forties with cropped hair opened the door to peer out.

'Rolo says hi,' I said.

'Come in.' He walked away, leaving the door ajar. I followed him into a narrow hallway with doors leading off it. 'Wait here.'

I closed the door behind me and stood in the corridor. After a couple of minutes the man reappeared with a large sports holdall. I could see from the way the veins stood out from his arms it was heavy. He dumped it at my feet. Then walked back into the room at the end, banging the door shut behind him.

I guess you don't want a receipt?

I swung the bag over my shoulder and returned to the van. The bag travelled in the passenger footwell where I could keep an eye on it.

Back at the club I found Rolo and he took me to the command centre. The memories of me kneeling down with a gun to my head spiked my adrenaline.

'Good lad,' he said, taking the bag from my grasp and placing it on the table. 'Do you want a look?'

'Yeah.' I stepped forward as Rolo ran the zip down. It was stuffed with rolls of bank notes; fives, tens, twenties.

'That, my son, is what it's all about. And come payday a slice of this will be coming your way.'

It was the largest bag of cash I'd ever seen. There must have been close to fifty thousand pounds. I had been used to seeing ten thousand here, twenty thousand there, but this was in a different league.

'Wow!' I said, much to Rolo's satisfaction.

'Go home and come back around ten o'clock in the morning. I've got another little job for you.'

Chapter 14

It was ten minutes to two in the afternoon and the Paragon club was closed. The neon sign above the entrance was dull and lifeless. A bookworm of a man wearing a leather jacket checked his watch and scurried across the road. He knocked on the door. It was opened by a short square guy sporting a double-breasted suit, one size too small for him.

'Can I help you?' he asked.

'I'm here to buy a car.'

'Certainly, sir, would you like to step inside?' The man did as he was told and entered the reception area of the club. 'Remove your jacket and raise your arms.'

The bookworm shuffled out of his coat and stood in his shirtsleeves with his arms raised, Christ the Redeemer style. The stocky man ran a black wand over his guest, the device remained silent. He ran the wand over the jacket and said, 'Thank you, sir, would you like to follow me?'

The bookworm wrestled a bulging envelope from the inside pocket of his jacket.

'That's not for me,' the stocky bloke said, before turning away and strolling down a short corridor into the main hall.

The bookworm followed him through a door and into the gloom of the nightclub. The enormous bar running down the left-hand side was in darkness as were the half-moon booths set against the walls. The chrome and glitz seemed to be subsumed into an all-pervasive grey. One booth seat was lit up by a single desk lamp.

Three round tables sat on the dance floor; an older gentleman with a thin comb-over was sitting at one and a man in a suit occupied the other. On the table, in front of the suited guy, was a laptop and camera.

Marshall beckoned to the new arrival and met him halfway across the floor. Four more men in suits were dotted around the room. There was no sign of the troubles of the previous day.

'Welcome. I hope you have a successful afternoon.' Marshall held out his hand. The bookworm handed over the envelope and Marshall walked off to sit at the illuminated booth.

'Please let me show you to your seat.' The stocky man waved his arm and guided the visitor to the vacant table.

At the far end of the club was a stage with a shimmering curtain draped as a backdrop. Two silver poles at either end stretched from the floor to the ceiling.

Marshall reappeared with the man's envelope in one hand and a bottle of Moët and a champagne flute in the other.

'This is in order. I've taken our door fee as agreed.' He placed the envelope on the table. 'And please accept this on the house… have a good afternoon.' He poured the bubbling liquid into the glass and left. Hanging around the neck of the bottle was a round token. Written on the token was *Mr Black*.

Marshall checked his watch and as the digits turned over to two o'clock he nodded to the guy sitting behind the laptop.

The stage lit up, and a man wearing a shiny suit walked over and jumped up onto it. He was lean and lanky with slicked back hair and an orange tan. He looked a bit like an eighties gameshow host, a black microphone taped to his cheek.

A large screen mounted on the wall burst into life, highlighting the man on stage with three blacked out head and shoulder icons on the right-hand side. The man sitting at the controls adjusted the camera.

'Good afternoon, gentlemen. I will be your host and auctioneer for this afternoon's entertainment. As promised, we bring you something different today, something a little out of the ordinary that we hope will be to your liking.' He waved his hands in the air like he was asking a contestant to choose a door.

'Now I need to go through a few points before we get started. We have five players today, two in the room and three online. We have ten lots, each one in pristine condition. This is a cash-only event. There are no lines of credit and all transactions must be settled in full on close of business. Failure to do so will result in you being blacklisted from future auctions and you will be subject to a penalty payment. Before we start I need to do a sound and visual check. Can everyone see and hear me okay?'

'Yeah.' A disembodied voice came through the huge speakers mounted either side of the stage.

'Yup, it's fine,' said another.

And another. 'It's good for me.'

The two men sat at the tables raised their hands in a polite, 'Yes'.

'That's wonderful. You know the drill; when you want to bid you say the name on your tag. The current bid price will be shown in the top right-hand corner of your screen. I will be the sole arbitrator of what the current bid is and who has made it. Is that clear?' There was another mumbling of agreement over the speakers.

'So, if you would like to sit back, enjoy your champagne and we will get the show underway. I would like to introduce lot number one.' The curtains behind him opened. 'This is a 2001 model with one careful owner. Never been in a race before and comes with a full service history. Doesn't require nitrous oxide to burn bright on the track. I think you will agree she has good lines with a cracking paint job. Who will start me off?' The room was silent. 'Come on, gents, we said we would be offering something special, and hére it is. Look at the bodywork. This one is built for speed. Who will give me two?' The number two flashed up on the top of the screen.

'Mr Red,' a deep voice boomed through the speakers.

'That's good. Now do I hear three?'

'Mr Blue.'

'Four, do I hear four from anyone?'

'Mr Red.'

'Okay, now we're rolling. How about five?'

'Mr Green.' The man with the comb-over held up his tag.

'Like it. We have five in the room. Do I hear six?'

'Mr Red – six.'

'Woah, that's more like it. I have a big six from Mr Red. Now who will give me seven?'

'Mr Blue, six and a half.'

'The bid is six and a half. Do I hear another seven? Any advance on six and a half?'

The room and speakers were silent. 'I'm going to call it, gentlemen.' The auctioneer danced about the stage like he was chasing chickens. 'Going… going… gone. Sold to Mr Blue for six and a half.'

There was a murmuring on the speakers and people reached for their drinks.

'Now we have lot number two. This one is the oldest model we have on the card today. Made in 1998. As you would expect she has a few more miles on the clock and has been to the races many times. She runs best on nitrous oxide but I am assured she will race okay without. This is a reliable runner with low maintenance costs. Who will start me off?'

Silence.

'I'll agree she's not in such good working order as the previous lot but will do the job. Who will give me two?'

Silence.

'No one? This has to be a welcome addition to any collection. Who will start me off with two?'

Not a murmur.

'Okay, how about one? Who will give me that?'

Nothing.

'Oh, come on, guys, this opportunity does not come around very often. Got to be worth one, who will give me a half?'

You could hear a pin drop.

The auctioneer turned to Marshall and shrugged his shoulders. Marshall nodded.

'Okay, moving on to lot three. This has to be the fastest one of the day. Made in 2003 with all the bells and whistles you'd expect to find. She has not been raced and is nitrous oxide free. Great bodywork. Guaranteed to turn heads. The bidding needs to reflect the quality of this model. I'm going to start at three. Who will give me three?'

'Mr Blue,' the voice echoed around the club.

'Mr Green – five.' The customer held up his tag.

'That's more like it. Who will give me seven?'

'Mr Red.'

'And now nine, who wants to own this for nine?'

'Mr Blue.'

'That's the ticket. What do you say, Mr Red? Do you fancy eleven?'

'Ten.' Mr Black held up his token and supped on his drink.

'That's what I like to see. Mr Black holds the bid at ten. Anyone for eleven? Get a load of what you're going to take away, gents. You won't find this quality anywhere else. Who's up for eleven?'

'Mr Blue.' The floating voice had an edge of frustration.

'Twelve, will anyone give me twelve?'

The room was quiet.

'Mr Black, do you fancy twelve?' He shook his head and poured himself more champagne. 'I'm calling it, gentlemen. Going... going...'

'Twelve, Mr Black.'

'Whoa! Just in the nick of time. Any advance on twelve? I have twelve from Mr Black, do I hear thirteen? Mr Blue are you in?' The speakers in the room remained silent.

'Going once... going twice... sold to Mr Black for twelve thousand pounds.'

And so, the afternoon rolled on, the champagne flowed and all the lots were sold. All, that is, except for lot number two.

Chapter 15

Bagley intercepted Kray on her way to the incident room. 'How did you get on with the Drug Squad?' he said, stopping her in her tracks.

Good afternoon to you too, tosser!

'We've been pursuing other lines of enquiry first. I wanted more information before I got them on board.'

'Like what?'

'Sorry?'

'Other lines of enquiry, like what?'

'We obtained a search warrant to the garage and recovered a computer and a bunch of financial records. We also interviewed the guy who runs the yacht club and tried to speak to Miriam Ellwood, but she was having none of it.'

'So, nothing about the drug connection, then?'

'The garage *is* part of the drug connection, you said it yourself. That's where he could be laundering the cash.'

'I asked you to get the Drug Squad involved and that's what I expect to happen. Is that clear?'

Kray cast her eyes to the ceiling. 'Yes, sir. Now if you'll excuse me, I need to conduct the initial briefing on the stab victim.' Kray skirted around Bagley and walked down the corridor.

'I've had a look at that case,' Bagley called after her.

'Oh?'

'I want you to handle it.'

'But sir, I know I was the attending officer but I thought, given that I have the Ellwood investigation, you would give it to Brownlow. I'm happy to kick things off, but I was expecting to hand this over.'

'I've examined the loadings and you have headroom to take this on as well. Colin has enough on his plate at the moment.'

'But…'

Bagley turned and walked away. Kray gritted her teeth.

Wanker!

She shoved open the door to the incident room, trying to hold her emotions in check. She had a briefing to conduct and couldn't betray the fact that all she wanted to do was dash after Bagley to kick him in the nuts.

'Good afternoon, sorry I'm a little late – I got nabbed by the DCI.'

In the room were three CID officers, including Tavener, who had been busy constructing evidence boards and briefing notes.

'Afternoon, Roz,' they said in unison, all of them aware that *ma'am* was not the term to use.

'This…' she pointed to a head and shoulders photograph on the board, 'is Thomas Weir. He was found by two passers-by in the early hours of this morning with his throat slashed. He died at the scene. Weir had been in trouble with the police in 2009 for causing an affray so we had his prints on file which enabled an early identification. It's our only piece of luck because the rest of the circumstances surrounding his death don't add up.'

'Roz,' piped up DC Louise Chapman, a woman in her late twenties wearing a tailored suit with her long brown hair pulled back in a ponytail. 'I know this guy, he works the door at the Paragon.'

'That's right, he does, or rather he did. I'll head over to the club when we're done to start asking questions. He lived with his girlfriend. She's been informed and will identify the body later today. I want one of you to be with her when she does and someone to examine his social media and phone records.'

'I'll pick both those up,' said DS Tejinder Gill, a dishevelled man in his early thirties with Brillo-pad hair.

'Okay. First priority: I want to know what Weir was doing in the alleyway.'

'Roz, reading the briefing notes, isn't this a street-mugging gone wrong?' asked Chapman. 'I mean, we found no possessions on him. Whoever killed Weir robbed him. Muggings tend to go one of two ways: either the assailant threatens the victim with violence unless he or she hands over their belongings, or, the mugger attacks the victim and robs them. And judging by the pictures and the initial forensics there was no struggle, so we must be looking at the second MO.'

'Yeah, I agree, but let's step through this,' Roz replied, standing next to the board. 'The first thing to consider is Thomas Weir was six feet one inches tall and weighed over fourteen stones, hardly mugging material. Also, he worked security at a nightclub, so we can assume he could handle himself and wouldn't be easily intimidated. So, I agree with the theory that he probably didn't see it coming. The assailant slashes his throat and allows him to die.' Kray pointed to the photograph of Weir sitting upright with his back against the wall and his legs out in front of him. 'He's attacked and slides down into this position. We can assume that at this stage the killer does not have Weir's valuables. So here is the first question: what is the easiest way to take the belongings from his pockets?'

'Roll him over,' said Tavener.

'That's right, but the killer leaves him in a sitting position and takes his wallet and mobile phone.'

'Perhaps they were in his jacket pockets so whoever killed him had no need to check the other pockets?' said Gill.

'But if you were going to rob someone you wouldn't check two pockets and call it a day. You'd check them all.' A murmuring went around the room. 'Also, Weir's legs are soaked in blood from his hips to his knees.' Kray pointed to another photo. 'The next question is: the blood flowing from his neck would run down his chest, so how did it end up on his thighs? I think he had his knees up under his chin when he bled out. Someone straightened his legs, maybe to check the front pockets of his jeans.'

'The blood patterns are consistent with the victim sitting in one place when he died,' said Tavener.

'Exactly. Now onto the third question: how the hell did he get there?'

'Maybe the killer swiped his keys and stole his car as well.' Gill was on a roll.

'Maybe. It's fifteen miles from his place of work to where he was found.'

'He could have taken a taxi?' asked Tavener.

'I want one of you to contact every taxi firm to see if they took a fare anywhere near Spencer Street,' said Kray. Gill raised his hand to accept the task.

'Someone could have dropped him off?' said Chapman.

'Yes, that's a possibility.'

'Perhaps he was killed for a different reason and it was staged to look like a mugging?' said Tavener.

'That's what I think,' said Kray. 'There are too many things that don't add up. I'll talk to the Paragon. Check out if he was working that night. They might be able to shed some light on why he was there.'

'I'll make a start on the house-to-house and check out the CCTV in the town, see if we get a hit,' said Chapman.

'I'll check out who owns the Paragon club and whether or not they have any other business interests,' said Tavener.

'Is there anything else?' Kray asked. A general shaking of heads followed. 'Okay, guys, we have a lot of ground to cover.'

Kray was eager to bring the briefing to a swift conclusion. She gathered up her things, bolted for the door and ran down the corridor to the ladies' toilet. She made the cubicle just as vomit burst from her mouth and slapped against the back of the porcelain.

Across the city Marshall was feeling sick for a different reason. Standing in front of Bernard Cross and being asked to account for yourself was a daunting enough task. But being asked to account for the loss of fifty-six thousand pounds was a suicide mission.

'Just run that past me again,' whispered Cross.

'The guy picked up the cash from Torville Road and was attacked. He had his throat slashed and died at the scene. When we found his body, the cash was gone.' Marshall's voice was croakier than normal.

'I thought that's what you said.' Cross was a small weasel of a man with grey hair and an immaculate taste in tailored suits. His cufflinks sparkled under the lamp which hung above the table. The restaurant was empty, except for the two of them, plus the nerve-wracking addition of two gorillas wearing suits, who were standing either side of Marshall. 'Was it a hired hit?'

'We don't know. Our men are all over the streets, but as yet, we've got nothing.'

'That's strange, someone generally knows something.'

'They do, but this time we're drawing a blank.'

'Fifty-six thousand pounds,' Cross mused to himself. 'Whoever did this deserves a spanking.'

'Yes, Mr Cross.'

'Do you think it's a retaliatory strike? We took out one of their guys a few weeks ago, is this tit for tat?'

'Until we find someone who knows, I can't tell.'

'Maybe, but it doesn't take a genius to put two and two together. We had intelligence suggesting they might muscle in on our shipment – we sent them a warning – they decide to retaliate. While relieving us of our money in the process.'

'I'm not sure, Mr Cross.'

'What are you doing to get my cash back?'

'We're out there shaking trees. Sooner or later we'll get a lead.'

'When you find out who did this I want to be present at the spanking, is that clear?'

'Yes, Mr Cross. I figured you would.'

'How is everything else going?'

'Good. We had a successful auction and moved all the merchandise, except one.'

'What are your plans?'

'The last one will go, we just didn't have the right clientele.'

'Okay, keep me posted.' Cross got up from the table and left via the back entrance with the two bodyguards in tow. Marshall took the opportunity to sit down and breathe, but his phone buzzed in his pocket just as he had gotten comfortable.

'Hey, boss, I think we might have a problem.' It was Dave Williams, one of the heavies from the club.

'I know we have a problem, Dave, we have fifty-six thousand of them.'

'Yeah, well, I think we've got another.'

'Go on, I'm loving all this bad news at the moment.'

'I can't tell you over the phone.'

'Don't fuck about, I'm not in the mood.'

'No, boss, I'm serious. Not over the phone.'

'Where are you?'

'I'm outside, I drove straight over.'

Marshall rose from the table and plodded to the front door. He went out into the street and could see Williams sat in his car. He opened the passenger door and slid in beside him.

'Well?'

'I just saw Trevor Huxley...' Marshall stared at him and said nothing. 'Boss, I said–'

'You must be mistaken.'

'No, boss, I followed him to make sure. It was Huxley all right.'

'You must have that wrong.'

'I wish I did. But it was him, I swear to it.'

'That's impossible. We killed Trevor Huxley and dumped his body in the sea.'

Chapter 16

Kray opened the glass door of the Paragon and stepped into the foyer. To the left was a small booth used to take entrance money and to the right was a half-moon desk to hand in coats. She walked through another set of glass doors into the club. The place was in semi-darkness.

'Hello!' she called. 'Anyone at home?' Her stomach rumbled from being empty, but at least she no longer felt sick.

A head popped up from behind the bar.

'Bloody hell, love, you're a bit keen aren't you? We're shut. Doors open at eight,' said a young black guy with cropped hair.

Kray opened up her warrant card. 'I'm DI Kray. I want to ask a few questions about a man who works here, his name is Thomas Weir.'

'Tommy, what the hell has he done now?'

'Was he working last night?'

'Erm, yeah, I think he was. I was on a rest day so didn't see him. But I think he was on.'

'Is there anyone here who can confirm he was at work?'

'Shit, he's done something, hasn't he?'

'Do you know him well?'

'Just work colleagues, really. He's a solid guy, good with the punters but he doesn't take shit from nobody. If you know what I mean?'

Kray nodded. 'Has he worked here long?'

'He was already here when I arrived and I've been here almost two years. Is he in trouble?'

'Is there someone else—'

'It's okay, Josh, I've got this.' It was Marshall. He strode across the dance floor, the clack-clack of his heavy shoes echoing off the walls.

'I'm DI Roz Kray.'

'My name is Eddie Marshall. I run the place. How can we help?'

'Was Thomas Weir working last night?'

'He was, or at least he was here for most of the night.'

'What do you mean?' Marshall invited Kray to sit at a table.

'He started his shift and then disappeared about ten o'clock. Left us short-handed so I'm not best pleased.'

'Does he have a habit of doing that?'

'No, he's a reliable guy. Not sure what happened, but he just took off without a word to anyone.'

'Did he have an argument with a customer?'

'Not as far as I know. He's a big hit with our clientele. Don't get me wrong, he can handle himself, but when there's trouble he's always able to talk people down. Can I ask what this is about?'

'Tommy was found dead in the early hours of this morning.'

'Shit, that's dreadful. How did it happen?'

'At this stage I'm not at liberty to say. Was there anyone who held a grudge against him or who might have got into a fight with him in the recent past?'

'No, no one. As I said, he was well liked.'

'Does he have a locker here?'

'No, but we have a place where the guys get ready for their shift. I can show you if you like?'

'That would be helpful.'

Marshall led Kray out of the main hall and up a flight of stairs. At the top was a small room with three rows of benches; a kitbag lay on a table in the corner.

'I think that's Tommy's,' said Marshall, nodding at the table.

Kray donned a pair of gloves and unzipped the bag. It contained a white shirt, a pair of black trousers and a black bomber jacket. 'Is this his stuff?'

Marshall glanced inside. 'Looks like it.'

'Don't touch this, one of our forensics team will be along to pick it up.'

'That's fine.'

'How did he get to work?'

'By car, I think.'

'Do you know the make and model?'

'No, sorry, I don't.'

Kray unzipped a pocket at the end of the bag and pulled out a set of keys. 'Do you have CCTV outside?'

'We have two cameras trained on the back, but nothing out front.'

'Can you let me have a download of the footage from both cameras for last night?' Kray handed him a flash drive.

'Yes, I can get that organised. Anything else I can help with?'

'I'm going to take a wander outside, I will be back shortly. Can you lock this door until the CSI team arrive to collect the bag?'

'Yes, that's no problem, tell them to ask for me when they get here.'

Kray nodded and made her way downstairs and out of the back of the club into the yard. There were several vehicles parked up and a row of bottle banks and rubbish skips against the wall. She looked up and could see the cameras keeping watch. Kray pointed the key fob at the vehicles and pressed the unlock button. Nothing happened. Outside, was a line of parked cars stretching the length of the road. She walked up the street, holding the fob above her head, repeating the process. After fifty yards the orange indicators of a blue Golf informed her she had found Weir's car.

Kray peered through the windows at the spotless interior. She clucked her tongue against the roof of her mouth in appreciation.

Mr Weir was a tidy boy.

Then she retraced her steps to the club with her phone pressed to her ear and requested a vehicle recovery along with a CSI to pick up the bag. Marshall was waiting for her with the memory stick in his hand.

'Here you go.' He handed it over. 'Did you find his car?'

'Yeah, it's parked outside. Any idea why he would have left without taking his vehicle? Someone give him a lift?'

'I'm sorry, I have no idea. As I said, we were not best pleased because he left us short-handed.'

'I'll be in touch, thank you for this.' Kray held up the stick and made her way across the dance floor to the front entrance.

'If you think of anything else, DI Kray, don't hesitate to get in touch.' Kray waved her hand in thanks. 'Oh, and by the way, we've been having some problems with the CCTV in the past few weeks. I hope it's downloaded okay.'

Kray stopped in her tracks and turned to face Marshall. He turned and walked away.

The traffic en route to the station was mercifully light. Kray churned over her conversation at the Paragon – she didn't like it. There was something about Marshall that sent her coppers' intuition into orbit.

He was too calm and too helpful. Smug bastard.

The phone rang, it was Tavener. 'Where are you?' he asked.

'On my way back, why?'

'I've got something to show you.'

'Sounds intriguing. I'll find you when I get to the station.' Kray continued to mull over her interaction with Marshall, and the more she thought about it, the more uneasy she became.

Twenty minutes later she was sitting in the incident room sipping a coffee. She handed the flash drive to Chapman.

'This is the CCTV footage shot at the back of the Paragon last night. Take a look at it to see if it captures Tommy Weir leaving the premises.'

'Will do, Roz.' Chapman beetled off with the memory stick.

'How did you get on?' Tavener asked.

'Weir was working last night and his car is still outside the club. He has a change of clothes in a bag which CSI are picking up. Apparently, he left work early but no one knows why. I met a guy called Marshall who said he runs the place but I don't trust him. What do you have?'

'I've been looking into where Weir worked. The Paragon club is owned by Bellville Entertainment, which is a limited company with a number of business interests; nightclubs, restaurants and gaming premises. It's owned by a chap called Bernard Cross who keeps a very low profile for a man who must have a sizeable personal fortune.'

'How does this help us with Weir?'

'Well, that's the thing, it doesn't.'

'So why are you telling me?'

'You know how you keep banging on about there are no such things as coincidences?'

'Yeah… and I do not bang on.'

'The name Bernard Cross rang a bell and I could not for the life of me remember where from. Then it clicked…' Tavener slid a sheaf of papers in front of Kray and jabbed at it with his finger. 'Bernard Cross is a member of the Blackpool Yacht Club. He owns the Marine Blue – remember the forty-foot cruiser that was in dry dock undergoing repairs?'

'Yes, I remember. What are you driving at?'

'Michael Ellwood gets washed up on the beach. Our working assumption is he was tortured and shot in the head while out at sea and dumped overboard. A second man has his throat slit in a knife attack, and just happens to work at the Paragon. Bernard Cross has the wherewithal to take Ellwood out to sea and he's the top man at the Paragon.'

'It's a tenuous link at best.'

'So, you're saying that's just a coincidence?'

'But aren't you forgetting one important point? The Commodore said the Marine Blue had been in dry dock for six weeks so it couldn't have been used to transport Ellwood.'

'No, I've not forgotten.' Tavener flipped over a few pages and pointed to an entry in the spreadsheet. 'This boat is also ocean-going and it's not in dry dock. I checked with the club.'

'Okay, so?'

'It's owned by Delores Cross – wife of Bernard Cross.'

Chapter 17

It was the summer of the year 2000 and I was fast becoming Rolo's go-to-guy when it came to running errands. Though the term 'running errands' gave my activities an innocent quality they did not deserve. It was a privileged position that enabled me to gain more and more insight into their operations. The Critchleys were the most successful gang in Nottingham, on their way to becoming one of the biggest in the UK. The stakes were high and rising by the day.

The effect on my cashflow was dramatic. Rolo held good to his promise that I would share in the profits. I had more money than I knew what to do with. It was hidden everywhere in my flat. I kept a meticulous record of every pound and never once did I consider skimming some off the top.

My influence in the team was growing. The other guys looked up to me, even Marshall. This was a rush, the likes of which I had not experienced before. Every day I came to work I got high on a heady cocktail of adrenaline and endorphins. Every day it sucked me further under. When I look back, the signs were there – I was losing it.

One time I was in the nerve centre dropping off another holdall bulging with cash when Rolo opened his desk drawer and pulled out his handgun. My senses went into overdrive. *What the hell was he doing?*

'Do you know how to handle one of these?' he said, handing it to me. It was a Beretta M9, one of my favourites.

'I reckon so.'

'Show me,' he said, with more than an edge of challenge in his voice.

I placed the weapon on the table and closed my eyes. 'Say go.'

'Go.'

I picked up the gun, ensuring the manual safety was engaged, and removed the magazine. Then I checked the chamber was empty with my little finger, pushed the disassembly button and rotated the latch to remove the slide. The recoil spring and guide rod were next, followed by the barrel. In twenty-five seconds, six components were lined up side by side on the table.

Keeping my eyes closed, I reversed the process, and thirty seconds later the M9 was back in working order, ready for action.

I opened my eyes to see Rolo grinning like a Cheshire cat. He leaned back in his chair and clapped his hands.

'That's impressive.'

'The army was good to me.'

Rolo rose from his chair. 'Come on, we've got a meeting to attend. Oh, and you'll need that.'

I slid the gun into the back of my jeans and covered it with my shirt. Rolo went downstairs, plucking a set of keys from a hook and exited the back of the club. The amber lights flashed on a big black Jag. He tossed me the keys.

'Where are we going?'

'Do you like Turkish food?'

'Erm, yeah.'

'Then get in and drive.'

I did as I was told and eased the luxury saloon out of the gates onto the main road. Rolo gave me directions as we went. We drove around in circles for what felt like ages then he said, 'Turn left into that side street, pull over and wait.'

He jumped from the car and disappeared into a betting shop.

What the hell is he doing placing a bet?

A couple of minutes later he re-emerged with two men.

Shit! The Critchley brothers!

Rolo piled into the front seat and the brothers slid into the back.

'Go back onto the main road and head into town,' Rolo said, not bothering to introduce the two new guests. I could hear faint mumblings coming from the back seat but for the majority of the next twenty minutes we travelled in silence.

'Stop here,' Rolo finally spat out when we were close by a parade of shops. We all got out and walked over to a Turkish restaurant that was marked with a big red sign saying *Closed*. The door opened as we approached as if someone had said abracadabra. The brothers filed in first, followed by me then Rolo.

A small man who looked as though he spent all his days in the sun locked the door behind us.

The place was long and narrow with a bar to the left and enough tables to seat about forty people. All but one of the tables were bare. The largest one was laid out with silver knives and forks and a bright white table cloth. The Critchleys were greeted by a tall swarthy man wearing a light linen suit. Two other men sat in a booth seat, each one chewing a toothpick. There was lots of handshaking and backslapping as the bloke in the linen suit showed them to the table set with silver.

Rolo took me by the elbow.

'Our job is to make sure they have an uninterrupted meal. I'll take the back of the room and you take the front. No one comes in or out. Got it?'

'Got it.'

'Who are they?' I nodded over to the two men sat in the booth seat.

'They are the Turkish equivalent of us.' Rolo walked to the kitchen end of the restaurant and took a seat at a table for two. I perched myself at the front. The thugs in the booth eyed us and gnawed on their toothpicks.

After a while the small man appeared laden with plates of food that he placed in front of the brothers. The smell was amazing and I automatically felt hungry. I watched as he continued to fill the table with plates. They tucked into the food, my mouth watering.

Focus, you idiot, focus.

After a while the small guy came over to me carrying two dishes.

'Afiyet olsun,' he said, placing them in front of me. One contained flat bread and the other a selection of mezes. Apparently Turkish gangland courtesy was alive and well.

I looked up to see Rolo enjoying the same treatment. I flashed him a smile and he shook his head – *don't eat it.*

We sat for two hours while the Critchleys and the tall Turkish man conducted business. As much as I strained my ears, I heard nothing. Suddenly they rose from the table and it was handshakes all round again. Given the amount of food they had consumed I thought we would be carrying them out in wheelbarrows. Rolo jumped up, as did the two men in the booth seat. I followed suit.

The small guy came over to clear away my untouched food.

'Git kendini becer.' My refusal to eat had not gone down well. He looked like he was going to stab me with a fork.

Ten minutes of theatrical goodbyes later and we were back in the car. We dropped the Critchleys off at the betting shop and headed for the club.

'Who were the two guys we were looking after?' I asked.

'That's not important.'

I tried a different tack. 'Did it go well?'

'It did.'

'It seemed to go well.'

We travelled in silence, then Rolo said, 'We have a shipment coming in soon.'

Jesus Christ, this is what I'd been waiting for.

'When is it?'

'We are still working out the finer details,' he lied. 'I want you on the team, you up for it?'

'You bet.'

In the weeks that followed I became increasingly involved in the preparations. The planning was run on a strict need-to-know basis. I'm not sure even Rolo knew the full picture. Every day we would have a list of tasks. Building the picture of what was going to happen was like constructing a massive three-dimensional jigsaw. A jigsaw with three crucial pieces missing: *what* was the shipment, *when* was it going to happen and *where*?

This was getting close. The problem was, I could feel myself losing my grip on reality. I was going under. And the further I sank into the underworld of the Critchleys, the more challenging it became to go home to Blythe. I tried to visit every month but the pace of the operation made it almost impossible.

I would kid myself that I was looking forward to going home; counting down the days in my head, but when it arrived I was a mess. A ball of nervous tension and anxiety would spin inside me. The weight of expectation always crushed the pleasure out of the time I spent sitting on my own sofa and sleeping in my own bed. Blythe knew it. We both knew it.

It was reasonable for her to expect that the man she married would walk through the door, but he seldom did. She got flashes of him, but for the most part I was going through the motions, trying to remember what a husband was supposed to do. The longer it went on the more lost I became. Both of us realised I was a walking façade which was tissue thin.

One night, when I was home for the weekend, Blythe said, 'I'm pregnant, you're gonna be a dad.' We were watching TV and had just finished dinner. I was basking in the afterglow of my medal-winning chilli when she simply came out with it.

I was thirty-two years of age and she was twenty-seven. We had been married for four years and had never expected kids to come along. Blythe had been told that she couldn't bear children after having fibrous growths removed from her ovaries. We had come to terms with that harsh reality and lapsed into our comfortable happiness – now we were fucking ecstatic.

And in that instant, everything changed.

After running around the lounge waving my hands in the air, occasionally stopping to kiss my wife, a burst of realisation stopped me in my tracks.

'That means…' I said.

'I know,' she replied.

'I'll need to make some changes.'

'I think that would be for the best.'

'I'll talk to them in the morning.'

'That would be good. What about…?'

'Yeah, that could be a problem. We're ten months in and…'

'They might tell you to…'

'They might. I'll see what they say in the morning.' We rarely saw the need to talk in complete sentences.

The next morning Blythe was proved right. They told me to complete my current assignment and after that they would get me out. They stressed the importance of the work I was doing and how they couldn't pull the plug so close to the climax. I agreed.

'A few more weeks, that's all,' I remember saying to her. 'Then I'll get a transfer and be home for you and our baby.'

'Okay.' She said it in a way that told me it was not okay. But what else could I do? I was slipping further away and we both knew it. The sooner I surfaced, the better.

The next day I went back to work and it was as if I had never been away. The lines were blurring badly and I had forgotten all about Blythe and the baby as soon as my foot crossed the threshold of my bedsit. I could feel myself being sucked under.

Who the hell am I?

Then I fucked someone I shouldn't have.

I'd love to say it was a spur of the moment thing but it had been brewing for months. And if it was only the once I could forgive myself the indiscretion – but it wasn't.

Natasha came out of nowhere, recruited as a dancer and table host to entice our more moneyed clients to part with their cash. She was of Eastern European extraction with that heady mix of old-style burlesque and Russian gymnast. It was a combination that was almost impossible to say no to. Actually, who am I kidding, it was *absolutely* impossible to say no.

I have no idea what she saw in me. I am reasonably good-looking but nothing special. She made a beeline for me and made it perfectly clear what she wanted. I later found out she had entered the country illegally and was looking for a meal ticket. Either way, we got it on, big style.

I told Rick about her in one of our daily debriefs. Well, when I say I told him, I kind of hinted at it. He didn't seem too bothered and changed the subject. I took that as his way of letting me know it was fine to carry on. So, carry on I did.

The trouble was Natasha came with a hefty price tag – she got my wife killed.

Chapter 18

I'm sitting in my car watching the back of the Paragon, taking stock of my position. One dead foot soldier and fifty-six grand in cash is not going to get me where I want to be. I need to get under the skin of the operation if I'm going to bring it crashing down, and that means gaining intelligence. Plus, perhaps inflicting a little disruption along the way.

The building has been in darkness now for around forty minutes. The clock on the dashboard reads 2.55am. I pull the blanket around my legs to protect them from the cold.

'I'm out of practice with this shit,' I mutter under my breath as the night creeps into my bones.

'You're telling me.' Jade blows into her hands and rubs them together. 'What are you going to do with the money?' She's sat in the back, her wide eyes staring at me through the mirror.

'Don't know yet, I'll think of something.'

'Thinking… Thinking? You're always bloody thinking!'

'If I rush into this, it's going to go wrong.'

'Fat chance of that! Not seen you rush at anything for years.'

'Yeah, well, I'm being cautious.'

'You weren't cautious when you sliced that guy up. That was good.'

'It served a purpose.'

'Yes, over fifty-grand.' Jade paused. 'You could buy some help?'

'That widens the circle. It's too risky.'

'It would mean you could cover more ground.'

'I know, but I'd be worried about keeping control, and at this stage, I can do without that.'

Jade nods and purses her black lips. 'You're going to hit them hard though, aren't you?'

'Yup, as hard as I can.'

'The bastards deserve a good kicking.'

I reach for the rucksack in the footwell, discard the blanket and step out of the car. The drizzling rain sticks to my face as I yank my hood forward and walk past the gates. There are two security cameras watching the yard but nothing at the side.

I skirt past the high wire fence securing the perimeter of the building next door. It's a solicitors' with offices on the ground and first floor. An alleyway runs between the two properties. I make my way to the end where another tall wire fence bridges the two walls, then rummage in my rucksack and pull out a set of cutters. The galvanized metal snaps as the jaws make light work of the links. In no time I'm peeling back the fence and squeezing through the gap.

To the side of the club is a set of stone steps leading down to a cellar door. I descend into the darkness, all the while looking for additional cameras. The door has a Yale lock. I put my bag on the floor and retrieve a small pouch and a pencil torch from the inside pocket of my coat. The torch goes in my mouth and I insert the L-shaped tension pick into the lock, followed by a Bogota rake. I jiggle the rake back and forth against the tumblers while maintaining a turning pressure on the lock.

Christ, this is taking far too long! Looks like freezing my bollocks off in the car isn't the only area where I'm lacking practice.

I can hear the tumblers clicking into place. Then the lock disengages and the door springs open. I check the interior of the doorframe to see if there are magnetic alarms fitted, but all is clear. I pack away my gear and edge inside. The thin torch beam scans around the bare brick walls, beer kegs and pipework.

There is a door set into the far wall. I make my way over and open it, a flight of stairs leads up to the nightclub. I make my way up and peep through a set of curtains at the top.

Shit!

In both the far corners I see the glow of red LED lights. The place is alarmed with movement sensors.

That's fucked it.

I can go no further. My search for information has come to a shuddering halt. I sit on the top step, mulling over my options, which are pretty limited, then return to the basement and find the fuse box. Inside are banks of breakers each with a code handwritten on the face.

None of them say 'switch off the alarm system'. And who was I kidding, any loss of power would set them off anyway. I'm stuck.

There's only one thing left to do, and that is to add a little *disruption*. I open up my bag and take out three glass containers, each one filled with a pale yellow liquid – petrol. Not enough to burn the whole place down but just enough to let them know I've been here and give them another headache. I place the jars on the concrete floor and look around for flammable material. In the corner is a stack of flattened cardboard boxes. *That will do nicely*.

I open the first jar and dribble the liquid onto the stack, allowing time for it to sink in. I remove the top from the second jar and place it on the floor next to the pile. I reach for the third jar when I hear a noise. A clunking sound coming from behind a closed door located in the opposite wall.

I stop and switch off the torch. There it is again – it sounds like metal being dragged across concrete. I bend down and grab the wire cutters.

The door has two deadbolts fitted, top and bottom. I eased them across. The scraping noise stops.

I inch the door open to reveal a small room about eight feet by six feet. The place is filled with women's clothing hanging from two free-standing rails. There is a second door at the back, it too is held shut with two deadbolts. I ease them across. There's a scuffling noise coming from the other side.

I fling open the door, holding the cutters above my head. The torchlight cuts through the darkness.

Now that's a game changer.

Chapter 19

Harold Biggs was nearing the end of his shift. For thirty years he had been ferrying folk around Blackpool in his cab. Taxi companies had come and gone but Harold kept on going, conducting his business with a smile.

His smile was particularly broad this week because in seven days' time he would be hanging up his driving gloves for good. He'd been planning his retirement for ages.

Despite the many years he had spent behind the wheel, three o'clock in the morning was always a struggle for him. He had never managed to get used to working nights and, with three hours to go until he knocked off, all he wanted to do was curl up and go to sleep.

The couple in the back of his cab were drunk as skunks. It was always a risk picking people up at this time – they might cause trouble, have run out of money or throw up in the back. These two looked pissed, happy and in need of their bed. Harold was only too pleased to be of service.

Harold and his wife had booked a cruise to celebrate his retirement. Ten days sailing around the Caribbean, eating and drinking themselves to a standstill. What a fantastic way to bring down the curtain on a working life.

Actually, it was a double celebration. One to commemorate his retirement and the second to celebrate thirty years of taxiing without having a single accident – an accolade for which Harold was immensely proud. Every week he would hear about this person having a prang or that person reversing into some inanimate object.

'Silly beggars,' he would say to his wife. 'Call themselves professional drivers. Some of these youngsters could hit something driving on Salisbury Plain.'

Unknown to Harold, his wife had bought him a beer tankard, complete with the inscription: *30 years and not a scratch*. A fitting tribute.

A young Asian woman bolted from a side street and dashed into the road. Harold's tyres screeched against the tarmac, trying to gain traction on the wet surface. The couple slid forwards and thudded into the front seats.

The Asian woman bounced off the bonnet, smashing her head against the windscreen, leaving behind a cobweb of shattered glass. She spiralled through the air, landing in a twisted heap about fifteen feet away.

In seven days' time, Mrs Biggs would present her husband with his tankard on the first night of their cruise. Well, she could hardly take it back to the store having had it engraved. And besides, she could still justify awarding him the commemorative gift on the grounds that it wasn't his fault. Harold, on the other hand, could do without the constant reminder sitting on the mantlepiece.

Chapter 20

The Critchley job was not going to plan. My promise to Blythe of having to stick it out for a few more weeks had turned into months, but I could tell we were getting close to D-Day. Rolo was jumpy as hell and kept disappearing without telling us where he was – the shipment must be imminent. Then it all went quiet. The hubbub of activity was replaced by a serene calm and Rolo looked like someone had confiscated his toys.

I asked him on numerous occasions what was happening and he would shrug his shoulders and say nothing. It was infuriating. Then one day, out of the blue, he called me into his office and said, 'It's been delayed, some fuck-up with the supply chain.'

'Oh,' I heard myself saying – my head was racing. 'I suppose it's business as usual for now then?'

'Yeah, pretty much.'

I was overdue a visit home and took the opportunity to grab a weekend away. The problem was, by now I had completely lost it. The affair with Natasha was out of control and the whole operation was approaching meltdown. I had tried to hide my decline from Rick but he could hear the warning signs in my voice. However, being this close to a massive win he was reluctant to hit the eject button. 'Hang on in there and stay focused,' he would say. So, hang on I did.

In truth, working for the Critchleys was exactly where I wanted to be; tripping out on adrenaline and burying myself deep inside Natasha whenever the opportunity presented itself. Which by that stage was every day and in more and more adventurous ways – I wasn't joking when I compared her to a gymnast.

I told Rolo I needed to visit my mother who was sick. Natasha blew a gasket when she found out because she wanted us to get away for a few days. In fairness, we had talked about taking a short break but I thought it would come to nothing – Natasha had other ideas. After a blazing row, I went anyway for a three-day weekend.

It was raining the night they came. Blythe and I were curled up on the sofa, she was absent-mindedly stroking her bump, which by now was showing above the waistband of her jeans.

I had mixed emotions: on the one hand I couldn't wait for this job to be over but on the other I didn't want it to end. I thought alcohol would dull my troubles, and had polished off a serious quantity of cans.

I went upstairs to take a pee and heard a knock on the front door when I was mid-flow. Blythe called up the stairs.

'There's a pizza boy at the door, have you ordered anything?'

The alcohol had numbed my senses. It took a while for what she had said to register in my brain.

'Don't open–' I yelled, as I heard the safety chain being dragged across and the click of the lock as it disengaged. Next thing, the door slammed hard against the hallway wall and Blythe was screaming.

I tucked myself away – still pissing like a racehorse – and ran to the top of the landing. I saw a man wearing a ski mask bundle Blythe into the lounge, followed by another bloke wearing the same gear, and carrying a baseball bat.

I launched myself down the stairs.

'Where is he?' one of the men was shouting in Blythe's face. 'Where's the fucker?'

She was hysterical.

I landed in the hallway and a third guy came out of nowhere knocking me to the floor. He took a swing with his bat and it smashed into the wall. Another swing. Another miss. I felt the wind of the bat sweeping past my face.

My right foot connected hard with his knee. He yelped with pain and fell on top of me. I yanked the weapon from his grasp and leapt to my feet. He was rolling around clawing at his leg. The end of the bat made an angry red circle in the centre of his forehead. He turned cross-eyed. I hit him again. A streak of blood erupted from the side of his head.

Blythe was screaming.

'Billy! Billy! No don't…'

She was on the sofa with the masked man holding a knife to her throat. I froze and the other guy smacked me across the shoulders with his baseball bat. I toppled over the coffee table. The next blow landed across my legs, sending a searing pain up my spine. I lurched forwards and drove my bat up between his legs. He screamed and doubled over, both hands clutching his groin. The next swing split the top of his head. I heard his skull crack open.

The guy with the knife yelled out; Blythe had broken free and was gouging his face with her nails. She was tearing into him. Blood was seeping through her fingers. I launched at him and missed my target and crunched the bat into the back of the sofa. He lashed out with his knife and sliced a deep gash across my arm, then bolted for the door.

I took chase but he was too fast. The last I saw of him, he was racing down the street on his scooter.

I went back to Blythe who was slumped on the floor.

'There's blood on the sofa,' she said.

'It's mine,' I said, trying to stop the bleeding from the cut on my forearm.

'I'm not sure it is, you know?' She removed her hand from her chest and blood glugged down her front. 'I think it's me.'

I tore off my shirt and scrunched it into a ball, holding it against the wound.

'It's all right, it's all right,' I said to her. 'Hold this tight while I get the phone.' I ran into the hall and dialled 999.

I spoke to a woman in the control room and told her we needed an ambulance, fast. I went back to Blythe to see her blood seeping through her fingers. I pushed my hand on top of hers.

'You'll be all right, you'll be all right,' I said to her over and over in an attempt to wish it away.

'I'm still bleeding!' she yelled, as I cradled her in my arms, trying to stop her struggling.

'The ambulance is on its way,' I said.

I remember hearing the thin, metallic voice of the woman in the control room. 'Sir, sir, are you still there?'

I picked up the phone with my spare hand. 'Yes, I'm still here. She's bleeding out. I can't… I can't…'

'I need you to maintain pressure on the wound, is your wife conscious?'

'Yes, yes, she's conscious.'

'Am I going to die?' Blythe said, looking at the bloodstain arcing its way along her chest and down her side.

'No, you're not going to die. The ambulance is on its way,' I repeated. I then squeezed my hand harder into the wound and a spurt of blood hit me in the face.

'Shit, now you're bleeding,' Blythe said, her eyes rolling back in their sockets.

'No, no, I'm fine. Stay with me, stay with me.' I reached for the phone again. 'Where the fuck is it?'

'On its way, sir, about six minutes away.'

'Tell them to hurry.' I looked down to see Blythe's eyes were closed. 'Fuck!' I dropped the phone and shook her for all I was worth. Blood sprayed out onto the sofa. Her consciousness jolted back.

'What? What is it? I feel so cold…'

'Keep talking to me, Blythe, keep talking.'

'Oh… err… I don't know what to say.'

'Anything, tell me anything!' I tore the cover from a cushion and jammed it in the hole. The control room operator's voice was sounding in the background. 'Sir, are you still there?'

Blythe's head lolled forward. I shook her. Nothing happened. I shook her again.

'What? What?' she came back. 'I feel so cold and so tired. I'm going to die, aren't I?'

'No, no, the ambulance will be here in the next few minutes.'

'But you can't stop the bleeding.' She gazed down at the crimson carpet growing around us. 'They have to save our baby.'

'Don't talk rubbish. You'll get through this when the paramedics get here.'

'No, Billy, I don't think I will. They have to save our baby.'

'You'll be fine, the baby will be fine.'

'Make me a promise…'

'Don't talk stupid.' Tears were streaming down my face as I pushed my hand against the wound for all I was worth.

'You need to promise me, you won't go after those who did this…'

'You're talking shit now, when the paramedics get here–'

'Shhh, listen. Promise me that you won't go after the ones who did this because they will kill you too. And I couldn't stand the thought of you dying.'

'Sir, sir, are you on the line?' the control operator said over and over.

'You have to promise me…' Blythe was pulling me down to her. 'Promise me…'

'Okay, I promise, I won't go after who did this. I promise.' My resolution split wide open and I began to sob.

Blythe cracked a smile. 'I love you.'

Her head rolled back, her eyes staring up at the ceiling.

'Blythe, Blythe, stay with me!' I shook her and her head boggled about. 'Blythe, for fuck's sake, Blythe!'

I laid her down on the floor and put my ear to her chest. Nothing.

I clenched my hands together to administer CPR, but as I shoved against her ribs blood erupted from the gash in her chest. My fingers went to her neck. There was nothing.

I picked up the phone. 'Where is that fucking ambulance?'

'It's a couple of minutes away, sir. What condition is your wife in now?'

I didn't hear the end of the sentence because I threw the phone to the other side of the room and went back to work on Blythe. I blew into her mouth and pumped her chest.

The ambulance arrived in twelve minutes, but it took nine minutes for Blythe to bleed out and die.

Chapter 21

I'm standing in my living room, staring out of the window at the early morning sun creeping over the houses opposite. My head is awash with the ramifications of what I'd found at the Paragon. It gives me so many options – but my brain refuses to click into gear. I need more coffee.

Jade is curled up, dozing on the sofa. Her hair is the colour of glacé cherries to match her lipstick. The grey and black eyeshadow daubed across her eyelids make her look like an extra from *The Walking Dead.*

'You don't have a plan, do you?' she pipes up, not bothering to open her eyes.

'I'm working on it.'

'You've lost your edge. Gone soft.'

'I'm thinking things through.'

'Is that what you call it? Not having a clue is what I'd call it.'

'I can do without this. And anyway, it's not that straightforward.'

'Really? Only if you overthink it.'

'Come on then, what do you think?'

'Bloody hell, do I have to spell it out?' Jade is on her feet now, prowling around the living room in her half-mast jeans and Doctor Marten boots. I take my cue; my turn to take a seat. 'Okay, first things first. They've identified Michael's body; how long do you think before that bitch sells you out to the police? She might even be spinning them the line that you killed him.'

'She wouldn't…'

'Are you for real? She wants your head on a spike and will do anything to get it.'

'No, I don't think–'

'I told you, you're going soft.'

'Stop saying that.'

'And what are you going to do when the coppers come calling? You may have hidden yourself away but you've not disappeared altogether. You need to get your story straight for when that happens.'

I pick up the camera and flick through the photographs that I took outside the club, trying to drown her out. Jade continues her rant.

'Listen to me, will you?' Jade is still stomping around. 'That's only half the picture, what the hell are you going to do about Marshall and the Paragon?'

I replace the camera on the table. 'That's what I'm trying to get my head around.'

'Get your head around what? Come on! Do I need to spell it out? There is a sports bag stuffed full of cash under the bed. You discover a woman being held in the cellar with all the hallmarks of being trafficked. And you're staring out the window like a bloody lemon – *thinking things through*? What is wrong with you?'

I get to my feet, go to the bedroom and drag out the kitbag. The smell of notes wafts up to greet me when I run the zip down.

'At-fucking-last!' Jade yells from the other room.

Twenty minutes later I'm standing in a queue waiting to be served. The guy in front of me is sending a package to Edinburgh and the woman behind the counter is intent on giving him the benefit of her experience of when she spent New Year's Eve there with her sister. He is too polite to tell her he doesn't give a shit. I huff my impatience but the woman is oblivious.

After several more minutes and our second trip down the Royal Mile, the man peels away and I put my parcel on the scales.

'Sorry to keep you waiting,' she says, in an overly friendly voice.

'I want this delivered by 9am tomorrow, please.'

She checks the weight, flips up the glass screen and I hand it over. 'Can you tell me what's in it?'

The question takes me by surprise. 'Oh, it's wedding invitations, you know the sort of thing – "please save the day".'

'Are they valuable?'

If only you knew.

'No, they're not.'

'Oh, that's nice. Is it your wedding? I do love a good wedding.'

'No,' I say, with as little emotion as I can muster. I don't have time to listen to her recount a wedding adventure with her sister. She looks put out. 'I'd like someone to sign for it when it arrives.'

She nods and says nothing.

'There's a premium for next-day delivery.'

'That's fine.'

She checks the address. 'You do know this is less than three miles away, don't you?'

'Yes, I know.'

'Okay, if you're sure.' She consults the courier schedule. 'We can get it there for nine o'clock?'

'Good, thank you.'

'That will be twenty-seven pounds thirty, please.' I hand over the cash and I watch as she slides the parcel along the counter. 'Here is your tracking receipt.' She gives me a slip of paper. 'You can use the web address to…'

I don't wait for her to complete her sentence. I nod another thank you and walk out.

That should put the cat amongst the pigeons.

Chapter 22

For the second time in the space of twenty-four hours Marshall found himself standing in front of Bernard Cross, the remnants of a half-eaten cooked breakfast on the table in front of him. Marshall was shitting his pants.

The restaurant was empty apart from the two muscle men flanking him on either side. They looked like twins with their tightly cropped hair and identical suits. Marshall was good with his fists, but he wasn't that good. One word from their weasel-faced boss and they would have him hacked into pieces and wrapped in plastic, destined for the bottom of the Irish Sea.

'I've been giving our unfortunate situation a great deal of thought,' Cross hissed. 'And I've reached the conclusion this has to be the work of the Berkleys. This is them upping the ante. We need to teach them a lesson. I told you someone needs a spanking.'

'You did, Mr Cross, but I'm not sure.'

'Have you gone muddled in the head? We kill one of their guys and they return the favour and kill one of ours. They raise the stakes by taking my money but that's not enough, so they break into the club, sling petrol around and take the girl. They are beginning to fuck me off!' Cross slapped his bony hands hard on the table, knocking his coffee cup out of its saucer. A dark stain spilled across the white tablecloth.

Any minute now that's going to be my blood, thought Marshall.

'Now I want you to tell me which one of the Berkleys you're going to bundle into the back of a van and bring here so I can watch you toast his face under the grill.'

'I'm not sure it is the Berkleys.'

'You are not making sense, Marshall. Can you not put two and two together these days?'

'I don't think it's them because we killed the wrong man.' Marshall's guttural voice tailed off to a whisper.

'What?'

'We killed the wrong man.'

'Are you telling me it wasn't Trevor Huxley?'

'Yes, that's right.'

'Then who the fuck did we feed to the fish?'

'His name was Michael Ellwood.'

'Who the fuck is Michael Ellwood when he's at home?'

'His wife identified the body yesterday. He's a guy from Manchester. He–'

'Let me get this straight. We abduct a guy, torture and kill him to send a message to the firm we believe are about to muscle in on our shipment. And now you say it wasn't him?'

'Yes, that's right. He looks the spitting image of Huxley and he was in the right place at the right time. So, we snatched him.'

'Didn't it register to you that it wasn't the right guy?'

'When we got him in the van things got a little rough and his face was pretty bashed up by the time we got him to the boat. He looked like him, I swear to God.'

'In your debrief you said he denied all knowledge of any shipment or being a member of the Berkley crew. That's not fucking surprising now, is it?' Cross pushed the table away and jumped to his feet. 'Well?'

Cross nodded and four strong hands seized Marshall by the shoulders and slammed his face into the table. They brought him up and banged him down again.

Cross returned to his seat and bent forward so he was eye level with Marshall. 'I understand now why you don't think it's the Berkleys. But what I don't understand is, if it is not them, then who the fuck is it?' He grabbed a handful of hair on the side of Marshall's head.

'I don't know,' Marshall sputtered, his face full of bloody tablecloth.

'No, and neither do I. But the good news is… that's what I pay you for. So, I'm going to do you a favour. Instead of letting Johnson and Johnson do what they do best and tear your arms and legs from their sockets, I'm going to let you walk out of here to find out what the fuck is going on. I want to know who killed Tommy Weir and stole my money. I want to know who broke into my club and I want the girl taken care of. She's a fucking loose end and I have a serious aversion to loose ends. Is that clear?' Cross released his grip and blew clumps of hair from his fingers.

'Yes,' croaked Marshall.

'Yes what?'

'Yes, Mr Cross.'

'Now say thank you.'

'Thank you, Mr Cross.'

Cross righted his coffee cup and topped it up. 'I trust everything is in order for the next shipment?'

'It is, Mr Cross. It's due in tomorrow.'

'That's good.' Cross leaned into Marshall. 'Any more fuck-ups and it will be your face toasting under the grill. Do I make myself clear?'

'Yes, Mr Cross.'

'Get him out of my sight.'

Johnson and Johnson manhandled Marshall to his feet and dragged him across the room as Cross's phone began to rattle on the table.

'Yes, Hazel.' Cross listened without saying a word, then waved his hand for the two heavies to bring Marshall back towards him. 'There's a Detective Constable Duncan Tavener wants to speak with me… you don't happen to know anything about that, do you?'

Chapter 23

Kray was sitting next to Chapman staring at the laptop, nursing her fourth morning cup of coffee. The screen was divided in two, each section showing a different view of the back of the Paragon club.

'This is Weir's car.' Chapman pointed to the image of a blue Golf travelling past the back gates. 'Timestamp is 7.32pm.' She pressed fast forward. 'Here, he's arriving at the club a few minutes later. Notice what he's wearing.'

'The same clothes he had on when he was murdered,' replied Kray, glued to the screen.

'Then at seventeen minutes past nine, this happens…' The black and white grainy images dissolved into a starburst of white noise.

'Shit,' said Kray.

'I checked the whole footage and it stays like that to the end.'

'That's fucking convenient.'

'Isn't it just.'

'Marshall's last words when I left was that they'd been having problems with the CCTV.'

'Either that or someone erased the recording.'

'Can you go to the Paragon and ask Marshall for the last three weeks' CCTV? Don't call ahead first, turn up unannounced. Stick with him while he gets it for you. If he gives you any trouble tell him we'll be back with a warrant.'

'Shall I say we've viewed this and the file was corrupted?' Chapman held up the flash drive.

'Yes, and when he says, "I told your boss we were having trouble with it", ask him which company he's using to get it fixed – see what he says.'

'Okay, Roz.' Chapman retrieved her jacket from the back of her chair and collected her things.

Tavener burst into the office. 'Roz, have you got a minute?'

'Sure, let's grab a coffee.' She drained the last dregs of the one in her hand.

They stood by the machine waiting for the dark fluid masquerading as coffee to fill the cup. 'What is it?' Kray asked, lifting the drink from the dispenser and pressing the buttons again.

'You know we were talking about coincidences?'

'Yeah, what of it?' Tavener hesitated. 'Do I have to beat it out of you?' Kray said, staring up at the towering Scotsman.

'I don't want to compromise your thoughts. I'd rather we take a ride to see for ourselves.'

'So, I do have to beat it out of you.'

'I want you to go with this, Roz.'

'Okay, what do you want me to do?'

'Come with me to the hospital.'

They left the station and piled into Kray's car, which was always a scary prospect for Tavener, having experienced it hurtling around corners on two wheels on more than one occasion. Thankfully, today, the blue lights were off.

They chatted about the case during the fifteen-minute ride to the Blackpool Victoria, but Tavener would not be drawn about what they were about to see.

They arrived at the reception for ICU and Tavener spoke to one of the nursing staff who directed them to a recovery ward. The smell of disinfectant and hand sanitiser made Kray want to gag.

In the corner bed lay a woman with a heavy bandage wound around her head. A clip was attached to the first finger of her right hand with a lead connected to a heart monitor. The graph on the screen showed a rhythmic heartbeat. The nurse drew a curtain around the bed.

'She's been unconscious since arriving at four thirty this morning. She has a fractured skull, a bleed on the brain and a compressed fracture to her left cheekbone. The rest of her injuries are mainly cuts and bruises. She's heavily sedated to allow the swelling on her brain to subside. I'm afraid you won't be able to talk to her.'

'Where are her clothes and belongings?' asked Tavener.

'They are in a bag in her locker.' The nurse indicated a cabinet at the side of the bed.

'Thank you. Is it okay if we stay a while?'

'Yes, that's fine. If there's anything you need, please come and find me.' She parted the curtains and disappeared.

They looked at the woman, dressed in a white and black floral surgical gown, her arms outstretched on top of the sheets. The left side of her face was a riot of yellow, purple and blue; the normal contours of her eye socket, cheekbone and jawline were unrecognisable, buried beneath a ballooned swelling.

Kray tore her gaze away and stared at Tavener with a 'what the hell are we doing here?' look plastered over her face.

'I'm waiting,' she said.

'I overheard a couple of uniform boys talking and made a few enquiries. This woman was admitted after being struck by a taxi. In his statement the driver said he was travelling at about thirty miles an hour when she ran out in front of him. He said it was as though she hadn't seen him. Apparently, after the collision, he saved her life. She wasn't breathing and her heart had stopped. He revived her by thumping her chest.'

'She's a lucky woman.'

'The paramedic's report says she's probably of East Asian origin and was muttering something when she was admitted. No one has been able to ascertain her identity or nationality.'

Kray looked at the labyrinth of tracks running along the inside of her arms. 'Looks like she didn't care much about hiding her addiction. Her arms are a mess.'

'She could be aged anywhere between sixteen and twenty-five. Possibly a streetwalker?'

'Maybe.'

Tavener reached inside the locker and pulled out the white plastic bag containing her clothes. He opened it up and studied the contents. 'That's weird. She has no money and no phone, and yet every item in this bag has a designer label. The T-shirt is Ralph Lauren, the jeans are Versace, trainers are Louboutin.'

Kray's curiosity was getting the better of her.

'Are you sure?' she asked.

'Take a look.' Tavener handed her the bag. Kray pulled out items of clothing and laid them on the bed.

'They don't smell so good,' she said. 'These haven't seen the inside of a washing machine in a while.' Kray picked up the T-shirt and examined the label. 'This is fake,' she said, rifling through the other items. 'They're all fake.'

'There's no coat or jacket. Do you think she's been trafficked and made a run for it?'

'Could be. You mentioned that the driver said she didn't see him. She could have been looking the wrong way when she ran out into the road. Many Asian countries drive on the right. How did you know about this?' Kray waved her hand across the clothes on the bed.

'I didn't. All I knew was a young Asian woman had been hit by a taxi.'

'So why are we here? At the station you said something about–'

'There's no such thing as a coincidence, right?'

'Right.'

'The taxi driver said she ran out of Francis Street… no more than 100 yards from the Paragon club.'

Chapter 24

The incident room was a hubbub of activity. Kray was on the phone, deep in a conversation that was not going well.

'Bloody hell, where've you been?' Tavener asked Chapman, as she bustled into the room, tossing her bag onto her chair. 'We were just about to send out a search party.'

'That was a ball-ache. Marshall had a right wobble when I showed up and wouldn't hand over the CCTV. He gave me some story about having to keep it because they were trying to identify some troublemakers. So, I did the next best thing, I watched it myself. Bloody tedious or what?'

Kray had one ear on the conversation in the office and the other listening to the protestations on the other end of the line.

'And what–?' asked Tavener.

Kray banged the receiver down. 'Welcome back, Louise. Let's take the opportunity for a quick update.' She stood in front of the board which was covered with photographs. 'Starting with Tommy Weir. I heard most of what you had to say, Louise – what did you find when you watched the footage?'

'Nothing. The CCTV at the club was fine, both cameras have been recording without a hitch. The only point in time when the footage was corrupted is the night Tommy Weir was killed.'

'So, Marshall was lying?' asked Kray.

'Yeah, I think so. He was not happy that I'd shown up unannounced, that's for sure. He started talking about us needing a warrant, so I told him we could do that if he preferred and we'd be back on Saturday night with a team of coppers to assist. He soon shut up after that.'

'Did he offer any explanation as to why the CCTV was working fine, when he told me there was a problem?' asked Kray.

'No, he didn't.'

'I said I didn't trust him,' Kray added.

'One piece of good news,' Chapman continued. 'The CCTV in town clocked Weir while he was driving to Spencer Street. I need to go through it to see if he picks anyone up or is followed by another vehicle.'

'And how are we doing with house-to-house?'

'So far, nothing. No one recognises Weir.' Chapman concluded her brief with a wave of her hand.

'Okay. Duncan, how did you get on?'

'I tried to get hold of Bernard Cross. His PA gave me the runaround, saying she couldn't locate him. She said he would call me back. But then, I get a call from his lawyer telling me Cross is keen to help with our enquiries, but any questions must be directed through him.'

'That's a bit heavy-handed,' Kray said.

'That's what I thought. I asked why and he said that Cross is a very busy man and feels our intervention will distract him.'

'I'll bloody distract him… What else do we have?'

'Tommy Weir's girlfriend has identified the body,' pitched in DS Gill. 'She's helping us piece together a profile of her boyfriend along with his possible movements in the hours leading up to his death. We're working our way through his social media history. I contacted every taxi company and no one had a fare in the vicinity of Spencer Street that evening. Not a pick up or drop off. There *is* one thing that jumps out though. When I went through his phone records there were four calls made to Weir's mobile between ten past eleven and half past eleven on the night he died. We ran the number and guess what? It was Eddie Marshall.'

'We need to talk to Marshall again – this time at the station. Let's see if a change of venue knocks that smug look off his face. Keep working with the girlfriend, there has to be something about Tommy Weir that would make someone want to kill him. We need to find it. Let's move on and talk about our other case – the mysterious Michael Ellwood. Duncan, you spoke to the Drug Squad.'

'I did and drew a total blank, I'm afraid. He doesn't show up on their radar either here or in Manchester.'

'So why flush chilli sauce up his nose?'

'I don't know, Roz. Maybe Ellwood wasn't into drugs, but whoever killed him was. We found nothing at his garage. I checked through his phone records and there's nothing out of the ordinary. Oh, and Miriam Ellwood continues to be unhelpful.'

Kray stabbed her finger at the photo of Miriam on the board. 'I think she's holding out on us. She knows more than she's letting on. Let's have another chat with her.'

'I've compiled a list of Michael Ellwood's business associates and friends,' Tavener continued, 'but so far everyone looks squeaky clean.'

'Okay, does anyone have anything else to add?' Three shaking heads stared back at her. The team went back to work. Kray stayed at the board, looking at the mugshots.

'What is it, Roz?' Tavener said.

'We have a murder victim washed up on the beach and a man knifed to death in an alleyway. On the face of it, two entirely separate cases. Why do I have this nagging feeling they're connected?'

'We have the link to Bernard Cross and the Paragon club.'

'Yeah, but it's a tenuous one at best. I spoke to a friend of mine who works in the magistrates' court. He said there's not a cat in hell's chance of obtaining a warrant to search Delores Cross's boat. We don't have sufficient grounds and, while that pissed me off, he had a good point – the only thing I could give him as factual evidence was, "Cross owns a boat". Which didn't carry the day.'

'It was a long shot.'

'This is beginning to bug me.' Kray waved her arm in front of the boards.

'Don't forget the young woman lying in the hospital bed.'

'I know, I'm sure she fits into this puzzle. We need to bring her into the picture somehow.'

'Bagley would never go for that; we have enough on our plate already.'

'That's true, but I got a—'

Bagley burst in.

'Roz, can I have a word please?'

'Yes, sure, I think we're done here. Okay, guys, you know what to do.' She picked up a file from her desk and followed Bagley down the corridor to his office.

'Where are we with the drug connection? I need to brief the ACC.'

'In a word, sir, nowhere. Ellwood doesn't come up on any of the searches.'

'Have you tried—'

'Blackpool and Manchester? Yes, sir. They both came up clean.'

'I don't buy it. This is a drug-related killing, mark my words.'

'The evidence would suggest otherwise. But something interesting came up.'

'Oh, what?'

'A young woman was hit by a taxi in town. She's in hospital with serious head injuries. Tavener and I went to take a look.'

'Why the hell did you do that?'

'It sounded out of the ordinary. She is of East Asian origin, no ID, no money, no phone. She's under sedation so we were unable to speak with her.'

'And you thought you'd stick your nose in? You do know we have a process for allocating cases, don't you?'

'I do, sir, but we were in the location so we thought…'

'How do you mean "out of the ordinary"?'

'Well I reckon she might have been trafficked.' Kray handed Bagley the file. He flicked it open and studied the photographs.

'You're barking up the wrong tree. I spent time in the Trafficking Unit when I worked in Nottingham and Manchester. The statistics are clear: trafficking that takes place in East Asia remains in East Asia. Countries such as Thailand, Malaysia, Laos, Vietnam, Cambodia tend to traffic people into the same region. A lot of the women are brought from the rural areas and sold in the city. They don't ship them into Europe, and they definitely don't ship them to Blackpool.'

'Yeah, I know that, but–'

'But what? She probably got mugged; ran out into the road and got run over. I don't see why we need to overcomplicate it.'

'Overcomplicate it? A young woman is lying in a hospital bed with a busted head and enough puncture wounds in her arms to embarrass a whole smack house and I think we owe it to her to explore all the avenues. Tell me the last time you saw track marks like that? What junkie do you know would do themselves that much damage?' Bagley glanced at the picture.

'Well?'

'That is the worst I've seen.'

'Exactly! And you know that traffickers use drugs to make their victims compliant. It forces them to toe the line. This…' she stabbed her finger at the image, 'is the result of someone injecting this woman – she's not doing this to herself.'

'I don't need a lesson in coercion techniques.'

'She was wearing counterfeit clothing.'

'Oh, come on, Roz, you can get knock-off goods on mail order these days. Check with Missing Persons before we start jumping to conclusions.'

'Something's not right.'

'When are you going to realise I don't run this department on gut feel and intuition? We step through a logical process using tried and tested police methods. I know you are part of the folklore around here, Roz, for cracking cases, but on this occasion you're wrong.'

Kray held her tongue, waiting for the penny to drop.

'This has nothing to do with trafficking but you're right about the track marks on her arm. She could be a drug mule?'

'Yeah, maybe.' said Kray.

'There's a drugs link to Ellwood, I'd stake my pension on it, and this woman looks like she has a drug connection as well.' Bagley stared at the picture while Kray held her breath. 'I want you to take this case, Roz, run it alongside the Ellwood investigation.'

Bingo!

'But I have a ton of work to do, what with–'

'Just do it, Roz. Just do it.'

Kray took the file from Bagley's hand, turned on her heels and walked out. She had to make a swift exit to hide the broad grin that was spreading across her face. She met Tavener coming out of the incident room.

'I've got a job for you.'

'What's that?'

'You need to get another evidence board.'

Chapter 25

Kray pulled her car into the visitors' bay and stepped out, grabbing her overnight bag from the passenger seat. She made her way to the foyer area and let herself in. The lift took her to the second floor and she slid the key into number twenty-four. She had butterflies in her stomach.

'Hi,' she called out, dumping her bag in the hallway and kicking off her shoes. The place smelled like a top-end restaurant. Millican had promised vegetable risotto followed by panna cotta and she had been looking forward to it all day.

'Hey, you're on time for once.'

'Well you said you'd be cooking something nice… this time.' They embraced each other, she kissed him on the mouth. She could taste wine on his lips.

'Cheeky sod,' he replied. 'I always cook you something nice. Are you up for a glass?'

'Yes, just a small one, I'm still trying to be good.'

He busied himself in the kitchen and returned with a chilled white wine. Beads of condensation clung to the outside of the glass. She plonked herself on the sofa.

'You're in a good mood,' Millican said.

'How do you mean?'

'You know… like… happy.'

'Now who's being a cheeky sod.'

'No, you do. You look… happy!'

'Well, believe it or not I think I might have had a good day!'

'Bloody hell, that's a first. Did Bagley fall under a bus?'

'No, no such luck. But I did make progress with the cases I'm working on and I left work on time. So, all in all, I'd say it's been a good day.' Millican slumped onto the settee beside her and she folded herself into his arms.

'Here's to having good days.' She held out her glass and they chinked a 'cheers'.

'You should have them more often.'

'No, I think one a year is quite sufficient.'

'Are you hungry?'

'Bloody starving.'

'Good, it'll be ready in fifteen minutes.' Millican heaved himself from the sofa and disappeared into the kitchen. Kray snuggled into the cushions and sipped her wine.

'How was your day?' she called out.

'Good,' he called from the other room. 'I had an article published.'

'Wow! I'm impressed, what's it about?'

Millican appeared in the doorway clutching a magazine. 'Listen to this… "It is well recognised that over the past four decades incidents of asymptomatic primary hyperparathyroidism have increased significantly. However–"'

'Hyperparathyroidism? Is that even a thing?'

'Of course it is. There's a really good bit here… "so the conclusion we can reach from conducting laboratory tests is–"'

'Is that reading pathology journals can significantly spoil an otherwise pleasant day.'

Millican feigned a pout. 'I take an interest in *your* work.'

'That's because I talk about it in plain English and not made-up words.'

'I'll fix dinner then.' He tossed the magazine at her from across the room and turned in a theatrical huff.

'I'm really proud of you.'

'Bollocks! Is that plain enough for you?' They both laughed.

Dinner was even better than Kray had imagined. Millican was a genius in the kitchen. She cleared the dishes from the dining room and loaded the dishwasher.

'That was amazing. Maybe you should write cookery books instead of pathology articles, I'm sure you'd get more readers that way.'

'You are pushing your luck, lady.' Millican wrapped his arm around her waist and pulled her close. 'Just you wait till I get you upstairs.'

'What arc you going to do? Read me some more from your journal?'

'Cheeky cow.'

'Don't squeeze me, I need a pee.' He wound his other arm around her and squeezed.

'Ohhh! Let me go before I wet myself.' Kray struggled free and legged it upstairs to the bathroom.

Sitting there, she could feel the butterflies in her stomach going berserk.

Tonight's the night.

This was going to plan. She had rehearsed what she was going to say and how she was going to say it. She ran through the little speech in her head again.

Chris, I have something to tell you. I've been meaning to tell you for a while and wanted to pick the right time. And now is the right time…

She reeled off a length of toilet roll.

Kray folded the tissue paper and wiped herself. A red smear caught her eye. She stared at it, her mind not computing what she was looking at. She took another length of paper and wiped again – same result.

She checked her underwear. Dark spots stained the material.

Fuck!

Chapter 26

I pull the car past the wrought-iron gates and park on the driveway. A dim light penetrates the fluted glass in the main entrance; other than that, the place is in darkness. I switch off the engine and check my watch, almost 9pm. I get out into the cold air and crunch my way across the gravelled courtyard, towards the light.

A tall pitched roof towers above me with ornate latticework decorating the edging. The stone plaque mounted high on the wall reads, 1863. The trailing greenery across the front of the property gives the place a vicarage-like feel. Which is no bad thing, I suppose.

I hear the chimes of a bell echoing somewhere in the hallway as I press the button. The dark silhouette of a figure approaches. The door opens.

'Are you Mr Ambrose?' I ask.

'Yes, you must be Richard Moss, we spoke on the phone. Please come in.' The man standing in front of me is middle-aged, dressed in a black suit, his white face highlighted against the gloom. He oozes a sense of melancholy from every pore.

I shake his hand and enter into the warmth of the house. The name Richard Moss came up on my internet search of garages in the Salford area. I have no idea who he is, or whether his car servicing lives up to his advertising claims. But tonight he'll do nicely.

'Thank you for seeing me out of hours, Mr Ambrose,' I say.

'That's fine, we try to be as flexible as we can. It is not always easy for people to get here during the day. I'm afraid ours is not a nine-to-five job.' His delivery is soft and low, almost a whisper. Boy, this guy is in the right job.

'No, I don't suppose it is.'

'My condolences on your loss.'

'Oh, err, Michael was a colleague. Well, less of a colleague more of a work friend. I run a garage in Salford Quays called Moss Autos, you may have heard of us?' Ambrose purses his lips and shakes his head. 'Michael and I used to send each other work – if I was snowed under I'd give him a call and vice versa.'

'His wife Miriam said they owned a garage.'

I nod my head and smile. He nods in return, minus the smile. The seconds tick by.

'Is it possible for me to…?' I ask, anxious to break the impasse.

'Of course, please follow me.' We make our way to the back of the hallway and Ambrose opens up a door leading to a long, dimly-lit corridor. There are doors leading off to the right and left. We reach the fourth one along. He pauses with his hand on the door handle. 'Due to the circumstances, the family have requested a closed casket.'

'I understand.' Ambrose opens the door, steps inside and ushers me in.

'If you need anything I won't be far away.' He crosses behind me and closes the door.

The room is lit by two subdued lamps, the walls painted cream, the carpet beige. A faint smell of furniture polish hangs in the air. Two chairs rest against one wall and two against the one opposite. Between them a pale brown casket is cradled on a wheeled trolley that's draped in white covers. The brass fittings seem to fluoresce against the dim lamplight.

I pull up one of the chairs and sit in front of the coffin, my head bowed. Tears well against my bottom eyelids and I reach up, placing my right hand onto the oak-veneered lid. I can feel the contours of the edging beneath my fingers, cool to the touch.

Tears roll down my cheeks and fall onto the carpet. My eyes become accustomed to the light and I watch the droplets lie proud on the surface before being absorbed into the pile.

My shoulders start to shake and I sob my goodbyes. Memories flash before me like a magic lantern show, each one a painful reminder of what has gone before.

I see the parade of care homes we visited, the look of glee on his face when he gained his apprenticeship and the look of sadness when I went off to war. I feel his hand squeezing mine; once when we stood at the graveside watching our father's ashes being placed into the ground and the second time when we buried Mum.

The memories come thick and fast, tumbling around in my head. They take me on a helter-skelter ride of the good times and the bad.

Suddenly, I'm back in my house in Birmingham, kneeling beside Blythe, screaming at her to wake up. I remember a pair of hands gripping my shoulders, pulling me away. A man dressed in green falling to his knees to take my place.

'The baby, the baby,' was all I could say. I have no idea what he said in return.

He put an oxygen mask over Blythe's nose and mouth then jabbed her with an adrenaline stick. The other paramedic went to work, resuming the compressions.

It was like watching everything in slow motion.

Five minutes later they stopped.

They patched me up, and when the police arrived I identified myself and gave them a potted version of events. I told them about the operation in Nottingham and about the Critchleys. I called Rick. He came straight over.

The coppers removed the ski masks from the two men who were lying on the floor. I recognised them from the club – both were dead with their heads caved in.

I later learned that Natasha had been suspicious of me going to visit my sick mother and had followed me. When she saw the set-up at home, she put two and two together and ran back to Rolo as fast as her shapely legs would carry her. I guess this was what Rolo was referring to when he said there would be the harshest of consequences if I broke the pledge.

I wanted revenge, who wouldn't? But I was embroiled in a massive police investigation that saw the Critchley operation shut down. Rolo and one of the brothers were sent to jail. The remaining brother was never charged and disappeared to live off his millions.

I was swept along in the enquiry which was a crazy mix of a murder investigation and a drug and money laundering case. And throughout, all I could think about was: *Who was the third attacker?*

Rick did his best to get me rehabilitated into the force but I couldn't risk that. I was still alive and sooner or later they would come looking for me again. Or at least that's what my paranoid mind kept telling me.

I had all the counselling that was going, but in the end I reverted to what I knew best and told them what they wanted to hear. Rick was a big support, right up until the time when he was told to move onto the next big case. Then he melted away, just like the others.

Every bone in my body wanted to wreak revenge but the promise I made to Blythe was the only thing I had left. Rick's parting gesture was to help me disappear – new name, new place, new job.

'If you're thinking of tracking them down – don't,' Rick had said. 'This is a fresh start, don't fuck it up.' And with his words ringing in my ears he was gone. I wasn't to see him again for another eighteen years. And now they had returned to take their pound of flesh in the form of my brother's life.

The vision of Miriam burst into my thoughts, her face snarling, spitting her words at me.

'Leave my fucking family alone! Come near us again and I'll kill you.' The image jolts me from my daydream.

There is a soft knock at the door. I rub my face with my hands and get to my feet. The door edges open and Ambrose is standing there in all his melancholy splendour.

'I just wanted to check you were…' he says.

'I'm fine, thank you.' I glance at my watch. 9.45pm. 'Oh, I'm sorry, I didn't mean to keep you so long. I lost track of time.'

'Don't worry, sometimes it takes that long. It's not a problem.'

'I'll be on my way. Thank you for being so accommodating.'

Ambrose moves to one side and I join him in the corridor.

'Will you be attending the funeral?' he asks.

'Umm, no, I don't think so.'

'Let me show you out.' Ambrose escorts me back to the main entrance and out the door. The cold air pricks at my face as I get into the car.

I didn't want to do that, but I needed to. I have no idea when the funeral will take place, but one thing I do know is… I won't be there.

'Do you feel better now?' asks Jade, her shock of blue hair complimenting her eyeshadow.

'Yeah, much better.'

I gun the engine and head back to the Paragon.

Chapter 27

Marshall walked across the pedestrianised area to the car park. The sprawling building in front of him was lit up like a small town. The umbrella above his head was to protect him from the glare of the CCTV rather than what was falling from the sky.

He was struggling to focus. That bloody copper had turned up and wanted to trawl through the CCTV. Christ knows what she reported back to the station. Marshall was sure that was going to return to bite him in the arse. He quickened his pace to fight against the cold. He was dressed in a cotton T-shirt when a thick overcoat would have been more in keeping with the season.

His face felt odd. His customary fringe had been swept back and the grey hair dye had aged him ten years. The goatee beard itched against his skin and the tinted spectacles made it hard to see in low light conditions.

The woman who had performed his transformation had been quick and professional, ensuring that when he held a mirror up after she'd finished, he didn't recognise the man staring back. He didn't balk at her £700 fee, after all, a breakdown of her invoice would read: Make-up – £15, keeping my mouth shut – £685.

Marshall weaved between the cars until he came to a red Ford Focus with the registration number that matched the one in his head. He reached under the front wing on the driver's side and pulled out the keys that were sitting on top of the wheel. He opened the hatchback. A holdall lay inside.

He locked the car and replaced the keys where he had found them. With the bag slung over his shoulder, he walked towards the entrance, the umbrella still blocking the view of prying eyes.

Marshall skirted around the side of the building and strolled down a pathway until he came to a concealed entrance. The lights from a hundred windows made it easy to find. The door was ajar, thanks to the stone wedged in the door jamb. Marshall folded his umbrella and went inside.

The place was in semi-darkness, with bare concrete walls and a set of steps leading up to the next level. Marshall stuck his head over the handrail to check the stairwell. It spiralled up to the top of the building. On the landing above he could see a green sign attached to the wall with the picture of a stick man running for a door. Above it was the word: Exit.

He yanked a set of blue scrubs from the bag and pulled the trousers over his jeans and slipped the tunic over his head. The name badge and lanyard read, Jason Bourne. He raised his eyes to the heavens, *surely not*? He rummaged around in the bag then kicked it into the corner under the stairs.

His footsteps echoed against the bare walls as he made his way up to the second floor. He put his ear to the door leading off the landing, took a deep breath and opened it. He stepped out into a long white corridor filled with bright, sanitised light and a handful of people. He checked his watch, it read 9.47pm.

Marshall made his way along a walkway that connected two buildings then turned left into a throng of people staring at signs and stepping out of lifts. Staring down another corridor and through a set of double doors he could make out his target.

A gaggle of people were crowded around a giant whiteboard filled with names and acronyms. The backs of their heads were nodding, the place filled with work-like chatter. The shift handover was in full flow. No one turned around.

A long desk separated the group from the general walkway and Marshall picked up a clipboard as he ghosted by. A half-round black ball housing the CCTV camera was mounted in the corner. He kept close to the wall to minimise his profile. The sound of call button alarms died away as he turned the corner.

Marshall kept his head down, glancing at the grey signs with blue lettering that were mounted above the doors: D1… D2… D3… D4. He looked through the glass in the double doors. The room beyond contained four beds, two of which were occupied. A woman dressed in a green uniform was standing at the side of one of them, topping up a plastic glass with fresh water from a jug. An emaciated woman lay asleep in the bed, her skin almost indistinguishable from the white of the sheets.

Marshall stepped away from the door and consulted his clipboard. He didn't know who Jerald Ross was, but the fact that he had DNR in big red letters at the top of the sheet didn't bode well for the bloke.

Come on, come on. He checked his watch – *shit, this is cutting it fine.*

He had wanted to farm out the job to a professional but the insistence of Bernard Cross that it needed to be sorted fast had made that impossible. He had also considered giving it to one of his boys but had quickly discounted that option. *If you want a job doing well, do it yourself.*

He peeked through the window.

Fucking hurry up!

The woman in green was standing at the sink, doing Christ knows what. He checked his watch again. Any minute now the place was going to be filled with people hoping to get through their shift with the minimum of fuss.

He went to look again. The door flew open and the woman in green busied her way to another side ward carrying her jug. Marshall put his shoulder to the door and slipped inside.

The old woman stirred in her sleep. Marshall ignored her. He was committed now. The woman in the corner was also asleep, though in reality it was a cocktail of drugs that kept her consciousness at bay. The large swathe of bandages wrapped around her head made her look like she was wearing a turban and the side of her face was bruised and swollen. A tube ran into her arm from a bag suspended next to the bed. The heart monitor silently kept time with every beat.

Marshall fished a syringe from his pocket and flicked off the cap, exposing the tip. He held it beneath the clipboard, his breath shallow, his senses on red alert.

He approached the bed, giving a quick glance over his shoulder. The canular inserted into the vein on the back of her hand had a second port. Marshall placed the clipboard on the bed and rotated her arm towards him to get a better shot. The needle pierced the membrane and the fluid coursed into her vein under the pressure of the plunger.

This would make her sleep.

Sleep forever.

Chapter 28

Kray found herself lying on a sheet of blue paper on a bed, staring at a blank blue screen. The front of her work trousers gaped open to reveal her belly and a small device was held tight against her abdomen with a blue strap.

A numbness slowly spread through her; that same feeling that had enveloped her while she was in Millican's bathroom.

'Are you okay up there?' he had called up the stairs.

Fuck, how long have I been here? Her grasp on time and reality had slipped – badly.

'Yeah, be down in a minute,' she had yelled back.

Come on, pull yourself together woman!

And pull herself together she did. Kray re-emerged as though nothing had happened. She adopted a warm and funny exterior, while burying the urge to get the hell out of there. She had feigned a headache and went to bed. A fitful night's sleep had done nothing to quell her anxiety in the morning. She left for work and, after making a few calls, had driven straight to the surgery.

Kray glanced across at the woman in the blue tunic who was busying herself donning surgical gloves. Her name badge read, Vickie Morgan.

'This will feel a little cold.' She squirted blue gel onto Kray's belly and moved the device over her lubricated skin.

Why the fuck does everything have to be blue?

Images leapt onto the screen, blurring in and out of focus as the probe did its job.

Kray held her breath.

Two hours earlier she had been sitting in the doctor's surgery telling, what looked like a fourteen-year-old boy, that she had found blood in her underwear.

'What colour was it?' he had asked.

Fucking blood-coloured!

She held her tongue and played nicely throughout the consultation.

'You've had a show. Spotting is very common and is usually nothing to worry about,' the doctor had said once they had finished.

'Usually?'

He had referred her to the maternity unit and her anxiety went through the roof when she realised it was the same hospital Chris Millican walked the corridors of on a daily basis.

'Does it have to be that hospital?'

'If you want to be seen quickly – yes,' came the blunt reply.

She consoled herself with the thought that the part of the hospital responsible for bringing new life into the world was at the opposite end to the part concerned with administering to the dead. The chances of her crossing paths with her boyfriend were slim.

Kray watched the picture on the screen change as Vickie swept the probe across her tummy.

'There, can you see? Baby is fine.'

Can't make out jack shit.

'Yeah, just about. Is that the heart rate?' Kray nodded at the bottom of the screen showing the number 134.

'How far along are you?' Vickie asked, her eyes glued to the image.

'I'm not really sure, maybe five weeks.'

Vickie scrunched up her nose. 'I think you're more like seven to eight. Have you not got a date for your scan?'

'Erm, no, not yet. I've been, well, you know, busy.'

Vickie nodded and smiled, but her face said it all. 'It would be good to get that booked.'

It was Kray's turn to nod and smile.

Vickie pushed a button on the machine and wiped the probe with a paper towel.

'Is that it?' Kray asked.

'It is, unless you have something else you want to talk through?'

'Err, no, no, I'm fine thanks.'

'Have a chat with your doctor about coming in for another scan. Probably around the twelve week mark.'

'Yes, I'll do that.' Vickie tore off a length of paper towel and handed it to Kray. She wiped the gel from her belly, fastened her trousers and swung her legs over the edge of the bed. The room began to spin. She gripped on to the mattress.

'You okay?' asked Vickie. 'Take a minute. Would you like some water?'

'Yes please.' The room swam in circles. Vickie handed her a plastic cup. Kray took a sip and immediately felt better. 'I didn't eat breakfast this morning.'

'That wasn't very clever, was it? You need to look after yourself.'

No shit.

The room stabilised and Kray stood up. 'Thank you,' she said, heading out the door.

'Take care,' Vickie chirped. 'Oh, and this is for you.' She handed Kray a small grey and black photograph.

'Umm…' Kray stared at it and screwed her face up.

'It's your baby.'

'Erm, thank you.'

What the fuck am I going to do with that?

Kray stuffed it in her bag and marched down the corridor, stopping at a vending machine to buy a bar of chocolate. She glanced at her watch. 10.25am.

I guess that can count as breakfast.

She chomped on the bar as she made her way out into the car park. As the sugar did its job she was in a world of her own, trying to process what she'd just seen. There was a person growing inside her. It had never felt more real.

'Roz! Roz! What are you doing here?'

She froze at the sound of the voice, then turned around to see her boyfriend's face creased up with confusion.

Marshall entered the back of the club and made his way up the stairs to the dance hall. He was still buzzing from the events of last night and had been awake since 5am. He couldn't wait to give a full report to Bernard Cross, hoping that his efforts would go some way to appeasing the weasel-faced bastard. If it did, it was difficult to tell. Having Johnson and Johnson breathing down his neck had taken the shine off it, but at least he hadn't got his face rammed into the tablecloth.

The club was a hive of activity with people polishing and hoovering for all they were worth.

'Morning, Eddie,' Josh called out from behind the bar, busying himself by filling the optics.

'Josh.' Marshall raised his hand.

'A package came for you,' said Josh.

'Oh, what is it?'

'Don't know. I left it in your office.'

'Cheers.' Marshall headed to the service stairs behind the stage. At the top he turned left and entered a small office, closing the door. Sure enough, a box was sitting on his desk. He opened the drawer and took out a pen knife. The blade made short work of the packing tape. He opened the flaps to reveal a piece of paper sitting on the top with a handwritten message scrawled across it.

I will call at 11am today.

Marshall peered inside to find the delivery contained oblong bricks wrapped in newspaper. He lifted one out, and using the knife, opened up the corner. His eyes widened. In no time, ten bricks were stacked on his desk, each one containing one thousand pounds.

Chapter 29

Kray's heart leapt into her mouth. She tried to swallow it back down.

'I didn't expect to see you this morning,' Millican said, kissing her on the cheek. 'What are you doing here?'

'Oh, err…' It took a while for her grey matter to get to work. 'My head is so full of these damned cases I wasn't concentrating and wound up in the wrong part of the hospital.'

'Where do you need to be?' He wrapped his arm around her shoulder.

Her brain finally woke up. 'Intensive care. There was a person admitted yesterday that's of interest to us. She was struck by a car and is in a bad way.'

'Bloody hell. You have taken a wrong turn. You're miles off.'

'Yeah, I know. Anyway, why are you here?'

'I couldn't park in my usual spot because they were repainting the lines and I ended up here. I left my wallet in the car, so had to come back. Do you have time for a coffee?'

'No, I need to get to the ICU.'

'Is it the Asian woman?'

'What?'

'The woman who was hit by the car – is it the Asian woman?'

'Yeah, it is. How do you know?'

'She was transferred to us early this morning. I'm not sure who–'

'Transferred to you? She's in the morgue?'

'Yes, I thought you knew. She died last night on the ward. I presumed that's why you were here.'

The scars across Kray's back ignited. 'No, I didn't know. Fuck!' She slammed her arms to the side of her body and turned away.

'I'm sorry,' Millican said, not knowing exactly what he was apologising for. 'I think she was suffering from a major bleed on the brain and–'

'I need you to do something for me.' Kray turned and placed both hands on his shoulders. 'Go to the mortuary and preserve the body. Don't let anyone touch it until I get there. Can you do that?'

'Erm, yes. Can you tell me what this is about?'

'I can't explain now, just do it.'

'Okay, okay.' Millican ran in one direction while Kray ran in the other. She snatched her phone from her pocket and dialled. Tavener answered.

'Hey, are you feeling better now? I got your message that you had a doctor's appointment this morning.'

'Never mind that. Get your arse down to the hospital and meet me in ICU. Ward D4.'

'Isn't that where we saw the Asian woman?'

'Get here as fast as you can and send a CSI unit. And get somebody to seize the CCTV footage on the ICU ward for last night.'

'Christ, Roz, what is this?'

'I'll explain when I see you.'

'Roz, are you running?'

'Fucking trying to.'

Kray dialled off and kept the phone in her hand as she belted into the hospital entrance. She took the stairs two at a time, constantly uttering the words, 'excuse me' and 'sorry'.

She burst through the double doors and ran past the nurses' station. One of them looked up. 'Can I help you?' Kray wasn't listening.

The doors to D4 banged back against their hinges, frightening the old woman in the bed half to death. Which, given her condition, was unwise, as she didn't need the help.

An orderly dressed in green was tugging the sheets off the empty bed in the corner. At her feet was the bag containing the Asian woman's belongings along with a yellow sealed bucket marked Medical Waste.

'Please step away from the bed.' Kray was panting like a seventies porn star. She held up her warrant card. 'I'm DI Roz Kray, can you step away from the bed please?'

The old woman let out a gargled shriek. 'Terrorist! Terrorist!' she yelled at the top of her voice.

Kray turned and showed her badge. 'No, madam, I'm a police officer.'

'Terrorist! Terrorist!' the old woman continued to wail, pulling the bedclothes over her head.

'What's your name?' Kray asked the man dressed in green scrubs.

'Jack, my name is Jack.'

'Okay, Jack, move to the other side of the room, away from the bed.'

'Terrorist! Terrorist!' came the muffled screams from the quaking mound on the bed.

Kray scanned around. 'Where's the drip?'

'It's in the bucket.'

'All of it? The tubes included?'

'Yeah, all of it. Look, all I'm doing is changing the bed.'

The ward sister shoved open the door, a slight but fearsome woman in her late forties wearing a dark blue uniform. 'What is going on here?'

The old lady let out another scream.

'I'm DI Kray.' She flashed her badge again. 'What happened to the woman who was in that bed? The woman with the head injury.'

The ward sister moved closer and whispered, 'She passed away last night.'

'How? How did she die?'

'From the injuries she sustained when she was struck by a vehicle. She's down at the mortuary. We will know more when–'

'I want you to clear this ward and seal it off. And I need to secure everything that is around the bed.'

'Why?'

'Never mind why. Can you do that for me?'

'Terrorist! Terrorist!' The old woman had found her voice again.

'And… tell her I'm not a terrorist.'

'Why do you want me to do that?'

'Because I'll need to interview her and she's not going to cooperate if–' Kray doubled over, clutching her side. 'Ooh… shit!'

'Are you okay?' asked the ward sister.

Kray straightened, then winced again in pain. 'It's just a stitch.'

'Are you sure?'

'Yeah, I'll be fine. A colleague of mine will be arriving soon, can you get this patient into another room while I–' Kray's phone buzzed in her pocket. 'Excuse me.'

Chapman's voice boomed down the line. 'Roz, the CCTV and ANPR have come back. I think we need to have another chat with Marshall.'

'Okay, I'm tied up at the hospital until Duncan arrives. Drag Marshall down to the station and I will meet you there.' She hung up and turned to the ward sister. 'Sorry about that. I need you to–' Kray doubled over again, holding her side. 'Fuck. That hurts.'

Marshall checked his watch – ten minutes to eleven. He went to the kitchen, made himself a black coffee and returned to his office, closing the door. He sat behind his desk and waited.

On the strike of eleven o'clock the phone rang.

'Hello.'

'Mr Marshall, Mr Eddie Marshall?'

'Yes, who is this?'

'That is not of consequence, Mr Marshall. What I want to know is – do I have your attention?'

'I received your package.'

'That is not what I asked – do I have your attention?'

'Yes, you do. What do you want?'

'That's what I like, a man who gets straight down to business.'

'I'm a busy man, Mr…?'

'You can call me Mr Jackal. Like in the book. I do enjoy a good book, don't you, Eddie?'

'Do I know you?'

'No, we've never met.'

'Do you want to tell me what this is about, Mr Jackal?'

'Of course. I am in the market to purchase some merchandise. Merchandise I know you stock on your shelves from time to time. Now, I am well aware there are procedures and protocols to follow to be able to make such a purchase, but you see, Eddie, I'm in a rush.'

'I'm not sure I know what merchandise you are referring to.'

'No?'

'No.'

'I believe you were careless enough to lose one the other night. Such a shame to waste such a precious resource. Does that help to jog your memory?'

'Look, Mr Jackal. I don't know what you're alluding to but–'

'I have a client who's willing to pay over the odds for your product. In return for a FastPass to the game. And he is, shall we say, very insistent.'

'Insistent?'

'My client is used to getting his way. You know how those people can be.'

'And what if I say no?'

'Mr Marshall, I am trying my best to make it easy for you to say, "yes". But in the event that you won't let my client play we will be forced to… well, let's just say the Paragon club will be looking for a new head of security. But we would much rather that didn't happen and you accept our goodwill gesture instead. What d'you say?'

Marshall picked up the nearest brick of notes from his desk. 'Is there more to this "goodwill gesture" than meets the eye?'

'There's plenty more.'

'Then I think we can do business, Mr Jackal.'

'Good.'

'How do I get in touch with you?'

'You don't. You will notice that the newspaper is taken from yesterday's edition of *The Gazette*. I regularly pass your club, that's how I knew what time you got into work. Stick a Post-it note to the inside of the glass on the front door and I will call you.'

'I can do that.'

'My client is impatient and would like to know the rough date of the next game.'

'Tell your client, soon. Goodbye, Mr Jackal.'

Marshall disconnected the call and immediately dialled 1471. The voice came back to tell him that the caller had withheld their number.

'Shit,' Marshall muttered to himself. He sat back in his chair and mulled over the conversation. This was certainly unusual and completely against every protocol their business had put in place. But on this occasion, he reckoned he could make an exception.

The goodwill gesture sitting on his desk would go a long way to salve his conscience.

Yes, that will do nicely.

Chapter 30

Kray had made it back to the station just in time to see Marshall sitting in the interview room with a face like a smacked arse. Chapman was sitting opposite, both of them cradling cups of coffee.

Kray took a seat and kicked off the proceedings. 'Just to reiterate, Mr Marshall, you are helping us with our enquiries and you're free to leave at any time. You can have a solicitor present if you wish?'

Marshall shook his head. 'No, that won't be necessary.'

'What happened to your cheek?' Kray noticed the abrasion under his eye.

'Oh nothing, it comes with the territory.'

'We have a couple of points which we are hoping you can help us with.'

'That's what she said.' Marshall cocked his head in the direction of Chapman. 'And while we're on the subject of being helpful... I don't find it helpful for this woman to enter my premises and commandeer my CCTV. It was not acceptable.'

'Do you want to make a formal complaint regarding the conduct of DC Chapman?'

Marshall thought for a moment. 'No, I don't.'

'Okay, then we'll press on. There are a number of aspects about the death of Tommy Weir that are bugging me, and one of them is cars.'

'Cars! Christ, I would have thought him being stabbed was more of an issue. But you're the copper, you know best.'

Kray ignored the gibe. 'Let's start with these...' Kray pushed a bunch of keys, encased in a plastic evidence pouch, across the table. 'Tommy's car keys were in his bag, do you remember?'

'Err, yes, I suppose so.'

'And Tommy's car was parked outside the back of the club.'

'Yes, so what?'

'The thing that's been bugging me is, if his car was at the club, how did he get to Spencer Street?'

'I don't know. All I know is he buggered off and left us short-handed. Maybe he got a lift or took a taxi?'

'We checked every taxi company and none of them have any record of dropping off a fare around that area.'

'Maybe he walked.'

'If he walked from the club it's fifteen miles, so that's unlikely.'

'He got a lift, then?'

'He could have. The other possibility is he took one of your pool cars.' Kray motioned to Chapman who slid a photograph across the desk showing four vehicles in the club compound. 'This was taken at 7pm on the night Weir was killed. You have a white Transit van, a small hatchback, an estate car and a saloon car all parked at your premises.'

'Yeah, so what? We make a lot of trips, run a lot of errands.'

'We checked, and all these vehicles are registered to the business, that's right isn't it, Mr Marshall?'

'They might be, I don't know.'

'HMRC requires the business to keep a log of when employees use a pool car. You know the type of thing – who is driving the vehicle, how many miles.'

'I called at your premises today, Mr Marshall,' said Chapman. 'And asked to see the log.'

'Woah! Why wasn't I informed of this?' said Marshall.

'Your employee showed me the log and it was blank for the night Tommy was killed. So, according to your records no one used any of the company vehicles that night.'

'I don't know. So, if none of the cars were used then Tommy must have got a lift from someone.'

'I suppose he could have,' said Kray.

Chapman placed another photograph on the table. 'This picture shows the small hatchback travelling south on Windsor Road at 9.45pm. It was taken at the junction with Sycamore Street. Which is one and half miles from where Weir's body was discovered.' Marshall stared at the grainy image. 'What was the car doing there?'

He pursed his lips and shook his head. 'Don't know. I run a club not a valet parking service.'

'Who was driving it?'

'How the hell should I know?' Marshall was going red in the face.

'I believe Tommy was driving this car. And if he was driving a company car that tells me he was on company business. Was Tommy running an errand for you, Mr Marshall?'

'No! He just up and left. I was furious.'

'We've looked through the footage from the camera on the junction and there is no record of it travelling back the same way.'

'I can't help you. It was a busy night and when Tommy did his disappearing act it was all hands to the pump. I didn't have time to keep track of pool cars.'

'It's very convenient that your CCTV at the club is corrupted at the very time this hatchback left the club and returned sometime afterwards.'

'I told you we had a fault.'

'But it would appear the fault hasn't affected any of the other footage. I know because I watched it,' Chapman said.

'What can I say, it's an intermittent fault.'

'So, you have no idea how this car came to be here?' Chapman said, pointing to the picture.

'Can't help you. I'm sorry.'

'When Tommy left you short-handed did you try to contact him?'

'Umm, yes, I think I did.'

'Here is a copy of the call history taken from his mobile. Do you recognise this number?' Kray pointed to an eleven-digit number on the printout. Marshall shook his head. 'Let me help you, Mr Marshall. This is your number. You called Tommy four times. Do you remember doing that?'

'Not especially, I was pissed off and wanted to know what he was playing at.'

'Four calls made between ten past eleven and half past eleven. Four calls in the space of twenty minutes. That's a bit excessive, wouldn't you say?'

'I was annoyed, I wanted to tear a strip off him.'

'And yet you didn't call him once between 9.45 and 11.10. Why was that?'

'I don't know, I was busy.'

'Then you receive a call from this number at 11:55. It's from one of your employees, isn't it? This number belongs to Josh Adams, the guy who works behind the bar. What did Adams say to you to make you stop calling Tommy Weir?'

'I don't know.'

'Did he tell you he'd found Tommy in the alleyway?'

'That's absurd.'

'Is it? He told you something that made you stop calling. By your own admission you were mad as hell and wanted to tear a strip off Tommy. So why stop after four calls, why not make it five or six?'

'I got bored.'

'Bored…? If you say so.'

'I've had enough of this.' Marshall stood up.

'If you could stay a little longer, Mr Marshall? I have a couple more questions.' Marshall slumped back into his seat.

'This photograph was pulled from your CCTV at 7pm and this is a picture nine hours later when the system repaired itself.' Chapman pushed two photographs towards Marshall, each showing the back compound of the club. 'What do you notice?'

'Erm, nothing.'

'This is like one of those "spot the difference" pictures. The same scene with the same four vehicles. Only in the later picture the vehicles are in different positions. Any idea why?'

'They were moved at some point during the evening. As I said it was a busy shift.'

'That's right, you did. And that's what made me wonder… if it was such a busy shift, how come all the cars were moved? Surely with Tommy going AWOL you needed people in the club, not moving cars around.'

Marshall shrugged his shoulders.

'Do you know what ANPR is, Mr Marshall?' asked Kray.

'What is this now, twenty questions?'

'It stands for Automatic Number Plate Recognition and it's a very cool piece of kit. It tracks vehicle movements on key roads. Do you know what we found?'

'Surprise me.'

'All bar one of your vehicles made the trip in convoy across the M55, down the M6 and across the A580 to Liverpool. The car that didn't make that journey was the small hatchback. What were you doing travelling en masse to Liverpool, Mr Marshall?'

'We had a team get-together at one of Mr Cross's casinos. You know, as a bit of a thank you to the boys.'

'In Liverpool?'

'Yup, we didn't stay long.'

'According to the ANPR you stayed just over an hour. Not much of an outing for the boys, was it?' Marshall shrugged his shoulders again.

'What's the casino called?'

'The Majestic.'

'And I have no doubt there are people who could verify you were at the casino?'

'Of course. Can I go now?'

'Just to be clear, Mr Marshall. You were pissed off because Weir left you short-handed at the club and yet you organised a works outing to a casino in Liverpool. Is that what you expect us to believe?'

'You can't be hard on the boys all the time. Good management is all about carrot and stick.'

Kray looked across at Chapman.

'That's all for now. I'm sure we will need to talk with you again, Mr Marshall. Thank you for your time,' said Kray.

'It's been a pleasure.' Marshall rose from his chair.

'Oh, one more question. Do you sail?' asked Kray.

'What?'

'Do you sail? You know, do you go on boats?'

'First you have a problem with cars and now you want to know about boats?'

'Well?'

'No, I wouldn't be seen dead on a boat. I hate them. Is that okay?'

'Thank you.'

Chapman ushered Marshall into the corridor. She returned a few minutes later.

'That was good work,' Kray said, sliding the photographs across the table.

'He's a slippery character. What do you think?'

'He's a lying bastard, that's what he is.'

'I think we rattled his cage, though. We need to keep tabs on him and see where he runs.'

'Interview his team from the Paragon, see if they corroborate his story, and pay the Majestic a visit.'

'Will do, Roz.'

Kray's phone buzzed. 'Kray.'

'I have a woman in reception wants to speak with you. She won't give her name.' It was Sybil Moore on the line, the Rottweiler who ran the reception desk with the efficiency of a FTSE 100 company.

'Oh, come on, Sybil, tell her this is not a place to play a game of "Who am I?" I'm tied up at the moment, find out her name and call me back.'

'Roz, I've been doing this a long time. If I can't get her name the first time, it's because the woman isn't going to give it if I ask a second. She seems agitated and insisted she would only speak with you. I've put her in an office.'

Fuck!

'Okay, Sybil, I'll be right down.' Kray ran down the stairs to the front of the building. Sybil stared at her over the top of her half-moon glasses and nodded in the direction of an office on the left. Kray acknowledged with a raised hand.

She punched down the door handle and strode into the small room, which was furnished with a round table and two chairs. One of them was occupied.

'Hello, Roz.'

'Shit!'

Chapter 31

'You need to talk to a man called William Ellwood, or at least that's his real name. What he goes by now is anyone's guess.' The diminutive figure of Miriam Ellwood sat with her hands clasped together in her lap, her thumb boring into the palm of her left hand.

'Who's he?' asked Kray.

'My husband's brother.'

'That name came up on our search but we've not yet interviewed him.'

'Yeah, well good luck with that. First you've got to find him.'

'Why would–'

'I told Michael he was dangerous, I said he should stay the hell away from him. I told him not to go!' Ellwood slammed her hand down onto the tabletop. 'But oh no, would he listen? Would he fuck! And now he's dead. I told him… I fucking told him…' She clasped her hands tight to her face and rocked back and forth, sobbing.

'Can I get you some water?'

'No, I don't want bloody water! I want you to find that shitbag brother-in-law and bring him to me so I can cut his balls off and ram them down his throat. Then… then…' She collapsed forwards with her head on the desk, crying hard.

Kray placed her hand on her shoulder. 'Miriam, take your time.'

Sybil appeared at the window in the door, having heard the commotion. She mouthed, 'Are you all right?' Kray nodded and brought her hand to her lips in the universal sign for a drink. Sybil nodded and beetled off. Time ticked by and Ellwood didn't move.

'I'm sorry.' She straightened up, wiping her face with her hands. 'Sorry… that keeps happening. One minute I'm okay and the next I'm behaving like a crazy person.'

'That's all right, let me know when you want to continue.'

'I'm fine.' Ellwood ran her hands through her hair and let out a deep breath. 'Now, where was I? Oh, yes, I need to apologise for the other day. I told you a pack of lies.'

'I know. Why don't you start again and tell me about William Ellwood?'

'Everyone calls him Billy. He and my husband were close, even though their lives went in different directions. They wouldn't speak for months, sometimes years, and then when they got together it was as though they had seen each other yesterday. They seemed to have this special bond between them, it was infuriating.' Ellwood seemed to drift off to a place where life no longer hurt. Kray waited patiently. 'That day, Michael travelled to Blackpool to meet up with Billy.'

'Why did he do that?'

'To be honest, I don't know. As far as I'm aware they just sat and chatted. I never asked Michael directly because I didn't want to know. When Billy got in touch I pleaded with him not to go, I begged him to stay clear. But he wouldn't listen, it was as though when Billy clicked his fingers Michael came running.'

'Had they done this before?'

'Yes, many times. For years we had no contact whatsoever, then bam! Billy got in touch out of the blue and he was back in our lives.'

'I don't understand, what's the connection with Blackpool?'

'I don't know that either. All I know is a couple of times a year Michael would tell me he was going to meet with Billy. There was nothing I could say to stop him. He'd simply disappear for the day and come back in the evening. We never spoke about what they did, or what was said – he didn't want to tell me and I didn't want to know. That man is poison and I didn't want him anywhere near us.'

'Why is he poison?'

Sybil arrived at the door with two cups of water. Kray got up and took them from her, passing one to Ellwood.

'Thanks,' Ellwood said, taking a sip. 'Do you ever look at someone and instantly know they're bad news? You know something isn't right with them.'

'More times than I would like.'

'That's how it was with Billy. The day I clapped eyes on him I knew he was trouble, I knew he was going to bring a world of hurt to me and my family. But Michael was blind to it, all he saw was his brother. All I saw was a dangerous man.'

'Why was he dangerous? Was he a criminal?'

'No, quite the opposite. He was supposed to be one of the good guys. But when I looked in his eyes all I saw was evil.'

'I don't get it. You're going to have to be more specific if I'm going to help you.' Ellwood stared at her hands, wringing them in her lap. 'Miriam why do you say—'

'He was an undercover cop.' The words tumbled from her lips as though an internal dam had burst.

Kray allowed the words to sink in. 'What sort of undercover work?'

'I don't know. I had the impression it was serious shit. He would disappear for months on end and when he came back he always looked like he was…'

'What, Miriam, what did he look like?'

'Cursed.'

'Cursed? In what way?'

'I don't know. It's the only way I can describe it. Yes, he was distant, yes, he was preoccupied and he took time to acclimatise when he came back, but that wasn't it. He looked cursed.'

'I don't understand, Miriam.'

'Like everything he came into contact with was going to get hurt. Like… Oh, I don't know – cursed! You need to protect me and my family.'

'Are you saying Billy Ellwood killed your husband?'

'Billy's a psycho but he'd never hurt Michael. There must be people who would want to do Billy harm, though.'

'Is that why your husband lost contact with him?'

'Partly. They lost touch when Billy went into the forces and then when he came out they picked up from where they had left off. Then Billy joined the police and went undercover. He would go away, then come back, then go away again. He lived in Birmingham at the time and we were in Manchester. Michael saw Billy whenever he could.'

'So, if it wasn't the job, then…'

'I don't know the full details. Billy was working on a case and came home one weekend on leave. The gang he'd infiltrated must have found out he was a cop and turned up on his doorstep. They attacked him and killed his wife.'

Ellwood sprawled on the table again, bawling her eyes out. Water slopped from the plastic cups.

'I'm sorry, I know this is difficult.' Kray placed her hand onto Miriam's arm.

'I didn't even know she was pregnant!' Ellwood pushed Kray's hand away and sat bolt upright up in her chair.

'I'm not following you.'

'They killed her. They burst into the house and stuck a knife in her and she bled to death. By the time the ambulance arrived she was already dead. Twenty weeks pregnant and I didn't fucking know.'

'Miriam, slow down, what are you saying?'

'And it's all down to him. It's all down to Billy-fucking-Ellwood. I lied to you last time because I didn't want you digging around. I was scared of what you might find. But you've got to help me now. I have two sons and he will get them killed. He's cursed, I tell you. Everyone he comes into contact with dies – I have to protect them.'

'How is he going to get your sons killed?'

'He turned up at the chapel of rest last night pretending to be someone else. The undertaker described him to me and I know it's him.'

'Billy visited the undertaker?'

'You have to find him. He's back in our lives and you have to stop him.'

'I will find him, Miriam. I promise. You say his wife was pregnant?'

'And I didn't know. Can you believe that I didn't fucking know?'

'Why would you know?'

'Because Blythe was my sister.'

Chapter 32

Miriam Ellwood spun the plastic cup between her fingers while staring down at the table.

'I told Blythe not to, and she laughed in my face. I begged her not to and she told me to mind my own business. We fell out about it. I pleaded with her, and said no good would come of their relationship. But she wouldn't listen. In the end she chose him and I lost my sister. We severed all contact.'

'When was this?'

'Twenty-three years ago. It was the only thing we argued about. Then almost five years to the day since I last saw Blythe, we get a phone call from Billy saying she was dead. Killed by a gang of men who broke into their house. It was then I learned about the baby. He was into some dangerous shit. It was inevitable that one day it was going to pile up against his front door. But instead of killing him, they killed Blythe. And now they've murdered my husband.'

'Who are *they*, Miriam?'

'The people who attacked Blythe. I reckon they've killed Michael to get at Billy.'

'How can you be sure of that?'

'I can't. But what would you think?'

Kray paused, considering the question. 'What was Billy involved in?'

'Don't know but it was dangerous stuff. After Blythe's death he went to ground and we never spoke of him. Then one day Michael tells me that he's taking a trip to Blackpool to see Billy. He was only telling me so I didn't think he had another woman. When he returned from his trips he was quiet and withdrawn. It took him a couple of days to return to his usual self.'

'You never went along too?'

'No. I would just sit at home waiting for him to come back. Every time I heard his key in the front door it was like a weight was lifted off my chest. He was home, safe. On the last trip he didn't come home.' Her eyes glistened with the onset of tears.

'What did the police say at the time of Blythe's death?'

'They closed ranks and it was all hushed up. There was an investigation but we never got straight answers to our questions. Three men forced their way into the house and Billy killed two of them. The third man got away… was never caught.'

'What happened to the gang that Billy had infiltrated?'

'I remember a couple of guys went to jail, but that's it. The gang was called the Critchleys and were a big deal at the time. The inquest was rammed with reporters, it was all over the news. We had to have a police escort wherever we went. It was a bloody nightmare.'

'And you believe these people killed your husband?'

'I don't know that for sure. All I know is, Michael meets up with Billy and is murdered in a fashion that's consistent with a gangland execution. You need to do some digging – then come back and tell me what *you* think.'

I'm sitting in my car, parked across the road from a large bay-fronted house with an integral garage and a wide sweeping driveway. The low privet hedge at the front has been pruned with precision. A small front garden is home to bushes and planted borders.

But I'm not here to admire the sleepy cul-de-sac. My long lens is trained at the leaded front window, beyond which is the dining room, where I can see Eddie Marshall sitting at the table finishing his lunch.

I followed him when he left his home early this morning and watched as he paid a visit to a restaurant that was shut. Despite the sign saying, 'CLOSED,' the front door opened as he approached and he went inside. He was there no more than fifteen minutes, then made his way across town to the Paragon. To my disappointment there was no Post-it stuck to the inside of the window.

Then to my surprise the coppers showed up and took him to the station. He was in there for the best part of an hour. For some reason he went home rather than return to the club.

A woman with blonde hair comes into view and starts clearing the plates away. She looks younger than him. I only get a partial glimpse of her. The camera goes click. She looks familiar.

She moves out of shot and I have a clear view of my target. He gets up and disappears. I pan the lens across the front of the house to the other window and watch as Marshall appears in the lounge, slumping down on the sofa.

'What's he doing?' Jade asks.

'Nothing, he's just sitting there. Maybe watching telly?'

'Tell me again, why are we here?'

'Gathering intel.'

'Gathering dust more like. How is this helping?'

'Sometimes it does, sometimes it doesn't.'

Jade throws herself back into the seat and folds her arms. 'You used to be so different. There was a time when you'd walk over there, knock on the door, and stab the bastard. There was a time when–'

'Shut up, Jade, I know what I'm doing.'

'Doesn't look like it to me. You need to get in there and kill him.'

'You know that's not an option,' I snarl through clenched teeth, trying to keep the lens still.

The camera goes click again.

'Don't tell me. *I made a promise.* You're such a pussy.'

'Shut it, Jade.'

'You were perfectly happy to slice the other guy up. What's the difference?'

'He didn't work for the Critchleys.'

'I struggle to see the distinction.'

'Yeah, well, you struggle with a lot of things.'

'Pussy.'

I watch Marshall put a phone to his ear. The woman comes into the room and he gets up, moves back into the dining room. His head is jerking back and forth in an animated conversation. He doesn't look happy.

The woman appears and he waves her away. The call is over and then he sits down, rubbing his chin with his hand. He leans forward, bringing both hands up to his face.

'What's he doing now?'

'Shhh.'

'Is he crying?'

'Be quiet, Jade, I can't quite–'

'Fucking hell. I mean… fucking hell. Can you see that?'

The image of Marshall blurs as my eyes fill with tears.

My camera goes click.

Back at my flat, I don't know what to do. My hands are shaking with rage.

'Look at it, look at it!' Jade is yelling at me from the other side of the room, marching around in her eighteen-hole boots, waving her arms in the air. Despite the Goth-like make-up, her face is flushed pink. The camera and lens lie on the table. 'Pick it up and look at it!'

I know she's right but I can't seem to get my arse out of the chair. I crumple forward with my head in my hands. My shoulders shake. The sound of sobbing fills the room.

'For Christ's sake, what is wrong with you?' she screams. 'You've wondered all these years; eighteen bloody years you've laid awake at night turning your head inside out trying to figure it out. And now you know! And all you can do is sit there?'

I catch my breath and wipe my nose on my sleeve. Both my fists are balled tight. I pick up the camera and press a button. An image of the bay-fronted property flicks onto the screen. I scroll through the photographs. I reach the one showing Marshall sat at his dining table, his hands covering his face. The next shot is of him taking his hands away. Between his fingers is a round disc. I click a few more buttons and zoom in. His left eye socket is closed and dark. The small disc between his fingers is a false eye.

My mind catapults back to that fateful evening when the pizza delivery bloke rang our doorbell; to the two men who tried to batter me to death with baseball bats; to the man in the balaclava who held a knife to Blythe's throat; to the sight of blood running down his mask as she tore into his face; to the post-mortem results that revealed skin and cornea under her fingernails; to the blood on the carpet as her life leaked from her body.

Marshall was the third man. The man who had his eye gouged so badly it had to be removed.

I'm staring at a picture of the man who killed my wife and unborn child. My head feels like it's about to split wide open. There is a rap on the door.

'Just a minute,' I call out.

'Are you expecting someone?' asks Jade, her face returning to the powdered white complexion she loves so much.

I shake my head and splash water on my face from the sink.

'No, no one.'

I dry off and open the door.

'Hi, Mr Wright, my name is Detective Inspector Roz Kray. May I come in?'

Chapter 33

'Are you okay? I can come back later if you'd prefer?' asked Kray, taking a seat on the sofa. The cold water had done nothing to hide the distress on Ellwood's face.

'No, that won't be necessary. It's been a trying time of late, I'm sure you understand,' he said, perching on the chair opposite.

'It must be difficult. Do you live here on your own?'

'Yes, I do.'

'I thought I heard voices?'

'How can I help, DI Kray?'

'What should I call you? Billy Ellwood or Billy Wright? What would you prefer?'

'Billy What-ever-you-like, is fine by me.'

'We are looking into the death of your brother, Michael, and I wondered if you would answer a few questions.'

'Yes, that's fine, I've been expecting you.'

'What happened on the day you planned to meet with him?'

'Before we start, who told you I was here?'

'You came up on our family search.'

'Really? I'm not sure I would have. I think it's far more likely Miriam paid you a visit and then you trawled through the archives looking for what had happened to Billy Ellwood. You then had to get the security lifted on my identity and went from there. Am I close?'

'Yeah, pretty close.'

'If we are going to do this, DI Kray, it will go a lot smoother if you're up front with me. Then I will feel more comfortable being up front with you.'

'Okay, that's a deal.'

159

'Michael and I met every now and again. I was afraid of losing touch altogether, so we played this elaborate game whereby I would send him a ticket to the cinema and he would show up. If he couldn't make it he would send the ticket back.'

'How often did you meet?'

'Two, maybe three times a year, always in Blackpool.'

'What did you talk about?'

'Anything and everything. I enjoyed hearing about how the kids were getting on and about his business. We didn't talk about Miriam, she was off limits.'

'How long had you been meeting up this way?'

'Five, maybe six years.'

'On the day you were supposed to see him, what happened?'

'Nothing. He failed to show up.'

'What did you do?'

'I waited, but heard nothing from him. So, I drove to his house.'

'Why didn't you give him a call?'

'When we got together he didn't bring a phone.'

'Why not?'

'To satisfy my galloping paranoia, I suppose. After what happened I didn't want his movements tracked.'

'You drove to his house to pay the family a visit?'

'Hell, no. If I'd showed my face Miriam would've picked up the nearest sharp object and plunged it through my heart. No, I hung around watching the house.'

'And what did you find out?'

'His car was there but he wasn't. The police turned up on numerous occasions and Miriam and the kids were in a right state. It was obvious something terrible had happened, so I kept my ear to the ground, but heard nothing. Then a body washed up on the beach and I put two and two together and figured it must be Michael.'

'Did you go to the chapel of rest yesterday evening?'

'Yes, I did. An Internet connection and a phone was all it took to find him. I didn't want to risk bumping into Miriam – it was the easiest way to pay my last respects.'

'Do you know the circumstances surrounding his death?'

'I assume he drowned…'

'I'm sorry to have to tell you, but your brother was shot and killed before he entered the water, and there were signs of torture.'

Ellwood's jaw dropped. He swayed in the chair, gripping the armrests.

'Torture?'

'Yes, I'm afraid so. Do you know of anyone who would want to harm your brother?'

'Jesus Christ, no! What do you mean torture?'

'The post-mortem showed signs of tissue damage to his nasal tract. We believe he had chilli and carbonated water forced into his nose.'

'What? That's a technique used by drug cartels – he was never into drugs.'

'Is there anyone who would want to harm your brother?'

'No. Nobody. He was just a regular guy with a wife and two kids. Jesus Christ!'

'We are trying to piece together his last movements but at this stage it isn't clear how he was abducted.' Ellwood stared at the carpet. 'One possible line of enquiry is that he was killed to get back at you for the undercover work.'

'Oh, fucking hell.' Ellwood bent forward, his head in his hands. 'It's possible, I suppose. But I've been out of that game for eighteen years, do you really think they would wait that long?'

Kray scribbled in her notebook. 'Can you tell me how you ended up in Blackpool?'

Ellwood straightened up. 'I was undercover in Nottingham with one of the biggest firms in the country, the Critchleys. They dealt in drugs mainly and I was in too deep. They rumbled me and came looking for their pound of flesh.'

'How did they rumble you?'

'From a tip-off. Anyway, one night they came calling and that's when Blythe was killed. I took out two of the attackers but the third man got away. Blythe had fought with him and had skin under her fingernails, but it came to nothing. After that I fell apart. Miriam blamed me for her death, and she was right – I blame myself. I tried to get back into work but I couldn't hack it and was pensioned off. That's when I decided to move and ended up here.'

'What happened to the Critchleys?'

'After the attack, our operation was holed beneath the waterline and the authorities swooped in on the Critchley brothers. I retreated into my shell and stayed there, nursing a bottle of whisky. What I do know is the elder Critchley brother took the fall, allowing the younger one to walk free. Their head of security – a guy named Rolo – went down, along with a few other guys. I'm told my testimony was critical. I only wish I could remember it. I hit the booze hard and to be honest the whole thing is a bit of a blur. I suppose somewhere in the dusty vaults of Nottingham Police HQ there is a case file detailing the whole sorry mess.'

'Just to clarify, the Critchley operation was where?'

'The Critchleys were based out of Nottingham, and we lived in Birmingham.'

'One of your attackers got away, didn't you want revenge?'

'I wanted it more than anything, but I made Blythe a promise that I wouldn't go looking for them. As she lay in my arms with her blood pooling around us I made her that promise. So, I could never go back on it. The only way I could deal with what happened was to run away and hide. That's how I ended up here.'

'What do you do for a living now?'

'Cash in hand jobs mainly, labouring and casual work.'

Kray gazed at Ellwood's tear-stricken face. His vacant expression told her time was up. 'Thank you for your time. I'm sure we will want to· talk to you again, Billy. Do you have a number where I can reach you?'

He reeled off his mobile and Kray noted it in her book. She stood up to leave and handed him her card.

'If you think of anything in the meantime, please give me a call, day or night.'

'I know the drill.' He opened the door.

'I'll be in touch,' said Kray. Ellwood nodded back. 'Oh, just one more thing; how did the Critchleys launder their money?'

'They owned four nightclubs, ideal for cleaning the cash.'

Kray wandered back to her car, the image of the Paragon raging in her head.

Chapter 34

Kray bustled into the incident room and was pleased to find it empty. There was too much ground to cover to have anyone sitting in the office. Her mobile was pressed to the side of her head.

'I know you have your hands full at the moment, Duncan, but I want you to look into something for me,' she said, tossing her bag down on the table.

'What is it, Roz?' Tavener replied.

'Ellwood had a brother named William who was an undercover cop. Back in 2000 he'd infiltrated a gang called the Critchleys who were based in Nottingham. They blew his cover and sent a three-man punishment squad to his house in Birmingham where they murdered his wife. Ellwood killed two of his attackers and the other got away. Dig out everything you can on the investigation; you might need to liaise with both police forces to get the full picture.'

'Yes, will do. Do you think this has something to do with the death of Michael Ellwood?'

'I don't know. It might have a bearing on the case. We need it ASAP. Ellwood said his wife had skin under her fingernails from when she was attacked. Find out if they conducted DNA analysis that resulted in a match with the suspect's. If you get any shit from Nottingham or West Mids give me a shout.'

'Okay. Oh, and by the way, when I interviewed the elderly woman at the hospital who shared the same ward as the victim, she confirmed that she saw a man enter the room dressed in blue scrubs. I'm not sure how reliable she will be though, because she also kept asking me, "Where's the terrorist?" Do you know what she was on about?'

'No idea.'

'Just thought I'd ask. Will get on to Notts straightaway.' Tavener hung up, his new marching orders received and understood.

Kray stuck a picture of Billy Ellwood onto the whiteboard and began drawing connecting lines.

Fucking terrorist, my arse.

Her phone buzzed.

'Hey, Tejinder, what have you got?'

'I'm at the Majestic casino in Liverpool and I'm afraid it's not good news.'

'Go on.'

'I've spoken to six employees who were here the night Weir was killed and each of them remembers Marshall turning up with his boys. They say they got here about midnight and left around one in the morning, which ties in with our timeline.'

'Shit,' Kray said, banging her hand on the desk. 'Can we lay our hands on anything to verify their story – CCTV at the club, perhaps?'

'If you're going to swear, Roz, now is the time. The CCTV at the casino has been out of commission for a week. The manager said I was welcome to check it out but he was pretty adamant it won't show anything.'

'Fuck it!' Kray spun on her heels. 'Take a look anyway.'

'Will do. The other thing is they remembered Josh not being there. Something about him missing out because they had sent him on an errand to buy bottles of Mumm champagne. They offered the information without being prompted.'

'This gets bloody worse. What's your take on it?'

'It was too scripted.'

'I bet it was. Okay, thanks for the update. Stay at the club and see if you can force any inconsistencies.'

'Will do, Roz.' Then he hung up.

'Bollocks,' Kray said, just as DCI Bagley wandered into the room.

'Ah, there you are,' he said.

'Afternoon, sir, I've just got off the phone with–'

'I've been talking to DI Brownlow, to find out how he's getting on. He told me that his house-to-house enquiries are taking longer than expected because you have pinched one of his officers.'

'Yes, that's right, I–'

'Do I have to remind you that I'm the one who allocates resources around here? And I do so on the basis of priorities.'

'No, sir, you don't have to remind me. Brownlow said the officer in question was spare.'

'Spare? Spare! Do we look like a department that has people spare?'

'I can only tell you what he told me.'

'And you didn't think it was worth running it past me first?'

'No, sir, it seemed a pretty straightforward move.'

'Brownlow now says he's short-handed.'

I'll fucking kill him.

'Sir, when I spoke to Brownlow he assured me–'

'Then I find out that you've cordoned off a ward in the hospital because it's now a murder scene.'

'That's right, sir, it's the Asian woman who–'

'I know who it is. This is the young woman with enough track lines in her arms to kill three people, who gets run over by a taxi and has a bleed on her brain. She passes away under the watchful eye of the intensive care unit and you think it's fucking murder? Am I missing something here?'

'That woman was the victim of trafficking. She was not just some druggy who simply ran out into the road.'

'Not that shit again. We had this conversation and I told you to pursue the line that she was involved in a drug connection with Ellwood. What evidence do you have that she was murdered?' Kray cast her eyes up to the ceiling. 'Come on, Roz, I want to know why we are burning resources investigating the murder of a woman who was probably going to die of her injuries anyway?'

'They killed her so she couldn't talk to us when she regained consciousness.'

'They? Who the bloody hell are they?'

'The people who trafficked her.'

'And who are these people?'

'I… I don't know.'

'That's right, you don't know, mainly because you're chasing your intuition again rather than sticking to solid detective work.'

'But…'

'But nothing, Roz. We've made zero progress with the Ellwood case, zero progress investigating the knife attack leading to the death of Tommy Weir and you now have us chasing ghosts by conducting a murder enquiry into a woman who died of her injuries in hospital. What the hell is going on?'

Kray's phone buzzed again. She glanced at the screen. 'Sorry, sir, I need to take this.'

'I suggest you answer my–'

'Hey, Duncan.' Roz turned her back to Bagley and paced to the other side of the room. She nodded but said nothing.

'Roz, I haven't finished,' Bagley called over to her. Kray continued to listen on the call. 'I won't tell you again, Roz. Hang up now,' he boomed. This time Roz did as she was told. 'I don't appreciate it when one of my team–'

'That was Tavener.' It was Kray's turn to interrupt. 'He's with the pathologist at the hospital. The young woman died of heart failure after her brain shut down.'

'See, I bloody told you.'

'Her brain shut down because her sugar levels dropped dramatically due to a massive spike in her insulin levels. The spike sent her into severe hypoglycaemic shock. The medical staff in attendance thought it was caused by her head wound and didn't test her blood. They were alerted when her heart monitor set off an alarm. By then it was too late. Forensics found traces of insulin on the canular stuck into her arm and the post-mortem confirmed a large quantity of insulin in her bloodstream. If the staff had given her an intravenous feed of glucose it would have reversed the effects, but they were unaware she had gone hypoglycaemic.'

'I don't understand, what are you saying?'

'She was killed with a massive injection of insulin. That's not all – there was another patient on the ward who recalls waking up to see a man in blue scrubs in the room.'

'So what? They're in and out all the time I would have thought.'

'She is a bit hazy on the time but she definitely remembers seeing a man.'

'Yes, but as I said–'

'At the time there were no male nurses on shift.' Bagley looked like someone had let the air out of him. 'So, is it okay if I keep the spare person?'

Chapter 35

Jade is charging about the flat screeching at the top of her voice. 'You were right. Your brother's dead because of that bastard Marshall, even the coppers think so!'

I'm sitting on the bed with the memory box nestling in my lap. Blythe had made it when she found out she was pregnant – a twelve-inch square cardboard box covered in pink newborn baby wrapping paper.

'We need to start collecting things early,' she'd chimed. 'A friend of mine only started hers after the baby was born and she'd lost stuff.'

The box now contains my memories of Blythe. Photographs, jewellery, perfume, a scarf – trinkets and keepsakes that remind me of her. I used to spray her perfume in the air and breathe in deeply; with my eyes shut it was as though she was sitting next to me. I could feel her presence. It was a stupid thing to do, the flood of grief that followed was too painful to bear.

Jade bursts in. 'Sitting here moping won't do you any good. You need to stick a knife into Marshall's good eye.'

'Give it a rest, Jade.'

'How much more provocation do you need before you get off your arse and sort it? Christ knows you're capable, just get out there and do it. I don't get it.' Jade is flushed in the face, the dark tattoos inked into her skin look angry.

'For pity's sake, leave me alone.' I pick up the box and hurry into the lounge to get away from her. She follows me. 'You know why I can't do that.'

'Yeah, I *know* why, but I don't *understand* why.'

'It's... it's... because.'

'Come on, what have you got to lose?' She grabs her hair and mimics pulling it out. 'You have no fucking life anyway! You go to work, eat shit food, watch TV and have the occasional wank. Hardly an enviable lifestyle. Walk up to the bastard and slice through his windpipe, then we can watch him gargle his last breath together. Wouldn't that be great? If you get caught and go to jail, so what? You can go to work, eat shit food, watch TV and have the occasional wank just as well in prison.'

'That's enough! I'm off for a drive.' I push past her and bang the front door closed behind me. 'And don't bother coming with me.'

I can hear her yelling as I hurry down the stairs to my car. I slam the door and breathe deeply, a welcome silence washes through my head. The engine cranks into life and I pull away from the kerb.

The urban scenery drifts by and I try to blank Jade's words from my mind. Life is never that simple.

Blythe was never supposed to die first, that was always my job. I was five years her senior and when the beer and wine flowed it was a topic that never failed to make its way into the conversation.

'You know you're going to die first, don't you?' she would say, giggling.

'Yes, if I get given the choice,' I would reply.

It made us laugh every time.

When we married we thought about having it written into our vows. It had a certain ring to it.

> *…in sickness and in health,*
> *to love and to cherish,*
> *till death do us part… only, you have to die first.*

We scrapped the idea. Blythe's family would have disapproved even more than they did already. When I think about it now – it doesn't make me laugh. I never got the choice to go first. One minute she was there and the next she was gone.

And therein lies the problem – nobody tells you how to be a man. If you're female there are a million different places where you can seek advice, each one telling you how to be a woman. The majority of it is a heady mix of toxic ideologies and conflicting advice, designed to perpetuate self-loathing, but at least it's there. At least women can choose.

If you're a man there's nothing.

Then, when you reach the age of thirty-something, you kind of work it out for yourself and the message is pretty simple: Go to work and look after your family. That's it.

There are nuances around the edges about love and fidelity, and not being a total dick – but basically that's it.

So, when as a man, you fail at fifty percent of what is a straightforward to-do list, it's tough to take. It leaves an indelible mark on your soul that no amount of living can wash away.

I only had to do two things and one of them I screwed up. The only thing I have left is a solemn promise, a promise I cannot break.

I find myself parked at the side of the road. Autopilot has kicked in and I'm staring at the front of the Paragon. I check my watch. An hour has gone by since I got away from the torment of Jade. I lift the lid on the memory box and lift out the scarf, breathing in her scent as deeply as I can. There are still faint notes of Blythe but the fragrance has gone, replaced mainly with the smell of old clothes.

I pick a photograph from the bottom of the box. It's not a holiday snap, or a picture from a raucous night out, it depicts a tiny person not yet born. The black, white and grey blend together to show a head, a leg, one arm and a rotund belly. All in glorious silhouette.

At the bottom is printed: Wed 1 March 2000 – 18 weeks. I remember it as if it was yesterday. We were both in awe of what we were looking at and Blythe gripped my hand as the nurse handed over the scan picture. We danced our way out of the maternity ward. We were so happy.

I look up and see movement behind the glass doors of the club. A dark shadow moving slowly. Then a square of fluorescent yellow bursts into view. It's a Post-it.

I shove the box off my lap onto the passenger seat and drive out of town. About half a mile down the road I swing into the car park of a hotel, get out and dash to reception. A tall, willowy woman with long hair and glasses greets me at the desk.

'Hello, sir, how may I help?'

'Do you have a public payphone?'

'Certainly, down this corridor following the signs for the Business Hub, and there are two on the left.'

I thank her and follow her directions. I find the phones mounted to the wall, lift the receiver, feed money into the slot and push the buttons. I hear a synthetic warble at the other end. It rings and rings.

Pick up, pick up.

'Hello,' a curt voice answers – it's him.

'Are you able to talk, Mr Marshall?' I ask.

'That was quick.'

'I find it pays to have eyes everywhere.'

'So it would seem.'

'Can you talk?' I hear the sound of a door closing.

'I can.'

'I hope you have good news for my client?'

'There is a new shipment coming in and we will be auctioning the merchandise tomorrow at the Paragon.'

'That doesn't give me much notice.'

'We prefer to operate on a just-in-time basis with the stock, I'm sure you understand.'

'Of course. My client will want to be there in person if that's acceptable?'

'That won't be a problem. There will be others in the room along with a number of remote customers. A door fee of five thousand pounds will be levied on entering the club and it is a cash only event. I will be checking the money myself on arrival and, of course, deducting our fee.'

'That all sounds in order. How does my client gain access?'

'Knock on the front door and ask to buy a used car. That will gain him entrance.'

'Can I assure my client that your operation has security and discretion as its number one priority?'

'You can. You can also tell your client that there is a ten per cent house commission on all purchases and another five per cent commission for me.'

'Is that usual?'

'The house commission is a standard charge, the one for me is… shall we say… another goodwill gesture.'

'My client is very grateful for his FastPass and would be only too pleased to show his appreciation.'

'We will see him tomorrow at 1.45pm. The auction starts at 2pm sharp.'

'Thank you, Mr Marshall.' The line goes dead.

Bloody hell. That went better than I anticipated.

I thank the woman behind reception as I leave the hotel and return to my car, sliding into the driver's seat. The scan picture has fallen onto the floor. I pick it up and place it in the box. Scrawled across the top, in my dead wife's handwriting, is the name, Jade.

Chapter 36

I arrive back at my flat, my head spinning with possibilities. Jade is curled up on the sofa, sulking.

'Where have you been?' she says.

'Out for a drive.'

'Did you stab him?'

'Don't be stupid.'

'I'm not the stupid one.' She jumps up and is in my face again. 'I'm not the one pussyfooting around. I'm not the one–'

'Change the record, will you?' I go through to the kitchen and switch on the kettle to make a brew. I can hear her muttering in the other room, letting her displeasure shine through.

Jade has been on the scene now for about thirteen years. She first showed up when I was in a drunken state on Christmas Eve. I was stumbling around trying to lock up for the night and heard a noise coming from the spare bedroom. I edged open the door to see a five-year-old girl dressed in Father Christmas pyjamas, getting into bed. A shock of black hair made her face appear translucent white in the semi-darkness.

'Has he been yet?' she asked, her brown eyes big and bright. She snuggled down under the duvet, pulling it tight under her chin.

The weird thing was, it was as though I had been expecting her.

'No, but he's on his way.' I walked in and sat on the bed. Her smiling face lit up the room. 'He won't come if you're not asleep.'

'But I can't sleep. I'm too excited.'

'So am I.'

'Have you put up decorations?'

'I have a small tree with baubles and tinsel.'

'Will that be enough? Will Santa come for that?'

'Yeah, Santa comes for a lot less. He visits children who have nothing.'

'That's because he's kind.' I looked into her eyes, could see Blythe staring back at me. 'I'd go to sleep faster if you stayed here with me.'

'Budge up,' I said. Jade moved over under the quilt. Only her face and fingers were visible. I lay next to her on top of the bedding and rested my head on the pillow. 'Is that better?'

'Yes.'

Within seconds she was drifting off to sleep, the sound of her breathing filling me with joy.

When I woke Christmas morning she was gone.

And so it continued. I wouldn't see her for months and then something would happen and she'd be there; lively and chatty, sporting her new-found fashions and latest hairstyles.

As the years went by she transitioned from a toddler to a teenager. The older she got, the darker her personality became. I know that's supposed to be the way, but this was different. It was as though her temperament was in sync with mine. The deeper I plunged into my own personal hell, the more she reflected it back at me.

Now Jade is with me most of the time. The problem is, she's constantly angry. She scolds me and goads me into doing something to avenge Blythe's death. I don't tend to think about it too much, but if I was a shrink I would say Jade is a manifestation of my grief and anger. She is the embodiment of my inner turmoil. But I'm not a shrink, so what do I know?

I drink my coffee, leaning against the kitchen worktop.

The options coalesce in my brain. Jade walks in.

'Now, that's what I call a plan.'

Kray was hunched over a speaker phone chairing a team conference call. She had just completed her account of the discussion with Ellwood.

'What do you think, Roz? D'you believe him?' asked Chapman.

'I think he went through a series of traumatic events, culminating in the death of his wife. We need to remember that at the time there was not the safeguarding protocols in place for coppers who went undercover like there are today. He looked a shell of a man, still trying to come to terms with what happened.'

'That's strange though, that when they met up, his brother didn't bring a phone for fear his movements would be tracked. It's like they were expecting trouble,' said Gill, his voice blasting from the speaker.

'I have to say I can't blame him, given what happened,' Tavener added. 'I would have thought paranoia was the least of his problems.'

'Have you had any success retrieving the case files from West Mids and Nottingham?' asked Kray.

'I'm getting them in dribs and drabs, Roz,' replied Tavener. 'So far, the documentation confirms Ellwood's account. I'm still going through it.'

'Okay, and what about the hospital?' she asked.

'We have a screen grab from the CCTV of a man dressed in blue scrubs who entered the ward where the Asian woman was being treated. It's being cross referenced with the database of employees. The picture is taken from above and shows him in semi-profile, so it's not great.'

'Okay, keep at it. Anything else?'

'Nothing has come up on missing persons, so we're no closer to being able to identify the woman.'

'Tejinder, what do you have?' asked Kray, searching for a scrap of good news.

'A big fat nothing, Roz,' his voice crackled. 'Everyone at the Majestic casino has the same story; Marshall and the guys showed up here, partied for a while and left. I'm wasting my time and will be heading back to the station after the call.'

'House-to-house? What do we have, Louise?' asked Kray.

'We've drawn a blank there too, Roz. No one recognised Weir's picture or saw anything unusual that night. And the social media trawl came up blank. Forensics have come back with a possible ID on the type of knife used. The blade had a sharp, smooth cutting edge on one side and a serrated edge on the other. Like a diver's knife.'

'Okay, that's something, I suppose.'

'But that's it, Roz.'

'Bollocks. When are we going to get a break? I'm convinced all three deaths are linked but we can't find the connection. Does anyone have anything to add before we end the call?' General murmurings of 'no' came over the speaker. 'Okay, I'll catch up with you when you're back at the station.' Kray thumped her finger down on the disconnect button and threw herself back in her seat.

Her mobile rang on the desk.

'Kray.' She listened to the voice on the other end. 'I'm on my way.' She gathered her belongings and hurried from the station. This could be the break she'd been waiting for.

Chapter 37

Kray was standing in the incident room staring at Bagley. She had decided in advance this was not going to be a meeting where taking a seat was required.

Bagley was slouched in a chair, fiddling with his tie, trying to stop himself from bursting a blood vessel. Kray had contacted Quade on returning to the station and had requested an urgent meeting. Quade had suggested Bagley should also be in attendance. He was sulking that she had gone over his head, denying him the opportunity to cream off any good news and deliver it himself.

'This is highly irregular, Roz.' He flushed red.

'ACC Quade said she would be here shortly.'

'I have other more important things–'

ACC Quade waddled in and crushed her arse into a seat. 'Afternoon both; I hope this is going to be worth my while because up to now it appears to be all downhill. The Chief is getting jumpy with the lack of progress and quite frankly, so am I.'

Glad we're entering into this in the right frame of mind.

'Hopefully, this will provide all of us with some much-needed good news, ma'am.' Roz was keen to get things moving. 'I'll get to the punchline first: I want you to authorise a raid on the Paragon club because I've reason to believe they are harbouring women for the purposes of trafficking.'

'Not this cock and bull story again?' Bagley could contain himself no longer. 'This is ridiculous, we don't have the resources to charge around town conducting operations on the basis of a whim. We've had this discussion and you're barking up the wrong tree. Will you stop this trafficking line of enquiry?'

'Is that in the same way as I was barking up the wrong tree when I thought the Asian woman had been murdered?' Kray was not going to be browbeaten.

'I do hope you're not wasting our time, Roz,' Quade interjected. 'Because I have not come here to listen to you two bickering. Sort it out, then get me involved, that's the way it's supposed to work.'

'Sorry, ma'am. If you would just hear me out,' Kray said.

'I'm waiting…' Quade replied. Bagley was fizzing.

'I've just had a conversation with Billy Ellwood and he told me that three nights ago he broke into the Paragon club.'

'What! Why the hell would he tell us that?' exploded Bagley.

'He believes the people who run the club had a hand in his brother's death. He broke in with the intention of gathering information. While he was there he discovered a woman was being held in a room in the cellar. She made a run for it and was knocked down by a taxi about two hundred yards from the club. I showed him a photograph of our murder victim and he confirmed it was the woman he saw that night.'

'This is more like it,' Quade said. 'Is he credible?'

'I believe so, ma'am.'

Bagley squirmed in his seat.

'Billy Ellwood told me that a new consignment of women is due tonight and they are to be auctioned off at the club at 2pm tomorrow.'

'How the hell does he know that?' asked Bagley.

'He wormed his way in and got an invitation.'

'This is absurd!' Bagley leapt to his feet. 'This is the word of a professional liar, a man who's spent his entire life concocting stories for a living. He's making this up to save himself from a charge of breaking and entering.'

'We haven't charged him, he volunteered the information.' Kray looked at Quade.

'Ma'am, there's more…'

Bagley was having none of it and marched up to the evidence boards. 'Let's get real here: we have Michael Ellwood who was shot through the head and washed up on a beach – no progress. Tommy Weir, murdered in an alleyway – no progress. An unidentified Asian woman killed at the hospital – some progress. I think we should stick to what we have in front of us, ma'am, rather than chase around in small circles because some ex-copper has an axe to grind.'

'Sit down, Dan.' Quade gave Bagley a sideways glance – he did as he was told.

'Dan is right, ma'am, we've been unable to make significant progress with the murders because we've been investigating them as stand-alone cases. I believe they are linked. And I believe the link is Eddie Marshall and the Paragon.'

'Who the hell is Eddie Marshall?' asked Quade.

'Marshall runs the club; he's the head guy. We've interviewed him a couple of times and he is a slippery bastard. Marshall and his team were caught on ANPR on their way to Liverpool on the night Weir was killed. He said they were going to the Majestic Casino but I think they went to Mersey Docks to pick up a delivery of illegal immigrants instead. I believe they conducted an auction the next day, but one of them didn't sell, and Billy Ellwood found her in the cellar when he broke in.

'I also believe that to facilitate that deal Marshall dispatched Weir to collect a sum of money. When he failed to return Marshall tried to contact him several times. He stopped calling when he received a call from one of his guys – I think that during that call Marshall was informed that Weir was dead. He has been giving us a right song and dance routine about the movement of the vehicles to cover his tracks. I also believe he ordered the death of the Asian to prevent her from identifying the club. Or he killed her himself.'

'Does Marshall have a link to Michael Ellwood?' asked Quade.

'In 2000, Billy Ellwood infiltrated a drugs gang called the Critchleys, who operated out of Nottingham. Eddie Marshall worked for them. On the basis of Ellwood's testimony at the time, the gang was decimated and I believe Eddie Marshall ordered a hit on Michael Ellwood as revenge for what Billy did.'

'Why did he wait eighteen years?'

'I don't know, ma'am, but I'm convinced Eddie Marshall is the key. He's the connection to all three murders. And we have an opportunity tomorrow to bring the whole operation crashing down around his ears.'

'It's an interesting theory, Roz, but it is just that – a theory. You have no evidence to back it up.' Bagley had his arms folded.

'Why would Billy Ellwood be telling us this?' asked Quade.

'When the undercover operation was blown, the Critchleys sent a punishment squad to his house. They attacked him and ended up murdering his pregnant wife. During the post-mortem they found skin and cornea under her fingernails. Ellwood is convinced it came from the face of the man that attacked his wife and got away.' Kray passed around the blown-up shot showing Marshall sitting at his dining room table, his ocular prosthesis in his hand.

'Marshall has a glass eye. Ellwood thinks he murdered his wife, Blythe.'

The rest of the day passed in a blur of frantic activity. Much to Kray's surprise Quade was willing to take a punt on her analysis and proposition. Bagley remained unconvinced and angry as hell. The fact that they were going to launch an operation against the Paragon club meant Bagley had his nose well and truly out of joint. Something she would, no doubt, regret at a later date.

Kray was feeling really proud of the way she had presented the case and had won Quade over with her weight of reasoning. This optimism was somewhat dashed when she overheard Quade saying to Bagley, 'Put it this way, whatever the rationale, if we don't do it and the press find out that someone had told us about the auction, we are in deep shit.' Which kind of took the shine off the afternoon. She tried to shove tomorrow to the back of her mind, but it wasn't working.

Kray arrived home to find the place filled with the classic aroma of Italian cuisine. How could Millican make the humblest of spaghetti bologneses seem like restaurant food?

'You don't seem yourself. Is everything okay?' he asked, as he put a handful of pasta into the boiling water.

'I've got a lot on at the moment,' she said, sipping her wine. 'Sorry if I'm a little preoccupied.'

'No, I don't mean now. I mean in general, you've been… I don't know… different.'

'I'm probably run down, I had that bloody water infection and I'm under the cosh at work. It's nothing to worry about.' She slipped her arms around his waist and hugged his back as he stirred the sauce.

Millican had called earlier in the day and asked her to come over to his place for dinner. She'd declined, saying that she had a big day tomorrow and needed a good night's sleep in her own bed – alone. But she was well up for him driving to her place to cook dinner, which for Millican meant a trip to the supermarket first.

He turned and pulled her close, kissing her on the neck. 'Are you sure you're all right?'

'Yeah, I'm sure.' She kissed him on the mouth. 'I'm fine.'

The pains in her belly had gone and the bleeding had stopped, however, the prospect of telling him about the baby was the furthest thing from her mind at the moment. She broke free from his embrace to set bowls and knives and forks on the worktop.

'You are a peasant,' he said, taking a spoon from the drawer and replacing one of the knives.

'I can't help it if I wasn't brought up posh and, anyway, I'll get that beautiful sauce down my front if I try to do the "wrap it in a spoon" malarkey.'

His phone rang.

'Here, stir this and don't let it stick to the bottom of the pan.'

'Whoo-hoo! Look at me cooking.'

He finished the call and furrowed his brow. 'Bollocks, I have to go. We had someone call in sick today which left me on call tonight. I need to dash, I'm afraid.'

'That's a shame. What am I going to do with all this?' She waved the spoon at the cooker.

'Eat it, I guess.' He hugged and kissed her. 'Sorry, I have to go.'

'I know – call you tomorrow, but it will be late in the evening.'

'Okay.' He gathered up his jacket and left, closing the front door behind him. Kray turned off the rings on the cooker and heaped herself some pasta and sauce into a bowl. The clock on the mantelpiece said 8pm. In twelve hours' time she would be organising a room full of coppers, explaining why they had to smash the front door of the Paragon club and what they could expect to find when they did.

The spag-bol tasted delicious, but it did nothing to quell the nervous tension raging inside her. Whichever way Kray looked at it, tomorrow was a big day.

Chapter 38

Kray was sitting in her car, parked in a side street one hundred yards from the Paragon.

Earlier, she had been on her feet in front of fifteen officers delivering one of the most important briefings of her career. After all, with three, possibly four murders hanging in the balance, not to mention the fate of goodness knows how many illegal immigrants, the stakes could not have been higher. She stared out of the windscreen, her palms sweaty, her stomach in knots.

Despite her best intentions she hadn't slept a wink. The details of each case swirled around her, keeping sleep well and truly at bay. She had spent the time gazing at the ceiling while rubbing her tummy.

The sun streamed into the car, heating up the interior. Tavener cracked a window down.

'Nice day for it,' he said.

'If it was pissing down with rain it would be a nice day for it. We need to nail this bastard. I want to look Marshall in the eye when we lock the cuffs on him – that's eye, singular.'

'You okay?' Tavener asked.

'Yeah, there's a lot riding on this.'

'I know, but the intel is good. We're in for a big result today.'

Kray glanced at her watch, five to two. 'Comms check,' she said into her radio. The teams sounded off, each one confirming they were in position, ready to hear the command – 'Go, go, go.'

Marshall was suited and booted and sitting in the club sipping a black coffee. The caffeine was definitely helping. Twelve hours earlier he had loaded his latest delivery from Mr Zhang into the Transit and handed over a briefcase full of money.

Jaded

The big gorilla in the overalls had been at Zhang's side again. Marshall had wondered why the guy chose to wear a boiler suit. Then, when he got close, he could smell grease and diesel oil. He obviously worked on the container ship in some engineering capacity or another.

Marshall had checked the manifest and found everything to be in order. They had ushered the women out of the container and into the van with a minimum of fuss; fourteen young women each with the same bewildered look on their face. Women who had braved the journey from Laos into Europe and across the sea into Liverpool – who were to be sold into prostitution and forced labour, not to mention the odd one destined for organ harvesting. Fourteen women who had put their trust in people, promising them a better life.

The journey to pick them up had been a ball-aching trip, because they had kept to the back streets and A-roads rather than use the motorways. It was worth it to avoid being captured by the ANPR system. Marshall drained his cup and checked his watch. Everything was ready, it was almost showtime.

Billy Ellwood was perched on a bar stool looking out of the window at the people walking by. His coffee had long since gone cold and the paper in front of him remained unopened. From his vantage point he could just see the front of the Paragon. This was the closest he dared get to the action. The club was shut. The front windows reflected the images of the people walking by. His eyes were everywhere, trying to spot a sign of the police operation that was about to unfold. He had no idea what time it would kick-off, but if it were up to him, he would crash through the doors at 2pm for maximum impact.

Kray picked up her radio. 'All units – go, go go.'
She and Tavener left the car and walked up the street. They could see the flood of armed officers dressed in paramilitary gear rushing towards the front of the Paragon. She knew there were

another two teams around the back doing the very same thing – one team for the cellar and the other to enter the building via the top landing. The tactical response leader gave the command and the front doors dissolved in a shower of glass.

'Police! Police!' the first man yelled at the top of his voice. There was a crash as they smashed through the inside door.

Josh leapt up from behind the bar. 'What the f–'

'Stand still with your hands where I can see them!' One of the officers levelled an assault rifle at him.

Other shouts of, 'Down on the floor, down on the floor!' echoed around the dance hall.

Kray entered the room, crunching glass under her feet, and looked around. Apart from the coppers and a couple of staff the place was empty. She ran to the staircase leading down to the cellar and collided with an officer coming the other way.

'Nothing, ma'am,' he said, as she pushed past him, her heart in her mouth.

Kray reached the bottom of the steps to find an officer emerging from a side room, the door hanging off its hinges. She pushed past him, scanning the concrete walls and floor – it was empty – as was the room beyond.

Kray dashed back upstairs to be met by Bagley standing in the middle of the dance floor shaking his head. Blood rushed through her temples with every beat of her heart. The radio in her hand gargled into life. 'Team Alpha – all clear.'

'Team Beta – all clear.'

Kray looked across at Bagley.

'What the fuck, Roz?' he mouthed. Kray spun on the spot looking at the empty booth seats against the walls. The guy from behind the bar was sat cross-legged on the floor with an officer standing over him.

Marshall appeared on the stage, dressed in a double-breasted suit, surveying the scene. He was tutting under his breath.

'DI Kray, good afternoon.' He walked to the front apron. 'This has to constitute police harassment, don't you think?'

Kray looked up at him, her breath short and shallow. Her head was spinning.

'What have you done with them?' she croaked.

Marshall simply stood there and laughed.

Kray felt a sharp pain in her stomach, then another, then another. She doubled over, clutching her side. She could hear Marshall cackling. The pain surged through her groin.

She felt warm and wet between her legs.

Kray's agonising scream filled the dance hall.

Chapter 39

Fluorescent strip lighting whizzed overhead as Kray was propelled down the corridor feet first on a trolley. She blinked as the bursts of light dazzled her eyes. Every now and again a face would stare down at her, filling her field of vision. A man and woman dressed in green marched either side, gripping the handrails.

She could remember bringing her hands up from between her legs in the club to find them covered in blood. The whole world went into freefall and she collapsed to the floor.

Next thing she knew, paramedics were trundling her into a waiting ambulance and gave her a shot of pain relief. The sound of the two-tone siren made her feel like she was back at work.

Kray raised her head to see she was still wearing her jacket and shirt but a thin blanket covered her from the waist down. Her hands were still a patchwork of red.

'Nearly there,' said the woman walking beside her. Kray turned her head to see she was carrying a plastic bag and a balled-up roll of grey paper towel. They banged through a set of double doors and stopped. The paramedic handed the bag and the towel to a woman dressed in blue, and then began to talk calmly while the nurse nodded.

'We are going to leave you here.' A man put his hand on Kray's shoulder and smiled. 'They will look after you.'

Kray felt woozy. The searing pain in her stomach had been replaced with a dull ache. A nurse came over and washed the blood from her hands using surgical wipes.

'Let's get you cleaned up a little. We need to move you onto a bed.'

Kray was wheeled into a side ward by two nurses.

The place smelled of antiseptic mouthwash and hand sanitiser. 'I feel sick,' Kray said, trying to lift herself onto her elbow. A nurse placed a cardboard bowl under Kray's chin just in time to catch the vomit. She coughed and spluttered. The nurse handed her a wad of tissues.

'Oh fuck,' Kray said, wiping her mouth. 'My baby, can you tell me—' The sentence was interrupted as her stomach heaved and a fresh mouthful of vomit landed in the bowl.

'Let me get that.' The nurse replaced the cardboard container with a clean one and handed over another wad of tissues.

'Can you tell me what's happened to my baby?'

'We're waiting for the doctor, she shouldn't be a minute.'

A woman dressed in suit trousers and a white blouse came in. All three huddled together over a stainless steel table in the corner of the room. Kray could see the ball of grey paper towel. Tears began pricking at her eyes.

She didn't need to ask the question again.

One of the nurses and the doctor left the room, taking the paper towel with them. The remaining nurse sidled over to where Kray was lying.

'I'm afraid you've suffered a miscarriage,' she said, in a flat, well-practised tone. 'We will need to examine you to be sure everything has come away.' Kray said nothing. She nodded as the tears ran down her cheeks. 'You'll probably be more comfortable on the bed. Do you think you can stand?'

Kray nodded again and lifted herself up onto her elbows. She twisted and swung her legs over the side. She was naked from the waist down. Her feet hit the cold floor and the nurse held on to her arm.

'You'll be better off in a proper bed,' she said, helping Kray to shuffle across the room. 'How about if we give you a wash first?'

Kray glanced down to see her thighs were discoloured with blood and dried fluid.

'Yeah, that would be good.'

'Is there anyone you need to call?'

'Umm, yes.' Kray tapped her hands on her jacket and found her phone. She pushed a couple of buttons.

The nurse helped her to lift her legs into bed and covered her with a sheet. She went to the sink to prepare a bowl of soapy water. Kray put the phone to her ear.

Millican clattered through the door, his phone ringing loudly.

'Roz, what is it? What's happened?' He looked at his phone and disconnected the call.

Kray stared at him, then at her phone and back again. 'But how?'

'You called me, saying something about being in an ambulance on the way to the hospital. You told me to meet you at Maternity.'

'Did I?'

'Roz, what the hell happened? Why are you here?' Kray held his gaze for a few seconds, then burst into tears. She held out her arms. Millican ran to the bed and hugged her. Kray sobbed into his shoulder, her arms pulling him tight.

'Roz, what's happened?' He gripped her shoulders and peeled her away from him. 'Talk to me.'

'I lost the baby.'

'What baby?'

'Our baby.' She spluttered into his chest.

'Our baby? You're pregnant?'

'I was, and now it's gone.'

'Shit! Are… are… you all right?'

'I don't know.'

'How… what?'

Kray broke away. 'I wanted to tell you, honest I did. But it never seemed to be the right time. And then when it was right I started bleeding and freaked out. I tried so many times to tell you… and every time…' She dissolved into gales of tears again, hurling herself into his chest. He wrapped his arms around her once more.

'It's okay, it's okay.' Tears flooded his eyes and ran down his cheeks. 'How long have you known?'

'A while.'

'A while? How far gone were you?'

'About eight weeks.' Kray took a tissue from her jacket pocket and wiped her nose. 'I was meaning to tell you – the other night when you were on call; the time when I had to attend that stabbing. And then… and then… and then I started bleeding.'

'Jesus Christ.' Millican held her, trying to hug the hurt away. 'You should have just told me.'

'I tried, honest I tried.'

'You should have just said, "Hey, guess what? I'm pregnant".'

'I wanted to choose the right time, I wanted it to be right… I wanted it to be… I'm so sorry.'

They rocked back and forth. It seemed like there was nothing more to say.

The nurse appeared by the side of the bed carrying the bowl of water and a towel.

'We need to conduct an examination to make sure everything is okay. The sooner we do that, the sooner we can make you more comfortable.'

'What sort of examination?' asked Millican, breaking the embrace.

'And you are…?'

'I'm her boyfriend.'

The nurse nodded. 'We need to do a pelvic examination and an ultrasound, to check the uterus is clear in order to prevent any infection. If not, we'll do a D&C which is a ten-minute procedure.'

The doctor and another nurse came in, wheeling an ultrasound machine.

'Would you mind waiting outside?' The nurse nodded to Millican. 'I'll come and find you when we're done.'

'Err, yes, of course.' He broke free from Kray's grasp and headed out the door. The nurse busied herself drawing the curtains around the bed. As the door closed behind him he could see Kray mouthing the word, *Sorry.*

He was rooted to the spot, trying to absorb what had just happened. All the time the same question rattled around his brain – *why didn't you tell me?*

Chapter 40

I'm struggling to keep to the speed limit as I head south on the M6 motorway. And having to listen to Jade ranting in the back isn't helping.

'I knew it, I fucking knew it. *Stick a knife in his neck*, I said. But oh no, you know best. *Let's get the coppers involved – let them do the dirty work.* Fat lot of good that was!'

'Piss off, Jade, pack it in with your *I told you so* routine.'

'But that's my point, I did fucking tell you. Why do you persist in ducking the issue?'

'You know why.'

'*I made a promise*,' she chants. I glare at her in the rear-view mirror, her heavily made-up eyes staring back at me from beneath her hooded fringe. She leans forward, draping her tattooed arms over the back of the seat. 'She stitched you up, that DI Kray. You gave her the inside track on something that you should have kept to yourself.'

'You agreed with the plan.'

'That's not the point.'

'Piss off, Jade, I'm not in the mood.'

The M6 gives way to the M5 and I'm forced to slow down because of the damned roadworks. As usual, no bugger is working on them. The events at the Paragon play over and over in my head. I saw the coppers congregating at the front entrance and watched them put the door in. I saw Kray scampering along the pavement and disappear inside. Then… nothing.

The time ticked by – I kept checking my watch – still nothing.

I'd been expecting to see a fleet of cars arrive to take the girls away to a safe house but all that turned up was an ambulance.

That was when my curiosity got the better of me and I left the café to get a clearer view of what was going on.

Two paramedics dashed inside, then one of them returned to fetch a trolley. I couldn't see the face of the person who was wheeled out. After a while the coppers left and drove away from the scene, then Marshall appeared at the front. It looked as if he was waving them goodbye. And that was it.

I ran back to my car and spent the next hour staring into the middle distance. I could feel the anger of eighteen years boiling to the surface, my knuckles white as I gripped on to the seat. I let out a scream of rage, slapping my hands against the steering wheel. That's when Jade showed up, spitting bile and fury in equal measure. I had a brief respite from her torrent of abuse when I visited the hardware shop but other than that she's been on full volume ever since.

I jolt back to reality and almost smack into the car in front as the traffic slows to a crawl.

'Fuuuck!' I yell at the top of my voice.

'The cops made you look a complete twat. Hanging on to an eighteen-year-old promise while all around you are laughing their bollocks off. You're a pussy, you know that, right?'

'I'm not telling you again.'

'Or what? What are you going to do? Report me to your new lady friend in the police? Because if that's the case I'll be perfectly fine. Fucking pussy.'

I slam on the breaks and swerve into the cones, bringing the car to a juddering stop. A cacophony of horns sound around me as drivers make rude hand gestures out the window.

I spin around in my seat, Jade recoils with her hands in her lap.

'You're right and I was wrong. Is that what you want to hear?' I spit the words at her. 'What the hell do you think we're doing here?'

'I don't know.' She avoids my gaze.

'I'm putting this right, Jade. It was a mistake to give the information to the police and I screwed up trying to keep the promise. Every day I torture myself about what happened to your mum, every day I play "what if" scenarios. *What if* I hadn't gone home that weekend, *what if* I'd smacked the guy holding the knife, *what if*—'

'What if you hadn't shagged that tart, Natasha.'

'Yeah, that too,' I yell at her. 'But I did and your mum died.'

'So did I.'

Her blistering comment punches me in the stomach. She has every reason to be angry.

'Yeah, you did and I have to live with that every day – every fucking day. So, don't give me a hard time about trying to do the right thing because I've spent the last eighteen years trying to do the right thing.'

'You've known all along what you needed to do.'

'Yes, I have, but I wanted to keep the last memory I have of your mum as pure as possible. I didn't want that to be as dirty and messed up as everything else in my life. Don't you understand that?'

'No, I don't. All I know is Marshall is walking about fit and well. When he should be spilling his blood around my feet while I laugh my tits off.'

'I know, I know. I will sort it, Jade, I promise.'

'Are you making another promise?'

'Yes, but this one's to you.'

'Shall I shut up now?'

'Yes, that would be good.' I reverse the car and force my way back onto the carriageway amidst the sound of protesting horns. The rest of the journey passes in silence, though it does nothing to curtail my rage.

I turn onto Holyhead Road and pick up signs for Handsworth Park. Sixty-three acres of landscaped grassy slopes, plus a lake and a cemetery that boasts the final resting place of the fathers of the industrial revolution and the founders of Aston Villa football club. At the time I wasn't aware of its heritage. All I knew was it had a copse of trees and bushes in the most northerly corner adjacent to the roadside properties on Hinstock Road. An ideal place to hide my trophies for a rainy day.

I park the car and retrieve my latest purchases from the boot. I should be more careful, avoiding the problem of prying eyes, but I'm way past caring. I find the spot – overgrown with brambles and undergrowth. I pull on gloves and rip the plants from the soil. I need to work fast.

The ground is soft and the edge of the spade slices into the earth. I shovel away, creating a rapidly growing mound of dirt. I strike something metal, then drop to my knees and scoop away the soil with my hands to reveal a green, corrugated piece of metal. I use my shovel to lever the metal box from its grave and heave it out of the hole.

The clasps have corroded and won't budge. The edge of the shovel makes short work of the rusty locks and I open the lid to reveal three packages wrapped in heavy-duty black plastic. I lift them out, placing them on the ground. Using my knife, I slit one of them and run my finger along the cold metal cocooned within. The plastic has done its job; my souvenirs from the Gulf are in good order.

Jade is beside me, staring at the packages. 'Remember you said that taking a life was fine so long as you've given the matter due consideration?'

'I do.'

'I think eighteen years is long enough.'

'I think you're right, Jade, I think you're right.'

Chapter 41

Bagley was taking the stairs two at a time while barking into his phone. 'I want everyone together in the incident room in fifteen minutes for a briefing. We need to regroup and formulate new lines of enquiry.'

'Yes, sir.' Tavener hung up and set about delivering his errand.

Bagley burst into the office suite on the top floor. He approached Norma Pettiford, the woman who guarded the diary of ACC Quade.

'Norma, I need to see the ACC, it's urgent.'

'She has someone in with her at the moment, I don't think it's important – would you like me to interrupt?'

'Thanks.' Bagley skirted around her desk and rapped on the door. He couldn't wait to impart the good news. He opened the door to find Quade having coffee with a man in a dark suit. 'Really sorry to interrupt, ma'am, but we have an urgent operational matter I need to discuss with you.'

'Oh, err, yes, okay. I think we're about done here. Do you mind, Derek? It's never a dull moment around here.' The man in the suit seemed fine about being kicked out, shook her hand and left. 'I wasn't expecting to see you until much later today.'

'And that's why I'm here, ma'am.'

'Go on.'

'There was nothing at the Paragon.'

'What do you mean?'

'At the club... there was nothing there; no illegal immigrants, no auction, no nothing.'

Quade leaned forward with her hands on the desk. 'Nothing?'

'Not a thing.'

Quade let out a deep sigh. 'The Chief's gonna go apeshit. I've been briefing him today about how we have a hotline of enquiry and intend to bring the murder cases to a conclusion. He made it perfectly clear that it was not before time. Now this! Kray was so convincing in her analysis.'

'We all know how convincing Roz can be, ma'am, but that doesn't make her right. I made my position perfectly clear. I had reservations about the whole operation from the start and now we have egg on our faces and are probably one mail delivery away from being sued for harassment. Not to mention having to pay for the loss of earnings and damage to the club.'

'I think, you might recall, we *both* had our reservations.'

'That's right, ma'am, we did.'

'What the hell am I going to tell the Chief?'

'Nothing yet. I'm getting the team together in ten minutes to get things back on track. We can't do anything about today's screw up but we can tell him what we intend to do about it. I don't go with this *all the cases are linked* bollocks. We need to tackle them separately.'

'Okay, I'll hang fire until you have your ducks in a row.'

'I'll see you later.' Bagley went to walk out.

'Erm, where's Roz? Why isn't she here to face the music?'

'She collapsed at the Paragon, not too sure what's wrong. They took her to hospital.'

'Shit, that doesn't sound good.'

'Maybe keeled over with embarrassment.'

Bagley made his way downstairs to the incident room where the team had already assembled. 'Okay, let's make a start,' he announced. 'Unfortunately, Roz has been taken ill and will not be joining us so I'm taking over the murder investigations.' Mutterings floated around the room. 'Today was a total cock-up so we need to regroup and crack on. So, as of now, we will adopt a fresh approach. I want us to start from the beginning with Michael Ellwood, looking for a drug connection. We need to revisit the house-to-house with Tommy Weir – somebody must have seen something. Someone knows what happened to him. I want a national alert put out to identify the Asian woman. I'm convinced she will turn up on a missing person's register somewhere. Find out who the person was at the hospital the night she died – it could be an abusive partner or her dealer.'

Tavener put his hand up. 'What about Billy Ellwood?'

Bagley nodded. 'Keep digging around in his past, there might be something there. And bring him in for questioning, I want to sit opposite him when he tells us why he led us on a wild goose chase today.'

'Sir, are we moving away from the theory that the murders are linked?' asked Gill.

'We are, from now on they're separate investigations. Is everyone clear?'

'Yes, sir,' was the collective response.

Bagley couldn't keep the smile off his face.

In a restaurant across town, a man wearing a shiny suit was standing on a makeshift stage. He was lean and lanky with slicked back hair and an orange tan. He looked like an eighties gameshow host. A black microphone was taped to his cheek.

'Good afternoon, gentlemen, I will be your host and auctioneer for today's entertainment. As promised, we bring you something different, something a little out of the ordinary which we hope will be to your liking.' He went through his well-rehearsed patter.

In the room were three men, each one seated at a well laid table, consisting of an ice bucket, a bottle of Moët, a large fluted glass and some canapés. A large flat screen TV and a set of speakers sat on a stand in the corner. The image of the auctioneer in glaring HD clarity beamed out at them. Down the side of the screen were six head and shoulder icons depicting the online guests.

The auctioneer continued his introduction. 'Now I need to go through a few points before we get started…'

Marshall was sitting at the back, his hand resting on a metal cashbox containing the door fees. Johnson and Johnson flanked the stage. There was one person missing from the event, the new customer who had so generously donated a substantial goodwill gesture for the privilege of taking part. There had been no way of contacting him or his go-between to inform them of the change of venue. Marshall assumed that the new boy would have clocked the coppers and done a runner. Never mind, there would be another auction in a few days – maybe he should give him a discount for the inconvenience.

'Before we start I need to do a sound and visual check. Can everyone see and hear me okay?' The man on the stage waved his arms about, it was almost kick-off time. 'So, if you would like to sit back, enjoy your champagne, and we will get the show underway.'

'I would like to introduce lot number one.' A young woman wearing a short minidress and high heels was brought from a side entrance and led to the stage. Her face was thick with make-up and her hair had been curled. Even the close attention of a cover stick couldn't hide the track marks peppering her arms. 'First one of the day, gents. This is a 1998 model. Never been raced but requires nitrous oxide to burn bright on the track. I think you will agree she has good lines with a cracking paint job. Who will start me off?'

A man sitting at one of the tables took a sip of his champagne and raised his token.

'I'll go three. Mr Red.'

'That's got us off to a flying start. Now who will give me five? Come on, gents, check out that bodywork. Do I hear five?'

'Five. Mr White,' said a voice through the speakers.

Marshall patted the cashbox – with fourteen lots on the card this was going to be a good day. Coupled with the earlier entertainment at the Paragon, this was going to be a great day.

Chapter 42

Kray disconnected the call. It was the third time she'd rung Millican and on each occasion it had transferred to voicemail. She was dressed in a hospital nightgown, lying in a bed in the side ward. The doctor had left over an hour ago and had given her the news that the embryo had been aborted cleanly and no further action was necessary. Her sickness had gone and she was feeling physically much better – her emotional state, however, was a very different story.

All she kept thinking about was the look on Millican's face when the realisation had dawned on him – *why didn't you tell me?*

As she lay there staring at the back wall she kept asking herself the same thing – *why didn't I tell him?*

The door swung open and in walked Millican.

'Where have you been? I've been calling you,' Kray said, raising herself up on her elbows.

'I know, I went back to your house to get these.' Millican handed over a bag containing clothes and toiletries.

'Thanks, but you could have answered your phone.'

'I needed time to think.'

'Oh.'

Millican sat on the side of the bed and held Kray's hand. 'What did the doctor say?'

'She said everything was clear.'

'That's a relief.' He leaned forward and kissed her on the cheek.

'The nurse said I can go home.'

'I didn't need this after all.' He held up the bag. 'Come on, let's get you out of here.'

The journey home passed in silence. Millican opened the front door and Kray shuffled inside. She felt like she'd been kicked in the stomach by a horse. She slumped down onto the sofa.

'I'll put the kettle on.' Millican busied himself with cups in the kitchen.

'I'm sorry I didn't tell you,' Kray said.

'When I bumped into you yesterday at the hospital, you were standing outside Maternity. What were you doing there?'

'I'd started bleeding and they sent me for a scan. The nurse told me everything was okay and said sometimes that happens.'

'Why didn't you tell me then? You had an ideal opportunity.'

'I don't know.'

Millican stopped making coffee and sat next to her on the sofa. 'Is it because you're not sure about us?'

'No, it's not like that.'

'Is it because you were deciding whether or not to keep it?'

'No, no, I was trying to pick the right time.' Kray flung her arms around him. He didn't reciprocate.

'I keep asking myself the same question: what would stop you from telling me? And the conclusion I reach every time is that you don't see our relationship as long-term.'

'I do, I do… please believe me.'

'I don't know what to believe, Roz. I thought we were good for each other, I thought we were going places. But if that were true you would have told me.'

'This is stupid, Chris, you know how much you mean to me.'

'Do I? Really? I'm not sure.'

'Chris, you've got this all wrong. You're in shock, I'm still in–'

'Shock! Of course I'm in fucking shock!' Millican jumped to his feet. 'My girlfriend announces that she's pregnant while lying in a hospital bed having just had a miscarriage. You robbed me of thinking I was going to be a dad. For however many weeks that lasted; you knew you were going to be a mum and you stopped me from knowing I was going to be a dad. You robbed me of that.'

'I'm sorry.'

'It was my baby too, you know?'

'I know.'

'Do you? Because that's a hell of a piece of information to keep to yourself.'

'I wanted to tell you, honest I–'

'Do you know I spoke to four different nurses and the doctor while you were in hospital and not one of them asked how I was? Not one.'

'They were focused on doing their job.'

'You didn't bother to tell me and they didn't care enough to ask. It's like I was relegated to the sidelines.'

'What? You're talking bollocks now.'

'It's about being kept out of the loop. And from what I can tell, I'm so far out of the loop I may as well fuck off.' Millican stood up and grabbed his jacket. 'In fact – that's a good idea. If you need anything, call me.'

'Where are you going?'

'Do you mind if I don't tell you right now? It doesn't feel like the right time.'

Millican stormed down the hallway and opened the front door to find Tavener about to ring the bell.

'Bloody hell, where did you come from?' Millican asked.

'I've come to see how Roz is. Is she in?'

'Yeah, she's in.' Millican pushed past Tavener. 'Did you know?'

'Know? Know what?'

'Never mind.' Millican darted down the steps to his car. Tavener watched him drive away and went inside.

'Hi, Roz. I thought I'd drop by to see how you are.'

'Yeah, so I heard.'

'What's up with Chris?'

'Can you do me an enormous favour?'

'Yes, what?'

'Go to the fridge and pour me the biggest glass of wine you can find, if you can't find a big glass, use a mug.'

'Wine? You were rushed to hospital in an ambulance today. Should you be doing that?'

'I should be carrying a fucking baby but that hasn't worked out so well. Just get it.'

Tavener's bottom jaw dropped open. 'A baby?'

'Yes, a baby. I had a miscarriage.'

'Holy shit. I'm so sorry, Roz.'

'Can you get me a drink, please?'

Tavener went into the kitchen and returned minutes later with half a pint of Sauv Blanc. He handed it over. Kray took a huge gulp.

'That tastes good.' She sunk back into the cushions. 'Sorry I swore at you.'

'Hey, if you can't swear at me who can you swear at?' Tavener said, sitting in the armchair opposite.

'Well, not Chris, that's for sure.'

'Has he taken it badly?'

'What he's taken badly is the fact I didn't tell him.'

'Oh shit.'

'The first he found out about it was at the hospital. I wanted it to be the right time, the right setting, but all I succeeded in doing is keeping him in the dark.'

'I'm really sorry, Roz. He'll be okay.'

'It took me weeks to get my head around the fact I was pregnant. I have to cut him some slack, he's only had hours to process the fact he was going to be a father – and now he's not.' Kray took another swig of wine. 'I fucked that bit up good and proper.'

'Once he's got his head around it, he'll be fine.'

'I hope so. Don't want to lose my baby and my boyfriend all in one day.'

'How are you feeling?'

'Physically, I'm okay.' Another chug of wine disappeared down her throat. 'Anyway, why did you drop by?'

'To see if you were all right.'

'What happened after the raid went belly-up?'

'We regrouped back at the station and Bagley gave us new marching orders.'

'Has he jumped in my seat?'

'You could say that.'

Kray shook her head. 'Bet he couldn't stop grinning.'

'He did seem pretty pleased with himself.'

'He's a dick.'

'I don't understand how it went so badly wrong.'

'I got carried away with what Ellwood told me. I joined up dots that weren't there and screwed up. But…'

'But what?'

'I believed him. When I was sitting across from him and he was telling me about how he had infiltrated Marshall's operation and how there was an auction, I believed him.'

Tavener said nothing. Kray looked at him over the rim of her glass. 'What is it?'

'Nothing.'

'You didn't just come here to see how I was, what is it?'

'You have enough on your plate right now.'

'Duncan, I can read you like a book. Now do I have to beat it out of you or are you going to tell me?'

Tavener opened his coat and pulled a sheaf of paper from his inside pocket. 'You know you asked me to dig up everything I could from Nottingham and West Mids about the Billy Ellwood case back in 2000?'

'Yes, what of it?'

'There was an obvious question hanging in the air: if Marshall was the third attacker, and the skin found under Blythe Ellwood's came from his face, why didn't they match his DNA?'

'That's the obvious question.'

'Turns out the evidence was compromised when the fridge it was being kept in developed a fault and stopped working. One hundred and sixty items of evidence were ruined.'

'A fridge going on the blink – that would do it.' Kray sat on the edge, leaning forward. 'Why are you telling me this?'

'It turns out the Nottingham force was trialling a new system whereby access to the evidence room was strictly controlled. Apparently, they'd come unstuck when they lost track of a blood sample which, in turn, led to a case collapsing. So they tightened up their procedures and the key to the room had to be signed in and signed out.'

'That's standard stuff.'

'It wasn't at that time. This is a copy of the log.' He handed Kray the wad of papers. 'The records show that the fridge was found to be broken on Tuesday 25 April. Which was the first day back after the bank holiday. Look at the entry on Friday 21 April.'

Kray flicked through the papers scanning the dates.

'Fucking hell.' Her eyes widened to the size of saucers.

Chapter 43

I finish writing fictitious names and addresses on lined paper and attach it to a clipboard. Dressed in an oversized boiler suit and peaked cap – I'm ready to go.

'I'm proud of you, Dad.' Jade smiles at me from the back seat. For the first time in years she looks pretty as opposed to angry.

'I got this. You wait here,' I reply, picking the cardboard box from the passenger seat. She nods in return. Stepping from the car, I cross the road and walk up the drive to the front door. My eyes are everywhere. I press the bell.

Through the frosted glass I can see movement in the hallway. I check around one last time – all clear.

'Can I help you?' A woman in her early forties stands on the doorstep in jeans and a white blouse, carrying a hand towel.

Fucking hell.

For a second, I forget my lines.

Her Slavic beauty hasn't dulled one bit.

'I have a package here for Mrs Bowden at number four?'

'Bowden? I don't think there's a Mrs Bowden living around here.'

'Oh, I'm sorry. Can you hold this while I check my delivery sheet? It's not heavy.' I hand over the box, then look at my clipboard before scanning the area around me.

'There are some new people who moved into–' She gets no further.

I slam my hand into her throat and drive her backwards into the hallway where she spills the box and towel from her grasp. The door bangs shut behind me as the back of her head thuds against the hardwood floor. Her eyes are bursting from their sockets, her mouth gasping for air. I roll her onto her front. A half scream is cut short when I force the towel into her mouth. Her teeth sink into my hand.

'Bitch!'

I rummage in the box for the rope and tie the towel in place, then bind her hands behind her back. She's writhing beneath me. The serrated edge of the diver's knife bites into her cheek.

'I will cut you unless you do as I say.' She bucks her knees in an attempt to throw me off. I press harder and draw blood. 'You're trying my patience.'

She freezes as the warm liquid runs down her face. I step off, grab hold of her collar and drag her into the lounge. Two minutes later she's tightly bound to a dining room chair.

I crouch down at her feet and look into her eyes. Blood is smeared across her face. I put my hands onto her knees; she flinches at my touch.

'Now all we have to do is wait.'

I go to the kitchen and fish a bottle from the fridge. My mouth is dry and the cold beer quenches my thirst. This is perfect.

'Eddie will be home in an hour, just enough time to relax and get to know each other, again.' I return to the lounge and switch on the TV, flicking the channels back and forth. 'Nod your head when I come to one you like.' Her eyes dart between me and the TV and back again. I raise the bottle. 'Cheers, Natasha. You're looking well.'

The clock on the mantelpiece reads 7.20pm when a set of car headlights sweep across the curtains.

'He's a bit early, maybe he knows you're entertaining guests.'

Natasha begins to yell into the gag. I walk behind her and wind my arm tight around her chest, the knife pressing into her throat. She goes rigid.

I lean into her. 'Shhhhh.'

The key twists in the lock and the sound of heavy footfalls fill the hallway.

Rob Ashman

'Hey, love,' Marshall calls out. 'I'm getting a beer, do you want something?' I hear him walk into the kitchen and the fridge door opening. There is a clink as the top comes off and bounces on the worktop. He comes into the lounge.

'Stay where you are, Eddie, or I will slice your wife's head off.'

The bottle slips from his grasp and lands on the carpet, spraying beer in the air.

'What the f–'

I can see his body tense, ready to fight. I pull Natasha in close and dig the blade into her neck. She lets out a muffled scream.

'Don't be stupid, Eddie. I'll open her like a Christmas present, I promise.' The blade digs into her flesh and she shrieks, her eyes wide and teary. He holds his hands up in a sign of surrender.

'Okay, okay. Don't hurt her. What do you want? I have money in the house – if you want money, you can take it,' he says.

I pull a set of handcuffs from my back pocket – another memento of a bygone life – and toss them over to him.

'Put one on your right hand. Do it!' He fiddles with the cuff and wraps it around his wrist. 'Now, sit on the floor next to the radiator and attach the other end to the pipework.'

Marshall looks around bewildered. 'Do it!' I yell at him. He scurries across the room and plonks himself against the wall. The sound of the metallic ratchet informs me the cuffs are secure. 'Okay, toss your phone over here.' He rummages in his suit jacket with his free hand and the phone wings its way across the lounge. 'Now remove your shoes and socks. Do it!'

Before long his footwear is lying on the other side of the room. I put the knife in my pocket and grasp hold of the back of the chair with both hands, tipping it backwards. I drag Natasha across the room and position her facing her husband, about five feet away. I take a seat on the sofa and remove the gun that'd been tucked into the waistband of my jeans. She lets out a muffled yelp.

'Now you can see each other better. This is nice, don't you think?'

'What do you want?' Marshall says, balling both his hands into fists. 'I told you I got money. It's upstairs.'

'I don't want your money, Eddie, because I already have it.' I allow the sentence to sink in. I can see the cogs whirring.

'You killed Tommy Weir.'

'I did, so I already have more money than you keep upstairs.'

'What do you want then?'

'I want you to answer some questions.'

'Questions? What are you, John Humphries? My guys are going to–'

I jump up and grab his wife. The tip of the blade puts a dimple in her cheek.

'You fucking hurt her and I'll kill you.'

'I don't think you will, Eddie.' I draw the point of the knife down her face, beads of blood break the surface. She yelps and tries to struggle free.

'Okay, okay. What do you want to know?' Marshall says.

'You're as bad as your wife. You don't remember me, do you?' I return to the sofa.

'Should I?'

'Eighteen years ago, we worked in a nightclub together. The guy running things was called Rolo.'

'Fucking hell, Billy.'

'Bingo! Got it in one.'

'You're a copper.'

'No, Eddie, I *was* a copper. But now as you can see, times have changed.' I brandish the knife in the air. Natasha pants, sharp breaths.

'What do you want to know?' he asks.

'Don't you think it's great we're all together again?'

'What do you want?'

'Does she fuck you like she used to fuck me?'

'What do you want!' Marshall yelled at the top of his voice.

'Steady on, I only asked. I need to explain the rules first.'

'Rules? What fucking rules?'

'I'm going to ask you two questions and you're going to answer them. If you piss about I'm going to hurt your beautiful wife. Is that clear?'

'You harm her–'

'Is that clear?' He glares at me. 'Okay, here we go – first question: did you murder my brother three weeks ago and dump his body in the sea? Second question: were you part of the punishment squad that showed up at my house and murdered my wife?'

I can see Marshall weighing up his options. What's he going to do? He was always one for bravado, always one for brassing it out. Will the fact that I have his wife at my mercy make a difference?

'I'm waiting…' I say. His face gives the game away.

'Fuck you!' he snarls. Natasha jolts in the chair, almost having a seizure.

'Are you sure that's the way you want to play this?'

'You're all talk, Billy. Always were.'

'And you're just the same, Eddie.'

'Fuck you.'

'Do you know that when you stabbed my wife it took her nine minutes to bleed out and die? And that was with me trying to stem the flow of blood.' I pick his phone off the carpet and hold it in the air. 'Now, we're not far from the hospital so I reckon they could get here in six minutes.'

'What the hell are you talking about? You've not got the bollocks for this.'

'Let's say seven minutes, just to be on the safe side.'

'Seven minutes for what?'

'So… nine minutes takeaway seven minutes is… You got two minutes to make up your mind. When you tell me what I need to know, I'll call 999 and the likelihood is Natasha will survive. Paramedics are much better trained these days. If you delay much longer than that, it will be touch and go.'

'Touch and go? Touch and go for what?'

I look at my watch and plunge the knife into her chest. 'The clock's ticking, Eddie, you've got two minutes.' I reach for a cushion. 'I'll do what I can to stop the blood.'

Chapter 44

Kray watched as the morning dew soaked into the hem of her trousers, changing them from grey to black. The dark clouds threatened rain. She tugged her coat tight around her body to protect herself from the wind coming off the Irish Sea, then crested the hill until a carpet of flowers opened up in front of her.

It had been several months since her last visit. She had always hated this place with a passion, but on this occasion the walk to the graveside felt calm and peaceful.

She wandered up the row of graves, stopping at the black marble headstone inscribed with the name, *Joseph Kray*. She unfurled a blanket and knelt down, taking a tissue from her pocket.

'Hey, how've you been?' She always started her one-way conversations with her dead husband in the same ridiculous manner. Kray knotted the tissue and wiped the recessed writing.

'I know I said I wouldn't be visiting for a while but I need you to do me a favour.' She cleaned the top of the marble, removing the grime. 'You remember the last time I was here and I told you about Chris? And about how we were getting on… and I wanted to make a go of it? Well, we made a better go of it than I anticipated and I fell pregnant.' Kray looked up at the sky, fighting back the tears.

'I know! All those months we tried for a kid with no result and… well… it just happened. It wasn't planned and it took me a while to get my head around it and then… and then… I fucking lost it. I had a miscarriage and that was it – no more baby.' She wiped tears from her face.

'I wanted to know if you would look after something for me?' Kray pulled the scan photograph wrapped in a clear plastic bag from her pocket. 'I got this when they checked me over at the hospital and I don't know what to do with it. I don't want to keep it because it hurts too much. I don't want to throw it in the bin because that doesn't seem right and I can't give it to Chris because… because… I have no idea if he still wants to be with me. I feel kind of stuck – so I wondered if you would look after her?

'That's right. Don't know why but I reckon it would have been a girl. Weird or what? God help her if she'd turned out anything like me, eh? She'd probably go and do something stupid, like get her husband killed.

'Anyway, I thought you might…' Kray fished a knife from her bag and plunged it into the soil at the base of the headstone. She cut an eight inch square of grass and lifted it away to reveal her gold wedding ring buried beneath. She picked it up, rubbed away the dirt and placed it back in the hole. She lay the photograph on top and replaced the square of earth, patting it down with both hands.

Kray swiped away the tears rolling down her cheeks. 'I've got some serious shit going on in work and I need to focus if I'm going to bring this bastard down. I'll focus a lot better knowing she's with you. Will you do that for me?' A breeze kissed her gently on the back of her neck. 'Thanks.' She patted the grass again and got to her feet. 'I gotta go…'

Kray put the knife in the bag, gathered the blanket under her arm and strode away. She gritted her teeth.

'And I am gonna take this bastard down.'

Kray walked into the small kitchenette at the station. Tavener had his back to her, making his first coffee of the day.

'Morning,' she said, touching him on the shoulder.

'Bloody hell, Roz. What are you doing in work?'

'Nice to see you too.'

'No, what I mean is–'

'I'm not going to sit on my arse at home given what you showed me last night. And besides, I need to keep busy.'

'Are you well enough? Shouldn't you be–'

'Yes, thank you for your concern, I'm fine. Now do you have enough for two in that fancy coffee maker of yours?'

'Sure.' Tavener pulled a second mug from the cupboard and depressed the plunger on the cafetière. He filled two cups.

Kray sipped at the hot liquid. She recoiled from the rim. 'What the hell is this?'

'Coffee.'

'Really?'

Tavener picked the packet off the counter. 'It says – *Lazy Sunday morning, gentle and easy-going.*' He looked impressed with his new purchase.

'Next time you go shopping, look for the one that says – *Kicks you in the arse, almost undrinkable.*'

'Not strong enough?'

'It's got no coffee in it.'

Tavener glowered at her. 'You're feeling better.'

'Yeah, well, I can't mope about the house.'

'What are we going to do?'

'We, Tonto, are not going to do anything. Leave it to me for now, I will shout when I need your help.'

Kray walked to her office considering whether or not to call Chris. She decided against it. He needed time to get his head around what had happened and her ringing him was not going to help the process. She was deep in thought when Bagley intercepted her.

'Bloody hell, Roz. What are you doing in work? Shouldn't you be–'

'You're the second person to say that to me this morning, sir.'

'Have you seen Occupational Health? I mean only yesterday you had a…'

'I'm fine. I want to be at work.'

'I'm not sure this is right, you know?'

'Oh, and how many miscarriages have you had, Dan?' She purposefully used his Christian name.

'Err, well, that's not the point.'

'I think it's precisely the point, so if you don't mind…' She brushed past him.

'I'm now Senior Investigating Officer for the murder cases. We have new lines of enquiry.'

'That's fine, let me know what you want me to do.' She disappeared into her office and closed the door.

Kray flipped open her laptop and started searching every database she could find. It was a little like trying to find a needle in a haystack but she was good at finding needles. The next hour went by in a blur.

Bagley poked his head around Kray's door. 'I've got a job for you. Tavener just got a call from the bloke who runs the boat club – apparently, you had a chat with him a few days ago. Commodore something-or-another – anyway, he wants to talk to someone and I have Tavener working on something else. Can you see what he wants?'

'Yeah, sure,' replied Kray.

'We've deprioritised that line of enquiry but we need to be seen to follow up anything that lands in our laps. It will be nothing, but I want you to take a look.'

Deprioritised? How can I say no?

'I'll finish up here and I'll take a run out.'

'No need for that, he's downstairs.'

Bagley disappeared. Kray logged out and picked up her notebook and pen, her head spinning with possibilities and conjecture. Her database search had only been a partial success and the burning question as she waited for the lift was… *How?*

She found the Commodore at the front desk and tried to drown out the song, 'Three Times A Lady' playing in her head.

'Good afternoon, Mr Bateman, you asked to see me.' Kray greeted him and shook his hand.

'I hope you don't mind me calling unannounced but I may have some information for you.' He was standing before her, every inch of him screaming, *Captain Birdseye*.

'Please, let's take a seat. How can I help?'

'I had a conversation with one of your officers about the Blue Lagoon, which is the vessel owned by Delores Cross. He seemed very interested in knowing its movements.'

'Yes, that's right, he mentioned it.'

'Well, I have to tell you that since you guys paid us a visit the whole club has been talking about nothing else. It's turned the place into a Miss Marple appreciation society with everyone playing the role of detective. Rumours and conspiracy theories are rife.'

'Oh, I'm sorry to hear that.'

'No, don't be – quite the opposite. The club bar has never been so full, no one wants to be left out of hearing the latest scandal.'

'But there's been no scandal.'

'I know, but that doesn't stop them making it up.'

For fuck's sake!

'You said you had some information, Mr Bateman?'

'A couple of our members, who own a boat called Sea Breeze, had an altercation with the crew of the Blue Lagoon.'

'An altercation?'

'Yes, we have strict rules about how boats manoeuvre in and out of the moorings, and on this occasion they almost collided. The Blue Lagoon was well out of order and a shouting match ensued, followed by a formal complaint.'

'Have you investigated the complaint?'

'We have.'

'And…'

'That's why I've come to you. Delores Cross isn't responding to any of our letters or emails and she is steadfastly refusing to engage.'

'I'm not sure that is a police matter, Mr Bateman.'

'I know that.' Bateman shook his head and his hat wobbled. 'What might be of interest is that the people crewing the Blue Lagoon were not members of the club.'

'They weren't?'

'No, the people from the Sea Breeze had a right stand-off with three men on the Blue Lagoon, shouting and bawling, they were.'

'When was this?'

'A little over three weeks ago, just before that poor man washed up on the beach. The talk in the clubhouse is about nothing else.'

'Who were they?'

'I don't know – I thought I'd come and tell you.'

Kray thought for a moment. 'Would the crew from the Sea Breeze be able to recognise the men again?'

'They might.'

'If we arranged for them to come down to the station, do you think they would look at some mugshots?'

'I'm sure they would.'

'I'll get that sorted right away. Can you give me the names of the people involved in the altercation?'

'They'll be delighted to help out. They were mad as hell. Apparently, one of the men used foul language, which was quite upsetting. Marjorie has been talking about nothing else since it happened.'

'Marjorie?'

'She was on the Sea Breeze. The guy was yelling at her, it got very personal.'

'Do you think Marjorie would be able to describe the man?'

'She wouldn't have to. She took his picture.'

Bateman fiddled with his phone then handed it to Kray. She zoomed in on the image.

Gotcha!

Kray spent the rest of the afternoon trawling through every database at her disposal. The overall picture was coming together slowly – *very* slowly. By the end of the day her eyes felt like someone had kicked sand in her face from staring at the screen.

Tavener came in, he'd been a busy boy too.

'What have you got?' he asked, handing over a coffee.

'A thumping headache.'

'Maybe this will help.' He slid a computer printout across the desk.

'Shit, where did you get this?'

'Off the system.'

Kray stared at her screen and then to the printout and back again. 'You could have found this an hour ago and saved me the trouble.'

'You needed me after all, Tonto.'

'Cheeky sod.'

'What's next?'

Kray explained what she needed him to do and left the office, carrying a thin folder. She took the stairs one at a time, arriving at the top floor. The secretaries had left for the day so there was no need to negotiate her way past Norma Pettiford. Kray tapped on the door.

'Bloody hell, Roz. What are you doing in work?' asked Quade.

'You're the third person to say that to me today.'

'Please come in. How are you?'

'I'm fine, ma'am.'

'Take a seat.'

'Ma'am, I need to talk to you.'

An hour later Kray rapped on Bagley's door. 'Have you got a minute, sir?'

'I'm a little busy at the moment, can't it wait until after we have the briefing?'

'That's just it, sir, I think this could be potentially sensitive and I'm not sure it's appropriate for the rest of the team.'

'Oh, what is it?'

'I spoke with the man who runs the yacht club.'

'The guy who showed up here?'

'That's him.'

'What of it?'

'He told me that a boat called the Sea Breeze had an altercation with one called the Blue Lagoon. Something about them leaving the jetty in a dangerous manner.'

'Is there a point to this?'

'The Blue Lagoon was crewed by three men who weren't members of the club and they had a shouting match with the people on the Sea Breeze. Anyway, one woman got so upset with their conduct that she took photos of them.'

'And?'

'Sir, I think the person on the boat is Eddie Marshall.'

'Not this again!'

'Bear with me a second. The altercation took place bang in the time window when we believe Michael Ellwood was abducted, taken out to sea and dumped overboard. When I questioned Marshall he said he wouldn't be seen dead on a boat.'

'How sure are you that it's him?'

'They are a little blurry, but it looks a pretty good match to me. The Commodore is sending me the photos so we can run them past imaging.'

'Bloody hell, Roz, do you know what you're saying here?'

'I know–'

'The Blue Lagoon is owned by Delores Cross. We trashed her husband's club yesterday looking for suspected illegal immigrants. His lawyer has already been on the blower twice. If we start going after his boat as well he's going to have a field day.'

'I agree, which is why I came to you. I'm not sure we should broadcast this new information until we have more evidence implicating Cross.'

'There is no evidence implicating Cross and all the photograph shows is Marshall on a boat. Hardly a smoking gun, is it?'

'I wondered if this was enough to get a warrant to search the Blue Lagoon. A good opportunity to get a CSI team on there, looking for evidence of Michael Ellwood.'

'On the basis of what? That Marshall lied to you about his dislike of sailing? I hardly think a judge is going to consider that sufficient grounds to grant us a copy of *Reader's Wives*, let alone a bloody warrant.'

'But if we find evidence that connects Cross to the murder cases then–'

'I'm telling you to drop it.'

'That's why I came to you first, rather than report it in the briefing.'

'And I'm pleased you did because we don't want anyone poking Bernard Cross with a pointed stick. But I'm telling you to drop this – move on – find something else to do.'

'You don't want me to progress the photographs?'

'That's right. Drop it.'

Kray returned to her office via the coffee machine. Her heart was thumping through her chest. The drink tasted awful but it kept her hands occupied. She checked her watch – counting down the minutes.

In the end she could wait no longer. Time was of the essence. She sunk the dregs from the bottom of the cup and set about her massive to-do list. The next few hours were crucial, she had to move fast. It was all about timing, and of late, her timing had been shit.

Chapter 45

Marshall screamed like a girl when I stabbed his wife, and began spewing confessions like confetti at a wedding – none of which were of any relevance to me. Once I'd calmed him down, promising to call an ambulance, he told me what I needed to know: *Yes*, he'd killed Michael and *yes*, he murdered Blythe.

The torrent of unburdening continued. He went on to say that Michael's death had been an accident, a case of mistaken identity – my brother was in the wrong place at the wrong time. They had meant to take out a rival gang member and my brother got in the way. I have to say, despite his protestations, the additional information made no difference. He was responsible, that was the bottom line.

I had the presence of mind to thank him for cooperating before I struck him over the head with the gun and rendered him unconscious.

I was grateful for the integral garage – without it I would have been struggling to get him into my car. I drove in and closed the garage door behind me before slumping Marshall into the back seats.

That was twenty minutes ago. Now I'm turning left off the Park Hall road, past the Best Western hotel and into the retail park. The place is deserted. I park at the back near the hedgerow. Marshall is moaning, which tells me he's coming round – excellent timing.

A patchwork of puddles reflects the halogen lights that ring the car park. Puffs of grey cloud scud across the sky, hiding the full moon, only to reveal it sometime later with a 'Ta-da' moment.

Jade is rubbing her hands together, fizzing with excitement. She gives me a sideways glance. 'What if he makes a run for it?'

'He won't, I've taken care of that.'

'And what about—'

'There's no sign of security, the van isn't here.'

'I've been looking forward to this.'

'Me too.'

I get out of the car and pop open the boot to make a last-minute check. I tick off the inventory in my head. It's all there. I bang the boot shut and open the passenger door. Seizing his feet, I yank Marshall from the confines of the car. He lands with a bump, slouched against the sill.

'Where the fuck are we?' he asks, his voice slurring. The welt down the side of his face has turned a furious shade of purple and yellow. His good eye is almost closed.

I lean down and shove the muzzle of the handgun under his chin. 'If you call out, I'll remove the back of your head. Is that clear?'

'Where's my wife?'

'She's probably tucked up in a hospital bed drinking tea.'

'Can you call the hospital, find out if she's okay?'

'Nope, that's not part of the deal. I said nothing about aftercare. On your feet.' I haul him upright, which proves to be a struggle. He wobbles about trying to get his balance. 'Walk ahead of me.'

He shuffles in bare feet around the front of the car and along the hedgerow. His hands are secured behind his back and I've tied his ankles together with a two foot length of electrical cable. His unsteady gait makes for slow progress, but that's fine, we don't need to be anywhere in a hurry. We've got all the time in the world.

We skirt around the perimeter fence until I say, 'Stop.'

'What happened to my wife? Did you call in time?'

'Stop worrying. They can work wonders these days.'

'I'm going to fucking kill you.'

I crack the gun across his face. The sight tears a three-inch gash in his cheek.

'Aghhh!' His knees buckle and I shove him into the long grass.

The high fencing consists of galvanised metal struts, riveted vertically to a frame. I push the head of the rivet and it pops out, landing in my hand. I repeat the process eight more times and swing the stanchions to the side. Many years ago, I drilled out the rivets and replaced them with dummies. To a bored security guard they look fine, and so long as no one removes the cable tie on the first strut, I have a ready-made swing door to use anytime I want.

I grab Marshall by the collar and drag him to the fence. 'Crawl through.' He does as he's told, blood falling from his face onto the grass when he shuffles forwards on his knees. I follow him and pull the bars back into place, then replace the dummy rivets.

Despite being in the open air there is a strange atmosphere that descends whenever I'm inside the compound. We pass the ironically-named Knightmare roller coaster, a rusted skeleton of a structure reaching up into the night sky. The screams and laughter have long since gone, replaced with an eerie silence.

I used to have a room in my flat dedicated to killing the man who had murdered Blythe. The promise prevented me carrying out my revenge for real but it didn't preclude me from acting out my darkest fantasy. When my demons got too much, I would retreat into my lair and not emerge until my bloodlust was satisfied.

Then it dawned on me that having such a room was not good, should I be visited by the cops – or anyone else for that matter. That's when I found Camelot, a disused theme park located south of Preston, close to the M6 motorway. It finally closed its doors to visitors in 2012 after coming bottom of the visitor attraction table and going downhill from there.

At first, it seemed only right that I should carry out my fantasies in the dungeon that still had human dummies manacled to the walls. But the place proved a magnet for those looking for the rush of wandering around the derelict attractions. So I widened my search and stumbled across a set of wooden buildings located in the top corner of the park. One of them was emblazoned with the name Bluebell Bottom. I have no idea what it used to be, but it's the perfect location for me to run and hide when my life spirals into the abyss.

Today is a big day, the Bluebell Bottom is no longer going to be the recipient of my blackest imaginations, today it's going to be the recipient of Eddie Marshall.

He hobbles along in front of me, dancing from foot to foot as the vegetation grabs at the soles of his feet. I jab the gun into the small of his back.

'Wait here,' I say, stopping at the back of the building. I reach down and prise away three planks of wood from the wall to reveal a gap big enough for me to squeeze through.

Marshall, on the other hand, might struggle. 'Get inside.'

He drops to his knees and eases his head and left shoulder through the hole. His movement is restricted by the cable tying his feet. 'You need to untie me, I can't–'

I stamp my boot into his ribs. He yelps with pain, and jackknifes, trying to protect himself. The next stamp lands on his protruding legs. I hear something crack. He yells out and frantically tries to caterpillar himself through the gap in the wall. I jump and land with my full weight on his ankle. The sound of small bones splintering echoes through the air. He jerks his legs through the gap, yelping in pain.

See, you fitted through after all.

'Fuck, fuck!' I hear him screaming inside. I poke my head in and order him over to the far wall. 'You fucking broke my ankle!'

'Move.'

I slip through and pull the wooden planks back in place, plunging the room into darkness. The noise of him sucking air into his lungs through gritted teeth makes him sound like a wild animal. I flick on the torch on my phone. Marshall shrinks away from the light. I yank on a metal ring that is set into the floor and a trapdoor yawns open. A four feet square black hole appears, the top few steps of a wooden staircase are visible in the torchlight.

'Get over here.' I shine the beam in his face.

'I can't fucking walk.'

'I'm not asking you again.'

'I can't push with my legs, you bastard.'

'Okay, let me help.' I walk over, grab the cable between his feet and heave. He slides across the wood, writhing around on his back.

'Agghh!' he screams.

I dump his legs through the hole, his body still prostrate on the floor. His false eye stares up at me while he squints through the other. I seize his shoulders.

'No, no, no. Please don't…'

I lift him and slide his protesting body through the hole. With every clunk, bang and scream my heart does a little jump for joy as he clatters down the flight of stairs. I shine the torch into the darkness just in time to see him pitch forward head first.

It's a long way down but looks like he made it.

Chapter 46

'This is a little unusual,' Bagley barked at Kray as he walked into the incident room. It was late and he had been on his way out the door when she requested to see him. 'Oh, good evening, ma'am, I didn't see you there.'

'Please take a seat, Dan, we need to run a few things past you,' Quade said, waving her hand at an empty seat.

'What's this about? Have I missed something?' he asked.

'I'm a firm believer that in this job there is no such thing as coincidences. Wouldn't you agree, sir?' said Kray, prowling around the room.

'What is this about?' Bagley asked again.

'Why did you fail to mention that you were involved in the original Critchley case?'

Kray was standing by the TV mounted on the wall, the remote control in her hand.

'What the hell…?' Bagley jumped back in his seat.

'When we found out Michael Ellwood was the brother of the undercover police officer Billy Ellwood, why did you fail to mention that you'd worked on the original case?'

'Err… how is this relevant?'

'You were part of the team who investigated the murder of Blythe Ellwood and you were also on the team that wound up the Critchley operation. Why didn't you mention that?'

'Err, I don't know. It was a long time ago. I was only a bit player in that investigation. I didn't think it was relevant.'

'The murder of Blythe Ellwood took place in Birmingham and the Critchley operation was based in Nottingham. It was a cross-force investigation. Do you recognise this?' Kray flashed a picture up on the screen showing a sheet of A4 paper covered in scrawled writing.

'No, should I?'

'This is a witness statement from Roland Eccleston, who ran the nightclub on behalf of the Critchley brothers. Do you recognise your signature at the bottom?'

Bagley went up to the screen and peered at the image. 'Yes, that's my signature.'

'Here's another witness statement, again bearing your signature – and another. In fact, you took a total of seven statements. Five in Nottingham and two in Birmingham.'

'I might have done, it was a long time ago.'

'I think, sir, you had more than a bit part to play.'

'I can't recall.'

'During the attack at Billy Ellwood's home his wife was stabbed to death and the post-mortem said they found human skin and cornea under her fingernails. When I interviewed Billy Ellwood, he was convinced that the third attacker was Eddie Marshall. He showed me a photograph of Marshall cleaning his ocular prosthesis. In other words – Marshall has a glass eye. Which would be in keeping with such an injury. But the police at the time could not use the DNA sample because it had been degraded.'

'Do we have to listen to this rubbish?' Bagley threw his arms in the air. 'This is a rehash of the fairy tale that had us chasing our arses at the Paragon club. This is bollocks.'

'Sit down, Dan,' Quade said.

Kray continued. 'The DNA evidence was compromised because the fridge in which it was stored developed a fault and stopped working. It was discovered on the Tuesday after the bank holiday. On the preceding Friday someone booked out the key to the evidence room at Nottingham police station. Do you recognise this signature?'

'This is rubbish,' protested Bagley.

'You booked out the key. What were you doing in the evidence room, sir?'

'How the hell should I know, it was eighteen years ago.'

'Without the DNA sample, Marshall was never arrested. There was a later report of a mass brawl at a pub where he lost an eye in a fight. The incident report confirms you were involved in that case as well, sir. Did you tamper with the fridge, causing it to fail in order to protect the identity of the third attacker?'

'That is an outrageous accusation! We should be out there, cracking real cases, not playing join the dots with things that happened years ago.'

'Continue, Roz,' Quade said.

'Earlier today I told you that the man who runs the yacht club had in his possession a set of photographs that showed Eddie Marshall on the Blue Lagoon. This is despite Marshall telling me he wouldn't be seen dead on a boat. I came to you with the information and you told me to drop it, even though the timeframe fits perfectly with what we believe happened to Michael Ellwood. You told me to drop it – three times.'

'Yes, that's right, because we had already covered ourselves in shit by smashing up Bernard Cross's nightclub, and his lawyer is baying for our blood. An operation you screwed up, I might add.'

'I never told you the Blue Lagoon was owned by Delores Cross.'

'What?'

'How did you know the Blue Lagoon belonged to Delores Cross?'

'You must have told me, or Tavener told me.'

'Nope, neither of us mentioned it. So, how did you know?'

'I must have read it in the case file.'

'Nope, it's not in there either.'

'Christ, I don't know, lucky guess I suppose.'

'What did you do after I told you about the photographs?'

'Erm, I went out for a drive to clear my head and think things through.'

Kray clicked the remote and a list of telephone numbers and times came onto the screen. 'This is the call log for Marshall's phone. You can see here there were three calls made to his number at 16.33. We traced the calls and they were made from a public call box in the Norbreck Castle hotel. Do you know where that is, sir?'

'Of course I know.'

'You should do, because this is a screen grab from the CCTV showing you parking in the car park of the Norbreck at 16.15. Can you tell us what you were doing there?'

'Do I have to go through this pantomime, Mary?'

'Answer the question, Dan.'

'I needed a piss, all right?'

'You were a ten-minute drive from the station and you chose to use the public toilets in the hotel?'

'I did, so what?'

'Marshall didn't answer his phone, so we also looked at the other calls made from the call box at the Norbreck. The next one went to this number…' Kray tapped the screen. 'This is the offices of Bellville Entertainment, a corporation owned and run by Bernard Cross.'

Bagley shook his head. 'This is all very interesting I'm sure, but—'

'And this…' Kray pressed another button on the remote and a video came up on the screen showing a boat with a gang of people swarming over it. 'Is the Blue Lagoon. Do you have any idea what these people are doing?'

'You seem to be the one with all the answers, enlighten me.'

'Looks to me like they're cleaning. Cleaning it to death. Now why would they be doing that?'

'I don't know – excess bird shit?'

'I think they are cleaning it to death because someone tipped them off that the boat might be subjected to a CSI examination. A suggestion that I'd put into your head an hour earlier.'

'That's nonsense. Anyone could have tipped them off.'

'That's true, but I only told you and the ACC.'

'What…?'

'And while we're on the subject of tip-offs, I could not get it out of my head that when I was sitting opposite Billy Ellwood he was telling the truth about the auction. I could see it in his eyes, I believed him. Here is the call log from the same public call box at the Norbreck, it shows a call to Marshall's mobile the night before the raid. It lasted twenty seconds.'

'This is fantasy land stuff–'

'This is a screen grab taken from the CCTV in the hotel reception – that's you, sir. Did you need another piss?'

Bagley was looking at the screen, his mouth slightly ajar.

Kray watched him squirm. 'There is one more piece in the jigsaw. We know Marshall worked in Nottingham in the year 2000, where did you work, sir?'

'You already fucking know.'

'That's right, you worked for Nottingham police, then you moved to GMP three years later. Guess where Marshall was based at that time…? He'd moved to Manchester to run Bernard Cross's security operation for his business interests in the city. Then Marshall gets a transfer to Blackpool, presumably to set up the people trafficking operation, and guess who follows him?'

'Have you finished?' asked Bagley.

'Yes, I think so, sir.'

'This is nothing more than a bunch of inflammatory accusations and flight of fancy rhetoric, Detective Inspector. You have no evidence to support any of your outlandish claims. It's all supposition and conjecture. You're doing what you always do – letting your overactive imagination run away with you.'

Quade got to her feet. 'I'm with Roz on not believing in coincidences and, if I'm to believe what you've been telling us, we have more of them than I can shake a stick at. I've heard enough. We need to pick up Marshall.'

'Already underway, ma'am.'

Kray crossed the room and opened the door. Two uniformed officers stepped inside. Her phone buzzed in her pocket, it was Tavener.

'Roz, I'm at Marshall's house. You better get over here fast.' He was out of breath.

'What the hell's happened?'

'It's like an abattoir.'

Chapter 47

I'm not homophobic, far from it. But the sight of a naked man lying spread-eagled on the ground does nothing for me. However, when that man has his hands and feet nailed to the floor and his name is Eddie Marshall I have to admit... I'm getting some kind of rush.

I was worried that the topple down the stairs had killed him. By the time I reached his crumpled body he was barely breathing and his pulse was weak. I straightened him out and after a little while he improved, though he still remained unconscious. This proved to be a silver lining because I had been wondering how I was going to nail the bastard to the floor.

I'm straddling a chair which I took from the cafeteria. It's one of those cheap plastic chairs that stack together. I only have one, but it does the job. I'm looking at Marshall with my forearms resting on the back. The room is damp with a high ceiling and all round wooden cladding. There are shelves and racking bolted to the walls. I think the place was used as a storage facility at one time. However, looking at the gradient of those stairs, how anyone could haul supplies up there is a mystery to me.

I have two camping lamps bathing the interior in yellow light, giving the room a flickering warmth. The rest of my toys are here; rope, electrical cable, plastic sheeting, petrol, pliers, knives, hand tools – you name it, I've got it. Everything a torturer needs for a good day out.

'When can we start?' Jade is skulking around, eager to get stuck in.

'There's no point if he's out cold. Where's the fun in that?'

'Can we cut his cock and balls off?'

'And have him bleed to death? That's way too quick.'

Jade is standing over Marshall, staring at his genitals. 'I think we should do it at some point.'

I nod my head. At least she's not yelling at me.

Marshall doesn't look good. His left eyelid has sunk back into its socket, where his false eye was knocked out in the fall. A tennis ball-sized purple bruise has come up on the side of his head, and I'm sure when I laid him out his shoulder looked dislocated. His ankle is black and swollen, so on reflection, I might well have broken it while helping him through the gap. Shame.

The six-inch nails that are hammered through his hands and feet have metal washers under the heads. I don't want to risk him tearing them through his flesh as he struggles… and he's going to struggle.

Marshall begins to make noises and moves his head from side to side. I pick up a bottle of water and empty it onto his face.

'Wakey-wakey.' He raises his head and coughs against the gag rammed into his mouth, then opens his eye and blinks. 'Time to wake up.' I tip the remainder of the water over him.

Marshall tries to move and that's when the pain surges through his body. He shrieks through the gag, his head flipping from side to side. He spots the nails and yells some more.

That's a good start.

'Now? Are we going to kill him now?' Jade is skipping around the room like she's at a barn dance.

'Patience, Jade, patience. This has been a long time coming, so we're not going to rush.'

Her face has that same look of eager expectation as she does on Christmas Eve. That childlike flush of excitement and joy.

'Oooo, this is going to be sooo good.' She clasps her hands together under her chin and does another little dance.

Marshall blinks at me – *Who the hell are you talking to?*

It galvanises him into more activity. Every move he makes is accompanied by gargled screams. I watch him writhe around, trying not to look too smug. I turn the ocular prosthesis around between my fingers, the blue-grey iris stares back at me.

'You dropped this.' My words galvanise him into more activity which is accompanied by more screams. 'The less you struggle the less it will hurt,' I say, going to the back wall and returning with a hand tool. 'Don't cause yourself any more pain than is necessary – that's my job.' I press the trigger and the sanding disc spins into action. The noise makes him go rigid, his head cranes forward to get a better view.

'The guy in the shop was a hive of useful information. Apparently, the disc spins at 10,000 rpm and the Lithium-ion battery lasts forever. The best thing about this one is it also takes a wire brush head and a grinding wheel for those stubborn parts. It only cost me sixty quid. Bloody bargain I reckon.' I hold the additional fittings up for him to see. 'How about if we give the sander a go first.'

'I love the noise that sander makes.' Jade is positively squeaking.

I kneel beside Marshall, his whole body quaking, then I straddle his stomach which causes him to arch upwards. The nails hold him firm.

'Oh yes, and before we start, I forgot to tell you. The answer to the question was ten minutes and thirty seconds.' He's shaking his head from side to side. 'That's how long it took Natasha to bleed out and die. It was great fun watching her blood soak into your lovely carpet. She did make quite a mess.'

The sandpaper disc tears into his nipple, shredding the skin into a bloody mess. He bucks and turns against my weight. I remove the tool to see a crimson arc of epidermis – the nipple and surrounding flesh are gone, now lying somewhere on the floor.

Marshall is going berserk.

'Fuck me, that's boss,' Jade yells, while cackling. 'Do the other one. Go on, do it!'

'Bloody hell, look at that. Took it clean off.' I snap the lever and the wheel detaches. I replace it with the cup-shaped wire brush. 'Let's try this one.'

'That's one mean-looking fucker.' Jade kneels next to me.

I hold the tool up and buzz it a few times and the brush whizzes round. 'I practiced with this one, and I can vouch for the fact it removed rust from metal.'

I press the trigger and plunge it into the left side of his chest, bearing down on him with my full weight. Blood and tissue erupt into the air. I can feel the spatter of skin landing on my face and going in my mouth. I'm aware of a stream of water jetting off to the side as he loses control of his bladder.

Marshall bucks and judders below me. His good eye rolls back in his head. I lift off and sit back. The brush head is dripping with blood.

'Fucking hell look at that hole!' Jade's eyes are wild with excitement.

'I should be wearing safety glasses for this one,' I say, wiping the debris from my face and spitting on the floor.

'Do his bollocks, Dad, do his bollocks!'

Chapter 48

'Cheers, mate, I really appreciate this.' I swing up into the cab, tuck my rucksack behind the seat and bundle the kitbag into the footwell. 'If you could drop me off anywhere near Birmingham that'd be great.'

The lorry driver heaves himself up into his seat. The springs complain as his bulk crushes them flat. 'That's okay. Let me know where.'

'I will. My name is Billy.'

The cab smells of old socks and lavender air freshener and the dashboard rattles as the engine roars. The driver clears the newspapers away and tosses them into the back. The breaks hiss.

'I'm Doug,' he says, checking his mirrors.

The beeping sound announces that we're on our way. When we're clear of the services Doug wastes no time and launches into a well-rehearsed speech telling me how shit the haulage business is and how he really wants to be a tree surgeon. The only qualification Doug has for this aspirational career move seems to be that he owns five chainsaws.

I tune out and let him ramble on, in my head I'm back in the basement of the Bluebell Bottom.

After two and a half hours Marshall's heart gave out. At least, I reckon that's what happened. Despite the floor being awash with blood and tissue, plus the occasional chunk of bone, I don't think he bled to death. I had to change the sandpaper disc twice because it kept getting clogged up. In the end I settled for the wire brush and the grinder wheel. I think Jade's favourite was definitely the wire brush – it flung shit everywhere.

Rob Ashman

I'd flayed most of the skin from his body and had decided it was time for a little heat treatment. The blowtorch made him dance and jigger like a landed fish; then he had some kind of seizure and that was it – game over.

I'd like to say I watched the life drain from his eye, but I was too busy making his flesh bubble. I missed that part. Jade was whooping and hollering, dancing around, waving her arms in the air. It was party time.

I turned to tell her he was dead, but she was gone. The place was silent but for the hiss of the blowlamp. We'd had our fun; it was time for me to go.

I left everything where it was and made my way back upstairs. The trapdoor opened up and a waft of cold air greeted me. I picked my way back through the park, taking care that no security had turned up while I'd been otherwise engaged, and arrived at the car. I looked like the scene from *Carrie*, the one where they tip the bucket of blood on her. I opened the boot and pulled out what I needed. In no time at all I was washed, towelled and wearing clean clothes.

The other benefit of the Camelot theme park is its close proximity to the Welcome Break service station at Charnock Richard. After a short walk I'd crossed the pedestrianised walkway that runs over the M6 to the lorry park located on the southbound carriageway. Half an hour later, I had myself a lift.

My time in the police had taught me that if you want to disappear there are certain things you must do: leave your credit cards and mobile phone at home, they are a beacon above your head; don't draw money from your bank account once you've left; don't contact friends or relatives because the authorities will be watching them, and avoid public transport.

When the coppers smash down the front door to my flat they will find my wallet, cards and phone on the bedside table, and as for not contacting anyone – that's easy – there is no one. Oh, and the bag lying at my feet will ensure I don't need to touch the money in my account.

236

I have to admit to suffering a pang of conscience when I was preparing to leave the flat for the final time. DI Kray seemed like a good copper and I didn't want her chasing loose ends, so in my wallet is a note addressed to her.

Roz,
When we spoke, I omitted to tell you one thing: I killed the man in the alleyway. I slashed his throat with a knife. He was one of Marshall's guys and I had to start somewhere. You're a smart woman and you'll figure the rest out for yourself. I didn't want you to burn valuable resources trying to track down his killer.
Take care.
Billy.

It seems only fair that I give her the heads-up.

'So, what about you?' Doug asks. I snap back to reality.

'Oh, err, my wife threw me out.'

'No way!'

'Yeah, she had an affair with some twat at work and told me to pack my bags.'

'Oh, man, that's shit.'

'I know. But that's the way it works, right? If I have an affair, I get kicked out; if she has an affair, I get kicked out. It's my bloody house as well as hers.'

'I know, mate, it happened to my buddy. You should have stood your ground.'

'I did and that's when she called the cops. She told them I was going to hit her and they escorted me out of my own house. I protested and they threatened to arrest me.'

'Typical, mate. Bloody typical.'

'So anyway, I think to myself, *bollocks to this, I've got friends in Birmingham. I'll be better off with them.*'

'I'm hearing you, mate. I've been divorced now for six years. Best six years of my life, I'm telling you.' Doug then proceeds to tell me in lurid detail exactly why they've been the best.

Doug and I rabbit on as the miles clock by. This is new territory for me, I'm making up my backstory as I go. The lies and anecdotes trip off my tongue and he's lapping it up. It's as though I've never been away.

I'm enjoying the new me. He seems a really interesting guy.

I feel lighter, as though the weight of eighteen years has been lifted from my shoulders. I've no intention of going to Birmingham. I'm heading for a quiet place in Devon where I'll lay low for a while, allow time for my hair and beard to grow and move on from there. I'm good at disappearing.

At the back of my mind I wonder if I'll ever see Jade again.

Somehow, I think not.

Chapter 49

Two days later

Kray nodded a hello to Norma Pettiford, who was guarding Mary Quade's office. Kray wrinkled her nose – the place smelled of fresh paint.

'ACC Quade is expecting you, Roz, go straight in,' she said, consulting her on-screen diary.

'Thanks.'

Kray opened the door to be greeted by Quade jumping up from behind her desk. 'Roz, glad you could drop by.'

'You wanted to see me?'

'Please take a seat.' Quade bustled around the desk and squeezed into one of the chairs at the conference table.

I bet that's going to be stuck to your arse when you get up…

'What can I do for you, ma'am?'

'I have a meeting with the Chief. What's the latest?'

'We found Eddie Marshall's body. The security firm who look after the Camelot site reported an abandoned car. We ran the number plate and traced it back to Billy Ellwood. Sniffer dogs found Marshall nailed to the floor in a basement of one of the properties on site. Fingerprints have confirmed it was Ellwood who used the power tool that killed him.'

'Any news on Ellwood?'

'Nothing. From what we can tell his belongings are still at his flat and he's disappeared. The clothes he wore when he killed Marshall are in his car. We're monitoring his bank account and we're going to put out an appeal.'

'That sounds like the right call. I've got an update for you: The Independent Office for Police Conduct and an internal investigation team are all over Dan Bagley. He's been charged and will appear in court tomorrow. There's bound to be a media circus when the news breaks. I wanted you to hear it from me rather than read it in the papers.'

'Thank you, ma'am, I appreciate the heads-up. The IOPC have already spoken to me and I've provided them with everything we have.' Roz got up to leave.

'Please sit a while, Roz. How are you finding the role of Acting DCI?'

'It's fine, ma'am. You may recall I did the role before, so it was the easiest move.'

'Yes, you did a good job last time.'

Shame you promoted a bent copper instead, then?

'Thank you, ma'am. As I said, it was the most straightforward thing to do, given the circumstances.'

'You know Bagley and I weren't friends. I knew him from work and that was about it.'

'Okay.'

'We met at police college years ago and our paths have crossed a few times, but I didn't really know him that well.'

'Your relationship, or otherwise, with Dan Bagley is of no concern of mine.'

'Now, I know we've had our slight differences in the past, Roz.'

Is that in the same way that America and Vietnam had a slight difference in the sixties?

'I think it's fair to say that.'

'But I want you to know that I rate you very highly and you have my full support.'

Kray wondered if this was the right time… she decided it was. 'I see things a little different, ma'am.'

'Oh?'

'My experience is you have never given me your support and have always chosen the word of DCI Bagley over mine.'

'That's because we have a chain of command that needs to be upheld.'

'We do, ma'am, and that is important but–'

'Do I have to remind you of the support I gave you when you came to me with the accusations against Dan?'

'No, ma'am, you don't. You supported me on that occasion and you gave me the green light to operate outside of the investigation – and for that I'm grateful. But that was only because the weight of circumstantial evidence stacked up against Bagley was so great that if it came out later that you had taken no action, you would be hanging in the breeze.'

'I'm disappointed that you see it that way, Roz. I've always had the utmost confidence in you.'

'It hasn't felt that way.'

'Anyway, that's water under the bridge.' Quade waved her hand in the air like she was swatting a fly. 'This latest situation means we will be looking for a new head of CID. We'll need to appoint a new DCI.'

'I figured that.'

'I want you to know, I will be running the selection board.'

'I thought you would, as you ran the last one.'

'You are a very strong candidate, Roz – a very strong candidate indeed.'

Kray stared into her lap, then looked up. Quade was smiling back at her, nodding her head with her eyebrows raised in a *do you get what I mean?* kind of way.

'That's good, ma'am.'

'So, I need to know, can I count on your application for the role?'

Kray placed both hands on the table and got to her feet. 'I've given this a lot of thought and I was going to drop by your office sometime later today.'

'Oh, why's that?'

'Because I wanted to give you this.' Kray fished an envelope from her inside pocket. On the front was written, *ACC M Quade*. She laid it on the table.

'What's this?'

'I took on the role of Acting DCI because I didn't want to let the team down. They have a heavy caseload and need someone in their corner, so I stepped up to the plate.'

'I realise that, Roz, you are hugely loyal to those around you.'

'Yeah, and that's the problem.'

'What problem?'

'I'm not sure that loyalty is reciprocated elsewhere.'

'I don't understand.'

'How can I put this… with the greatest of respect, ma'am… shove your job up your arse. I've obviously written it in more flowery language in the letter, but the meaning is the same.'

Quade's mouth dropped open. 'But… but…'

Kray turned and walked out.

'Roz, you were asking if the ACC had any time in her diary today,' Norma Pettiford called after Kray. 'Do you still need an appointment?'

'No, Norma, I think we're done.'

Chapter 50

One year later

Millican pushed open the door to the pub and stepped to one side, allowing Kray to shimmy her way in. The place was brash and noisy, with music blaring from speakers the size of armchairs, and clusters of pretty people standing at the bar.

'Oi up!' Tavener galloped over and enveloped her in a bear hug. 'I wasn't sure you'd be able to come.'

'Get off, you great lump.' Kray shoved him away and slapped him on the arm.

Tavener shook hands with Millican.

'How you doing?' Millican asked.

'Bloody pissed by the look of it,' answered Kray.

'Come on over, I hope ya wearin' ya drinkin' troosers.' The more drunk Tavener got the more Scottish he became. He put a giant paw on Millican's shoulder. 'Great ta see you.'

Kray scuttled along behind. They reached a gaggle of people in the corner, where two huge ice buckets were sitting in the middle of the table, overflowing with bottles of beer, fizz and white wine. A huge cheer went up when they saw Kray.

'Bloody hell, Roz. I didn't know you were coming along.' Gill came over and gave her a more gentlemanly hug.

'Hello everyone!' Kray shouted over the cacophony of sound. 'We got back a few days ago and weren't sure if we could make it.' This prompted a great deal of backslapping for Millican and more hugging for Roz.

Louise Chapman sidled over to Tavener. 'You going to top me up?'

He pulled the bottle of fizz from the icy water and emptied it into her glass. 'Who'd have thought it, Roz? Me… a Detective Sergeant.' He raised the empty bottle in the air.

'Congratulations, Duncan, you deserve it,' Kray said.

'Don't praise him too much, Roz. If his head gets any bigger he won't get his ears through the door.' Chapman reached up and kissed Tavener on the cheek.

Kray raised her eyebrows.

Tavener leaned over. 'A lot's happened since you've been away.'

'So it would appear.'

'Anyway, enough about me, how about you two?' Tavener said, handing over two bottles of beer. Kray looked at hers and handed it back.

'What am I supposed to do with that?' she said.

'Sorry.' Tavener poured her a glass of wine the size of a fish bowl.

'Our Europe trip was amazing.' Millican wound a tanned arm around Kray's shoulder. 'We travelled around, catching planes, renting cars, stopping in hotels and having a good time.'

'How long were you there?' asked Chapman.

'Four months.'

'Bloody hell, no wonder you both look so well.'

'We decided to splash out with some of the money from the sale of my house,' Kray said, taking a large swig of wine. 'If you're going to do it – do it properly. Cheers everyone.'

They raised their glasses and the four of them chinked.

'Hey, wait a minute!' yelled Chapman. 'What's this?' She lifted Kray's left hand to reveal a ring on her third finger. 'You sneaky bugger.'

'Oh yes, and somewhere along the way, we got engaged,' Millican said.

'That's fantastic.' Tavener was in bear hugging mode again and grappled Kray and Millican into a clinch. 'I'm so pleased for you both.'

'Yeah, we're pretty pleased about it as well.' Millican struggled free and shook Tavener's hand.

'That's marvellous, a double celebration,' said the big Scotsman.

Chapman planted a kiss on Millican's cheek and dragged him away to tell the others.

'Thanks for coming,' Tavener said.

'It's not every day my little protégé moves up the ranks.' Kray raised her glass again.

'I miss you,' he said.

'Bollocks.'

'No, I do. It's not the same without you. No one threatens to beat me up or tells me to fuck off.'

'You'll find someone else to annoy.'

'Did you know Brownlow retired?'

'I'm not interested.'

'Bagley got sent down. By all accounts he'd been on the take for years. The Critchleys started off by blackmailing him over some recreational drug use and then brought him onto the payroll. Bagley and Marshall were joined at the hip; wherever Marshall went, Bagley followed.'

'I said I'm not interested.'

'Ellwood disappeared into thin air. It's like he's fallen off the face of the earth. Not a trace.'

'I'm still not interested.' Kray poured more wine down her throat. 'What about Quade?'

'I thought you weren't interested.'

'Do I have to beat it out of you?'

'Ha, she's still there. Larger than life.'

'Larger than any life I know.'

'Do you wish you were back?'

'Christ, no. Well, maybe a little, but don't tell Chris. I've got an interview for a new job on Monday.'

'Doing what?'

'Fraud investigation for an insurance firm.'

'So, if they have any serial killers making false claims they send for you?'

'Very funny.' They hugged each other. 'I'm proud of you.'

'Do I get an invite to–' Tavener stopped, aware there was another person standing next to them. 'Good evening, ma'am.'

'Good evening.' It was Mary Quade. 'Hi, Roz, I hope you don't mind, I heard you were here.'

'Hi, Mary, I guess bad news travels fast.'

'Don't worry, Duncan, I'm not going to stay,' said Quade.

'Would you like a drink, ma'am?' he asked.

'No, I'm driving, thank you.'

'How about a soft drink?'

'I'm not staying. I've come to see Roz.'

'Me? Why have you come to see me?'

Quade took Kray by the elbow and led her to one side.

'I'll come straight to the point. I need your help.'

'To do what?'

'We've got a problem.'

'We? I don't think *we* have a problem.'

'Okay. I have a situation with a case and could really use your help.'

'What sort of case?'

'A murder investigation.'

'You're asking me to come back?'

'Well, maybe, how about–'

'I'm flattered, but the job takes its toll. It demands that you sacrifice a lot and I've sacrificed more than most; my physical health, my mental well-being, my dead husband and my unborn child. Plus, it almost robbed me of the chance to make a new life with Chris and I cannot risk that happening again.'

'I agree, it's not without its challenges, but–'

'Mary… if you were drowning I'd throw you a breeze block. My first answer still stands – stick your job up your arse.'

Acknowledgements

I want to thank all those who have made this book possible – My family, Karen, Gemma, and Holly for their encouragement and endless patience. Plus, my magnificent BetaReaders, Nicki, Jackie and Simon, who didn't hold back with their comments and feedback. I'm a lucky boy to have them in my corner.

I want to thank my ARC Group who have shouted about my books and made me blush with their unwavering support.

And last but by no means least, my wider circle of family and friends for their endless supply of helpful suggestions. The majority of which are not suitable to repeat here.

44611387R00153

Printed in Poland
by Amazon Fulfillment
Poland Sp. z o.o., Wrocław